M000214936

The Heretics of De'Ath

ALSO BY HOWARD OF WARWICK

The Domesday Book (No, Not That One)

The Chronicles of Brother Hermitage:
The Garderobe of Death

The Chronicles of Brother Hermitage

The Heretics of De'Ath

Howard *of* Warwick

First published in 2014 by
The Funny Book Company
Dalton House
60 Windsor Ave
London SW19 2RR
United Kingdom
www.funnybookcompany.com

Reprinted 2019

Copyright © Howard Matthews 2014

The right of Howard Matthews to be identified
as the Author of this work has been asserted
by him in accordance with the
Copyright, Designs and Patent Act 1988.

All rights reserved.
No part of this publication may be reproduced,
stored in a retrieval system or transmitted,
in any form or by any means, electronic, mechanical,
photocopying, recording or otherwise without
the prior permission of the publisher.

A catalogue card for this book
is available from the British Library.

ISBN 978-0-9929393-0-4

Cover design by Double Dagger
Typeset by Lodestar Editorial

CONTENTS

The Daily Orders

The original manuscripts from which this tale is drawn
naturally follow the daily life of the monastery.
(It is only to be expected that Brother Hermitage
would record events against this reference.)

For those unfamiliar with this pattern, a short guide is
provided below, taken, we believe, from a contemporary
source. A less than devout one, it seems.

Matins: *Midnight*
Midnight! If you wake up in chapel, it's probably Matins.

Lauds: *1 o'clock*
You've only just nodded off after Matins.

Prime: *6 o'clock*
That's morning 6-o-clock!

Ladye Masse: *8.30*
Can't we have five minutes to ourselves?

Magna Missa: *10 o'clock*
There's that ruddy bell again.

Sext: *12 o'clock*
Well, we were up at midnight, so why not midday?

Vespers: *6 o'clock*
Just what you need after six hours work.

Compline: *7 o'clock*
A joke, surely?

Matins: *Midnight*
Is that the last Matins again or a new one?

September 1066

After Vespers

ND THUS I REFUTE THE PROPOSITION in all its blasphemous impudence. I say yes, the Lord did get sand in his shoes during the forty days and forty nights in the wilderness. Any other belief is HERESY.' Brother Ambrosius hurled the final word into the rafters of the refectory.

Young Brother Hermitage who was in the front row – or who, more accurately, *was* the front row – nodded with admiration and respect as the elderly bulk of the orator sat down in exhaustion. The argument had been long and complex, and despite a warming fire which made this the most comfortable place in the whole monastery, only three monks remained alert at the end of the four-day exposition. And that's allowing a very broad definition of 'alert'.

Hermitage was surprised the official opponent in the debate had given up after only the first five hours. He said he was retiring to his chamber for private prayer and took the novice Thabon with him. Their prayer was pretty vigorous, judging from all the grunting noises. Thus there were three contemplations on the case of Brother Ambrosius.

He glanced at the others to encourage their reactions. First was Brother James, and his was clear and instant.

'Oh, bugger,' he muttered, 'back to the garden.'

Hermitage frowned, but recalled that interest in the debate was an exeunt from daily labours. He smiled, trust Brother James.

Casting the old monk's carefully constructed arguments to another mind in the room, that of Brother Francis, meant they fell not so much on stony ground as on extremely large boulders. All of them stupid. His response was the same as always.

'What?' he said, as if accused of something distasteful.

Hermitage shook his head lightly in disappointment, not at the reactions of his Brothers, which was frankly no surprise, but at the loss they suffered through not engaging with this marvellous topic.

Leaving them to their own devices, Hermitage returned to the pose of those in profound thought, or profound boredom. He hunched almost double, propped his elbow on his knee and buried his face in his left hand. Thus he demonstrated deep concentration, or that he was dozing off.

Hermitage was so excited he could not have slept, even if he had been up all night writing a short summary of yesterday's proceedings – which he had. After a while he raised his head and lifted his bright and wakeful eyes to the massive and complex timbers of the roof. He stroked his chin and began to order the many significant ideas accumulated over the last four days. He considered the argument had weight and a certain beauty, although the premise that sand was a work of the Devil was perhaps a weak spot. Most impressive was the passion of Ambrosius for this rather obscure area of theological research.

Deep in his own thoughts, carefully constructing his observations and responses, Hermitage failed to notice that Brother Ambrosius was looking around in some agitation and anger. With a strangled gasp, the old man suddenly clutched at his chest.

The Lord above, perhaps having heard all that he needed, spared the world from further debate by recovering Brother Ambrosius to his bosom. Far from having the opportunity to respond to any questions Hermitage might have come up with, the poor man stopped responding to anything.

Hermitage also failed to notice that Brother James, alert to the ways of the world, looked around to confirm that no one else had noticed this event and slipped quietly out of his seat and away into the darkness.

Hermitage thought on in quiet satisfaction, relishing a rare opportunity for intellectual activity in this austere institution. The monastery in De'Ath's Dingle had a sparse population and provoked little interest from senior figures in the Church – in fact, it hardly attracted any attention at all. That this debate of Conclave was assigned here, while literally a Godsend to Hermitage, was a sure sign the result was of absolutely no interest to anyone.

The all-pervading ambience of isolated misery explained why it was some time before the dark of the autumn evening brought another monk to the great hall to light the sconces. Only then was the blindingly obvious fact of Brother Ambrosius's death revealed.

Sconce lighting at De'Ath's Dingle was a serious and sombre duty, to be completed with quiet devotion. It was a privileged task, given to those who would not use the opportunity for frivolous discussion with other monks, or as an escape from the natural labour of life. It was not meant to be a pleasure and so the Prior, Brother Athan, was the perfect choice. He had told Hermitage on many occasions that the unending toils of this life were a precursor to the hereafter, where things would be really tough. It was accepted wisdom that the man wouldn't take pleasure if it was carried by a flea and injected into him.

Even Brother Francis, who knew very little, had learned to move away from Athan when he saw him coming. He followed his instincts now, looking round in apparent puzzlement at where James had got to and why Ambrosius had stopped talking.

As Athan entered, Hermitage turned towards the distant door and saw surprise on the monk's face. Athan didn't like surprises. Apparently it was only a short step from a surprise to a joke, and then where would we be?

'Brother Hermitage,' Athan boomed.

'Yes, Brother.' Hermitage stood and responded loudly.

'What have you done?'

'Erm.' This was not what Hermitage had expected at all. Some cutting remark about the debate being a waste of breath perhaps, or the oft repeated accusation that Hermitage was a self-indulgent enthusiast. What had he done? He hadn't done anything. Yes, he'd been thinking deeply, but that counted as doing nothing as far as Athan was concerned. He gaped a little, hoping that there would be some further explanation.

'Brother Ambrosius,' the new arrival barked. As if this was sufficient explanation.

'Erm,' Hermitage repeated, uncertainly.

'Brother Ambrosius is dead,' Athan said, never one to beat around the bush. Beat the bush maybe, set fire to it as a sinful luxury, but on all occasions get straight to the point.

Hermitage wondered who Athan meant for a moment. There was a Brother Ambrosius at Peterborough, but why would Athan be concerned with that? He glanced back at the large shape of the old monk who had so recently completed his argument, and considered. He did look a bit dead now it was pointed out, but that couldn't be. Surely nobody died just like that. He had seen dead people, and was sure they hadn't sat down in a chair to do it.

Dead bodies were the result of run-of-the-mill domestic mishaps. Usually they'd been chopped up, or mangled by some piece of machinery or a horse's trampling hooves. Ambrosius looked quite normal: very still and rather staring, but apart from that normal. His pose in the chair was a touch more slumped and the look cast solidly on his features was of outrage, which was a bit odd considering he had just finished his debate.

The longer Hermitage looked the less normal it became. Ambrosius didn't move. At all. His huge chest and stomach no longer made their wheezing way in and out, and he hadn't farted or belched for at least a minute.

Hermitage looked around the room to see if there was anything that might account for a death. Across the length and breadth of the chamber he didn't really know what he was looking for. There was certainly no horse or suspect machinery.

'Are you sure, Brother?'

'Yes. I'm sure,' Athan snapped. 'Don't go anywhere,' he added, pointing a finger at Hermitage

Hermitage hadn't been going to.

Brother Athan strode across the room as if it were insulting him by being in his way, and peered closely at the defunct monk.

'Yes, definitely,' he spat into the room, as if accusing Hermitage of something.

'Oh,' Hermitage replied, 'that's strange.'

There was a pause while Athan did some glaring. Only Hermitage felt pauses needed filling.

'We must pray for the departed, although it's a bit too late for unction *in extremis.*'

Then Hermitage was puzzled. He liked being puzzled.

'I wonder when he died.' He puzzled away.

'Oh you do? You've been here for his entire pointless ramble, the best part of a week. You've given the old fool your undivided attention, and you wonder when he died?' The older man had suspicion in his voice. He also had it in his look, and probably had some spare in his habit should it be required.

'Well, I didn't notice anything, and as you say, I've been here all the time.' Hermitage blinked in the face of the inevitable consequences of this statement. He had never learned the technique for hiding his light under a bushel when situations got awkward. He was incapable of keeping his mouth shut.

Athan paced back to where Hermitage was standing and took up his usual position, just too close to be comfortable. As he did so Hermitage squirmed under the gaze, every stain and ragged thread on his well-worn habit calling out for punishment.

Hermitage faced his Prior. His bright blue eyes were wide and honest. He smoothed the unruly lock of chestnut hair that tufted from his tonsure, despite the best efforts of the barber. The open and fresh expression that sat perpetually on his handsome and even features bolstered the intelligent enthusiasm, bubbling like a fresh spring from every pore.

'You make me sick,' Athan said. 'You were here all the time, and so?' He gave Hermitage a moment to answer, a moment which went over the head of the enthusiast like a heron in a hurricane.

'And so how do you explain a dead monk and you in the same room?' Athan screamed helpfully.

'I was contemplating the argument and preparing to raise a few questions,' the younger monk answered honestly, wondering why Athan was so excited.

'Raising the Brother himself would be a miracle, never mind getting any answers,' Athan waved his arms at Ambrosius. 'I walk into the room of a most important debate of Conclave and find a dead body with you leering over it.'

Hermitage was offended. 'I wasn't leering over it. I wasn't anywhere near it. I didn't even know it was there.' He paused as he thought of something else. 'Anyway, what do you mean important? You've always said the debate…'

'You were the nearest one.' Athan cut Hermitage short. 'I want to know what you're up to.'

'I'm not up to anything.'

'You were engaged in the debate.'

'Well, I was listening,' Hermitage said, wanting to be strictly accurate. As usual.

'He was talking, you were listening?'

'Yes.'

'Now he's dead, you're not.'

'Well, yes.' Hermitage really couldn't see where this was going.

'Very suspicious. You have ruined the Conclave.'

'Ruined the Conclave?' The accusation knocked Hermitage back a bit.

'Yes, you idiot. The reason Ambrosius was here in the first place?'

'I know what the Conclave is, Brother. I just never knew you had an interest.'

'Of course I have an interest in what is important to the Church.'

'But you said this debate was a complete waste of time and the lives of those who would fritter away their minutes listening to the interminable drivel of a demented old man.'

'Don't quote me back at myself, Hermitage. I might get annoyed.' Athan thumped his fist into his palm for emphasis.

'I'm still not sure I follow, Brother,' Hermitage said, so meekly that lambs would have lain at his feet.

'Ambrosius's ramblings were just that. It doesn't mean that the decisions of Conclave are not of vital importance to the future of the Church.'

'But I thought you said the Conclave itself was a steaming pile of...'

'And now Ambrosius is dead, this particular decision cannot be made and you seem to be in the middle of it. That is extremely serious.'

Hermitage blundered on. 'I think you may be exaggerating a little, Brother. The wilderness footwear issue is not of mainstream significance. Obviously in Matthew caput four reference is made to stones in sandals, and while Ambrosius's point about the existence of demons is granted, there is doubt that they should be manifest upon the body of...'

'No, no, you fool. It's no good you carrying on the debate with a dead monk, is it?' Athan gestured once more at the slowly stiffening Ambrosius. 'The major problem is how this vital Conclave can resolve itself.'

'Vital?' Hermitage had thoroughly enjoyed the debate, but even he wouldn't have called it vital.

'Vital,' Athan emphasised the word. 'The vital debate is halted because there is a dead Brother in a room with only you in it.'

'But I hadn't noticed,' Hermitage pleaded. 'He must have simply died. He was old. Perhaps the exertion of the debate was too much for him.' As he spoke, he reflected that it hadn't really been much of a debate. Arguing with three monks, none of whom answered back, could hardly be described as testing.

The message was not sinking in, so Athan trod on it a bit harder.

'That will be of little comfort to the Abbot, will it?'

Now the blinkers of enthusiasm were torn from Hermitage's eyes by the overhanging branch of mortality. The wheels on his cart of fervour cracked on the stones of self-preservation, and he wanted to go to the privy. Understanding flooded through him from brain to bowels, and his mouth opened and closed a few times of its own volition.

Hermitage had chosen the Benedictines as they were a very flexible order. Yet this Abbot considered flexibility something to be frozen solid, preferably into some sort of weapon. He was a man of severe countenance, severe habit and a severed leg from some accident long ago. He nurtured great bitterness – and his only spark of generosity was to nurture it so well that it could be shared with everyone around him

'The Abbot?' Hermitage swallowed hard. 'The death of a Brother is a regular occurrence and we simply give the Abbot the old habits. I don't see why he would want to be involved now,' was the rather pathetic argument he came up with.

He waited for Athan's response and watched. The pockmarks and lines on the man's face seemed to squirm under the intolerable pressure of reasoning, while already small and pinched eyes tightened further. Athan drew in his breath and delivered his riposte.

'He wants to be involved, because he does.'

'But the other Brothers will bear testimony to the situation,' Hermitage whined slightly.

'Other Brothers?' Athan's voice lightened to a point in which Hermitage detected a hint of pleasure.

He looked around the room and noticed there were no other Brothers.

'I think you'd better come with me, young Hermitage. The Abbot will want to determine how the death came about and what to do to you. I mean with you.' Athan thought for a second. 'No, I mean to you.'

He helped the young man up by the elbow, if using the grip of a blacksmith to drag someone along can be called helping.

As the pair walked out of the room, exchanging the glow of the large fire for the cold of advancing evening, Hermitage offered a short prayer for the departed. It seemed the prayers of those under suspicion are incapable of ascending to the ears of the Lord. This one must have rebounded from the refectory roof and landed on Brother Ambrosius, as the corpse chose this moment to slide gracelessly to the floor, cracking its head on the flagstone.

Hermitage jumped and spun hopefully, expecting to see Ambrosius fully recovered and dribbling his familiar smile. He winced when he saw what had happened. Even Athan drew in his breath as if sharing the pain. Hermitage muttered a short blessing. Athan added his own contribution.

'Well, if he wasn't dead before, he is now.'

Hermitage grimaced.

'To the Abbot,' Athan said, with what passed for glee.

Hermitage cast a final glance at Ambrosius, being quite clear that he would prefer a night in the company of a corpse than half an hour with his Abbot.

Caput II

Day One   After Matins

RUDGING THROUGH THE WINDING WAYS of the monastery at De'Ath's Dingle, Hermitage's grim forebodings of a meeting with the Abbot were encouraged by his surroundings.

Stone. Just stone. Stone everywhere. Dull, grey, monotonous, repetitive, unending, tedious, soul-destroying stone. The Abbot considered a piece of moss or a splash of lichen an outrageous frivolity to be scrubbed away immediately, day or night.

Hermitage knew those entering the cloistered life should be sombre and serious, but the stone of De'Ath's Dingle made Brother Athan look like a jester on mushrooms. If the material didn't get you down, the construction certainly would. Apart from being so bad as to be dangerous, the masonry had been designed to concentrate attention inward, to the spiritual world.

Not that there was much evidence of the mason's craft in De'Ath's Dingle. Stone piler-uppers would be more descriptive. They may have heard of mortar, but had certainly not sullied their hands with the stuff.

Lord William De'Ath, who left his name to the land and his money to the Church to ensure a kind reception for his soul in the afterlife, was probably hammering on the lid of his tomb even now, anxious to kick some monastic backsides. A fellow of great cheer and joyfulness, he moved to England simply because he liked it, bringing his wealth from France. William purchased the Dingle because, as he put it himself in his bequest:

'It is the most beauteous spot upon God's earth and shall have a monastery put upon it so that praise shall be given to the ends of time for the wonders of His gifts. The holy men who come here shall delight in the blessings of His nature and rejoice with all about and bring good cheer to all.'

That all William left his only son was a semi-decrepit stone quarry went some way to explaining the turnout of events.

Then there was the Abbot himself. As far as Hermitage could tell, he was a man of no humour whatsoever. Any sign of it in others was stamped on with his heaviest boot, specially kept in his chamber for the purpose. Piety and misery should be everywhere, and it should emanate from the Abbot's study.

The monks stood together outside the Abbot's door. Hermitage was shaking slightly, while Athan strangled a smile that dared to twitch into the corner of his mouth. Brother Athan hesitated for a moment before knocking. Nobody knocked at the Abbot's door out of choice — they were all brought there, occasionally conscious.

'Wait,' the Abbot's voiced pierced the evening gloom. Hermitage and Athan waited. And waited.

'Yes,' the Abbot barked.

'What?' Hermitage was startled to hear the voice again as he realised he had drifted off into a daze. Goodness knew how much time had passed. It was certainly very dark now. Brother Athan was standing exactly as he had. Hermitage thought he enjoyed the needless wait they had been forced to endure.

'Yes' was not an invitation to enter, however. Hermitage was about to push the door open when he was pulled back by Athan's horrified glare.

'There has been an incident in the Great Hall, Father. Brother Ambrosius is dead,' Athan called.

'Hardly an incident, Brother,' Hermitage piped up, 'he simply died, that's all.'

'Who spoke?' blasted from the room as if the Abbot was standing next to them. Hermitage recoiled as the voice hammered his ears.

'I have Brother Hermitage with me. He had something to do with the death,' Athan laced his reply with accusation.

'I...' Hermitage began.

'So Ambrosius is dead. Deal with it.' The screaming Abbot had now lowered his voice to a loud shout.

'There will be repercussions, Father. It was in the middle of the debate.'

'Well, not strictly the middle. More like – ' Hermitage muttered this time, rather quietly, and so Athan simply hit him on the head, rather firmly.

The noise that came from the room at this news was probably human. Hermitage thought it unlikely the Abbot had a large, sickly yet still violent polecat in there with him, vomiting up last week's meal of putrid mouse, but he couldn't be sure.

'So we can expect visitors,' the Abbot spoke through teeth which Hermitage, even from this distance, could hear were clenched.

'I fear so, Father.' Athan sounded meek. 'It is likely that the Bishop, as Conclave Master, could not let such an event go without further information. If the debate was not concluded, it would have to be taken forward by another.'

'If anyone could be found who has any interest in this rubbish,' the Abbot huffed with contempt. 'Get in here.'

Athan pushed at the door and led the quaking Brother Hermitage into the room.

Hermitage was rational enough to understand that the monastery of De'Ath's Dingle was an expression of the destruction of human joy and the direction of the mind inward to contemplate its own decay, misery and ultimate destruction. He saw that this chamber was its soul.

Stone could be fabricated into inspiring representations of the divine. It could be used to ford rivers. It could be broken into small pieces and thrown at people. In the Abbot's chamber the very fabric of the building had given up hope of ever achieving anything; it was just waiting for Judgement Day.

After a few moments of disorientation, Hermitage realised the room was not quite square. Its walls were neither quite parallel nor level. The ceiling was not quite all there, allowing the rain to drip reluctantly in when the wind was in the right direction, which it almost always was. There was a large fireplace in one corner, but it had never been used for anything so sinful as generating heat. If a fire had been lit in this room the flames wouldn't dance, they would form a cortege.

As he glanced around, Hermitage found one thing which did lighten the place. A tapestry hung across the inside of the door and Hermitage looked to it for some relief from the unremitting gloom. As he gazed, he realised what it was a representation of, and looked away very quickly.

He had seen his Abbot only once, when he first arrived at De'Ath's Dingle, and that had been an unpleasant experience. He naturally assumed that the fellow before him was some plague victim on the verge of death. Highly infectious, no one had bothered to give him any clean clothes or feed him. Or show him where the privy was. It had been an awful shock to discover that this was the Abbot. Other monks told him not to worry too much as the Abbot kept himself to his chamber.

He hadn't realised exactly what that meant until now, and judging from the smell, the Abbot had rather let himself go since their last meeting. In fact he had let himself go several times, in different parts of the room.

'So,' the unpleasant accumulation of Abbot's habit spluttered into the room, 'what have you done, Brother?'

The kick on Hermitage's shin from Athan told him that he was permitted to speak. He hesitantly looked into the wizened face of the gnome-like being in front of him.

'I, er, I was simply engaged in the debate of Brother Ambrosius when it appeared that he was dead.' Hermitage found him-

THE HERETICS OF DE'ATH

self clasping and unclasping his hands and hopping gently from foot to foot. He tried to stop.

'It appeared? Where did it appear from?' Brother Athan said as he stood by the side of the Abbot and took over the argument.

The Father hunched a little further forward on the three-legged stool which was the only furniture in the room, and looked as if he was listening intently – or was going to sleep. Hermitage imagined that the Abbot did not sleep, far too indulgent. Anyway the Angel of Sleep probably wouldn't take him.

Hermitage wasn't sure whether he was talking to the Abbot or the Brother, and so tried to address both.

'Well, Brother Athan entered the room and pointed out the fact,' he explained, his head twitching backwards and forwards.

'So you had been in the room all along, and had not noticed that the person you were debating with was in fact dead? Rather a one-sided discussion, don't you think?' Athan's sneering sarcasm was a familiar friend to Hermitage.

'No Father, I mean yes Brother, I mean I wasn't the one debating with him. I was concentrating on some counter arguments to Brother Ambrosius's proposition and was distracted by my own thoughts.' Hermitage was distracting himself with his own fidgeting, so he tried really hard to stop.

'You were thinking. That's why you didn't notice an old man die in front of you?' Athan's tone implied thinking was akin to throwing a baby down a well.

'He had reached the end of the argument and so had stopped. I think it must have been soon after that he died. I mean he didn't stop mid-sentence if that's what you were thinking.'

'We had better leave it to the Abbot to decide what he was or was not thinking, Brother,' said Athan with a mixed tone of triumph and disdain.

'So the argument was concluded?' This was the Abbot who

seemed to care not a donkey's bottom about the fate of Ambrosius.

'Certainly Ambrosius had put his complete opening case, I believe,' Hermitage answered warily.

'How long did it take him?' the Abbot demanded.

'Er, four days Father.'

'Ha, the abridged version. Well at least if the argument was done we can all rest in peace.' There was a very slight movement from somewhere in the Abbot's habit which could be mistaken for relaxation.

'Did Ambrosius then respond to your questions, Brother? Was the case put forward by his opponent?' Athan was back in the fray.

'No, Brother. As I say, I was formulating my points and the opponent in the debate was missing when you came in.'

'Bugger,' said the Abbot.

Hermitage was now being ignored, for which he was truly grateful. He quickly concluded he didn't want to be ignored too long in this room; he was worried what it might do to him.

'An inconclusive debate,' said Brother Athan, as if it mattered.

'Not necessarily,' the Abbot replied.

Hermitage detected some other debate going on here.

'If the case had been put, and there was no refutation, then the debate is ended.' The Abbot obviously wanted this to be the conclusion.

'In favour of the motion?' Athan seemed astonished.

'Why not?' said the Abbot. 'Who honestly cares about opposing Ambrosius's senile ramblings?'

'Father,' Athan now seemed a little agitated, 'as I understand it Ambrosius was arguing that the Lord did get sand in his shoes during the days in the wilderness.'

'I am sure the Lord was quite capable of such an unremarkable feat,' the Abbot responded.

In other circumstances, at another time, Hermitage would

have smiled at the pun. But smiles had no place here.

'But if that is the case then he must have suffered the normal discomforts of mortal man.'

Hermitage was about to butt in and say that wasn't the point at all. The briefest of pauses allowed him to remember where he was, who he was and who he was with. He said nothing.

'His life and ours are ones of great suffering, Brother. As is right and proper.' The Abbot nodded; this idea clearly gave him some pleasure.

Athan remained anxious and ground his teeth – normally an indication that his anxiety would soon seek physical release. As Athan would hardly lash out at the Abbot, Hermitage took half a step away.

'Whatever the outcome of the debate. Father, we have no record of the conclusion. The Conclave could not declare it closed one way or another.' Athan shrugged a 'none of this is my fault; I'm only trying to help' kind of shrug.

The Abbot remained silent and still, but somehow Hermitage could tell he was thinking deeply. As an Abbot, the conclusion of the debate was in his hands. He could declare a decision and make the record say what he wanted. He wondered why the two men were so concerned with this topic. He thought Father Bergius's debate on whether scourges should have thorns in them or not would be more to their taste.

'The Conclave must be informed then,' the Abbot concluded with what seemed like a shiver.

Athan relaxed visibly. 'And then there is the question of Brother Hermitage's involvement in the death.'

'Hardly involvement, Brother,' Hermitage found the courage to protest.

'At the very best you were there when a Brother died and simply left him to make his own way to the hereafter. That's negligence. At worst you've committed some horrible sin about which we can only guess.'

Hermitage did feel bad at this. Athan had a point. Poor Ambrosius had been in a room with a fellow monk at the time of his passing, and he had been no fellow at all. He lowered his head, accepting the reprimand with his usual humility.

'And so some punishment is in order,' Athan said with relish. He was always going on about punishment. Hermitage accepted there should be just desserts for his abandonment of Ambrosius; trouble was, Athan's desserts were always so extravagant.

'This is such a serious matter that I had better lock you up while I think what might be best.'

Now that was worrying. Athan never needed time to think up punishments. Normally inspiration came naturally.

Athan directed his justification to the Abbot. 'I can hardly accept that he was ignorant of a dying Brother.'

'Brother Hermitage is ignorant of so many things,' the Abbot responded.

Hermitage found this rather hurtful. He knew pride was a sin, but privately he thought of himself as rather bright. Which, compared to the population of De'Ath's Dingle, he was.

There was more. 'I find it quite conceivable that he could be in the same room as the Heavenly Host and fail to notice.'

'But he must be held to account for events.' Athan was shocked that the Abbot could think otherwise.

'I have a suitable task in mind for our inattentive initiate.'

Athan raised his eyebrows and Hermitage shook. Some of the Abbot's reprimands were probably waiting for sinners at the Gates of Hell. Just on the inside. The two men waited with very different hopes.

'The Conclave must be informed. Hermitage shall travel to Lincoln.'

Well, that didn't sound so bad.

'On his own.'

Oh.

27

'And report to the Bishop.'

Oh dear.

'Now.'

Hermitage looked out of the hole in the wall that passed for a window and saw the dark of night waiting to envelope him. He couldn't see the murderers and ruffians, but he knew they were out there.

With no signal of any sort Hermitage could recognise, the discussion was over. Athan herded the young monk out of the Abbot's presence. As they left, the door closed, returning the old man to his daily routine of doing nothing and hating it. Hermitage realised the Abbot's seat was positioned so the focus of his attention was on the tapestry behind the door. Now he knew why the Abbot looked like he did.

Hermitage stepped slowly from the door contemplating this latest turn of events. He thought about how his arguments could be rehearsed for the new debate, how saddened he was that Brother Ambrosius would not see the outcome from this world, and how right the Abbot had been to conclude the debate was unfinished. Most of all he thought it a shame that he wouldn't have any involvement in events. He'd be dead at the side of the Lincoln road.

'So, Brother? You do know the way to the Conclave, I assume?' Athan's voice tried to do sweetness and light, but it couldn't.

Hermitage could only shake his head slowly.

'I shall prepare a message to make sure you get things straight while you pack.' He took a step back, probably to admire the effect of his words.

'I've heard it's thirty miles,' Hermitage whimpered.

'Then the sooner you start, the better chance you'll have of making it,' Athan said brightly.

'Perhaps I could take...' Hermitage was trying to think quickly what he could take; perhaps several other monks.

'A stout stave if I were you.' And with that Brother Athan was gone.

◆   ◆   ◆

Hermitage knew that the monks of the time were expected to be regular travellers. The peripatetic pilgrim monk was common, but a lot tougher than Hermitage. Hiding in the bushes while a gang of peripatetic bandits went by was not one of Hermitage's talents.

The journey here from his last monastery on the Lincoln coast had been a ghastly experience, even though he was accompanied part of the way by a band of his fellows on their way to Lichfield. Strangely, after a few hours of lively discussion on a variety of topics they decided that they didn't want to go to Lichfield any more. In fact some of them didn't want to be monks any more.

His state of panic at the thought of travelling to Lincoln was such that his packing consisted of a small devotional volume and a spare pair of sandals.

Thus Brother Athan found him, sitting on his cot, twiddling his thumbs and staring at the wall.

'Come, Brother.' Athan waved him to the door.

Hermitage looked up, rather absently noticed Athan, and stood. He followed the older monk through the twisting turns of the monastery towards the main gate, not quite believing what he was about to do. Only when they reached the exit from the monastery did he find his voice.

'Perhaps, Brother, it would be better if I delayed departure until dawn.'

Athan opened a small gate set into the larger defensive door, which itself stretched above their heads and vanished into the darkness of the keep.

'Oh, look,' he said, 'that's handy.' He gestured towards the eastern horizon, just lightening with the first rays of the new day. 'I hope you packed enough food,' he added as he thrust a parchment into Hermitage's hand, bundled the monk out of the door and closed it firmly behind him. From inside what suddenly seemed a warm and comfortable home, Hermitage heard Athan's familiar tones.

'Oy, Barnard, come here. I've got a job for you.'

Hermitage turned to face the road. 'Food?' he thought, as he realised that no, he definitely did not know the way to Lincoln.

Caput III

Day Two   Prime

o,' Brother Hermitage thought, on the dawn of a not-very-brave new day, 'I shall address this problem as I would any other, by considering the information available.' He then started talking out loud to himself. Hearing a voice helped a bit, even if it was only his own.

'It is thirty miles to Lincoln and I have heard it said that a brisk man can walk at three miles in one hour. Therefore thirty miles should in fact take me no longer than ten hours. I shall be there before nightfall.' He did genuinely feel better as a result of this and strode purposefully along the dirt track leading from the monastery gates.

The ambience of the Dingle of William De'Ath threw itself on his senses, driving all thoughts of difficulty from mind. Dawn lit up a million sparkling drops of glass-like dew, festooned upon an army of delphiniums, which marched the eye into the heart of a ravishing wood. A speckled carpet of gold and brown leaves furnished a room of unbelievable grandeur, with magnificent firs and oaks for walls and a canopy of spectacular colour for a roof.

A light autumnal mist softened the view and deadened the air. Gentle sounds of the waking birds had almost a physical presence, dancing among the woods. The path was the only real thing in the world: the rest was too fantastic for truth. With a heart light at the sights and sounds before him, while at the same time heavy that he would disturb, and then lose this vision, the monk stood in rapture before the glory of God's nature.

The beauty was almost unbearable when a pair of pigeons swooped down from one of the trees, settled in the middle of the

31

path and began gently cooing to one another, searching amiably for the first of the day's food.

It seemed unnatural when the figure of a man appeared out of the mists along the track and disturbed the birds, making them rise and fly along a couple of feet above the ground. It was blatantly and definitively horrible when another man appeared from behind a tree in the pigeons' path and smashed one of them back to the ground with a large stick. He stood chuckling at the fluttering and now deformed bird, before picking it up by the legs and waving it at head height.

'You'd think the bloody things would learn to fly up, wouldn't you?' he exclaimed towards Hermitage, before he and his friend padded back into the mist to start plucking the first of their day's food, scattering the dew and trampling the flowers as they went. A lone pigeon landed and searched for something its small brain told it had been there a moment ago, but which seemed to be missing now.

Hermitage felt much the same.

With a heavy sigh at the contradictions of the world, he set off on his journey, leaving behind the fragile beauty of the Dingle, the unbreakable presence of the monastery and the intransigent nuisance of mankind.

His distraction was such that he failed to notice two figures emerge from the monastery gate behind him and step softly in his path. They were not monks, and one of them was rubbing his ear as if someone had just hit him.

Twenty nine and a half miles short of his goal, Hermitage hit a problem. A crossroads.

He was proud of his train of thought. 'The sun is in front of me and rising, therefore that is east. I know De'Ath's Dingle to be north of Lincoln, and so the correct road is to the right.'

The figures who were following paused in puzzlement. The tall, rotund one turned to the slight, weasel-like one and shrugged. They made themselves comfortable in a dry culvert just to the side of the road and waited.

Only a few minutes later Hermitage's road bent so sharply that, as the sun vanished behind a rising fog, he realised he was heading west. He wondered about following the trail. He also wondered about turning round and going back to the cross-roads. He wondered whether the other roads had bends in them. Finally he wondered about dying in the middle of nowhere and being pecked to pieces by crows. After this particular wonder he had a bit of a sit down. Eventually he leaped up and cursed himself for being a fool.

'Curse you, Hermitage, for being a fool,' he said to a hopeful-looking crow. 'Why follow the road? You are not a cart; you can walk where your legs will take you, head south and all will be well.' A brief thought about the lamb that strayed from the path crossed his mind, but he felt sure that wasn't meant to apply to such a literal situation as this.

It took Brother Hermitage several hours to discover he knew less about finding his way across open country than he did about finding it along well-marked roads. The mist was now thick, he had no clue where he was, but he was definitely cold, wet and not a little angry at his situation. He reasoned that his best option was to simply sit still, wait for the sun to re-appear so he could get his bearings and set off once again.

He chose the bank of a small stream as a resting place. The water course emerged from the mist to his right and wandered off again to his left with a much better idea where it was going than Hermitage. The ground was damp and boggy, but at least it was landmark of some sort.

✦   ✦   ✦

As night fell, Hermitage wondered about being pecked to pieces by owls.

✦   ✦   ✦

The following dawn found him looking with sinful thought at the descent from the trees of a solitary pigeon.

He stood up in the cold morning air and stretched the weary damp out of his bones. Standing on tiptoe, he scanned to the east for any sign of civilisation which might indicate a useful direction to take. He was shocked to find none whatsoever.

A much greater shock awaited his westerly scanning. He had only turned a quarter of the way round when the bulk of the monastery imposed on his view, and forced him to crane his neck upwards to see the tops of the walls.

Hermitage didn't say anything; he wasn't the type to say anything. Most other types would have had several things to say, all of them very rude. Any other type would probably have danced up and down on the spot trying to kick anything that came within range while tearing out lumps of their own hair and shouting obscenities.

His circumnavigation of the monastery of De'Ath's Dingle had taken a whole day and a night, and had brought him to a point just under his own cell window. He recognised a stream as the water course which flowed into the monastery from the west as a relatively clean supply from the nearby spring. It came out of the east as a sewer. It was in the latter that he had spent the night.

Hermitage picked himself up and started to brush himself off, before realising he was getting the stuff on his hands. He set off back to the track. Dawn at the gates on this day seemed to have lost a lot of its magic, so he simply strode purposefully down the track, through the woods and kept straight on at the crossroads.

His invisible companions had become so comfortable in their culvert that they didn't even wake at his passing.

His newly found faith in the path laid before him was rewarded as the day grew older and one or two figures appeared, using the route just like normal people. Also like normal people, they crossed the road to walk on the other side from the smelly lunatic, who had obviously been given a monk's habit as some act of equally lunatic charity. Hermitage was firmly back in his normal frame of mind when he realised that he had let at least ten people go by without asking one of them whether he was on the right road or not.

A few 'excuse me's' later, which prompted those approached to hastily back track, avoid the path or just plain run away, Hermitage managed to get in the way of a very well dressed man who was absorbed in thought.

'What?' The man simply jumped with surprise as he realised that he had nearly walked into someone. He looked closely and seemed to recognise a monk. He then sniffed the air and serious doubt crossed his face.

'What do you want?' he demanded, a very nervous look settled on his face.

'Tell me, my son, is this the right path to Lincoln?' Hermitage asked.

The man relaxed a bit. He still wrinkled his nose at the smelly habit, but Hermitage's manner settled him.

'No. Er, I mean yes.' The man seemed rather careful and cautious, and looked at Hermitage as if the monk was about to do something surprising and unpleasant.

'Well, which?' said Hermitage, feeling both irritated and ashamed at his irritation.

'I mean it is the road to Lincoln, but not the way you're going.'

Hermitage's heart fell. Not back past the monastery again.

'Is it the way you're going then?' he asked.

'Yes. Er, no.' The man was clearly not terribly decisive.

'If you could direct me, my son, I would be most grateful and no longer detain you from your journey.'

The man lightened considerably at this.

'Right,' he said, 'back the way you came for about half a mile.

There's a single track goes off to the right through the wood for a few yards and then you're on Ermine Street. Turn right, straight on and that's it. Lincoln.'

'Thank you, my son.'

As he strode off, he glanced backwards to see that the man had found something fascinating in a nearby ditch. He was giving it all his attention and looked as if he might be there for some time.

The sun now rose firmly into the sky with no sign of the mist of yesterday. It warmed Brother Hermitage's face so that he paused for a moment, closed his eyes and let the heat soak into him, dispatching at least some of the memories that remained from the night before. His task was clear and he would set about it with a will. He would also set about it with a pace as his habit had started to steam slightly and he wanted to let the smell waft behind him.

Back at the interesting ditch the man was approached by two more strangers.

'Did you see a monk go by?' a fat man with a swollen ear demanded.

'Yes,' the man responded warily, 'he's headed for Lincoln.'

'About bloody time,' a stick-like companion said, and they sped off.

The man frowned and rubbed his chin before wandering along after all of them.

✦   ✦   ✦

The directions given to Hermitage seemed accurate enough, and he found the single track through the woods without any problem. Emerging from the far side, he came upon the great artery that was Ermine Street. Or rather the Ermine Street that had once been a great artery. When the Romans left they took knowledge of road building with them. They also took all the maintenance instructions.

Striding along amongst the potholes, Hermitage was given a wide berth by every other traveller. He pretty much had the road to himself. Passing through a wooded area, where the trees met overhead to create a tunnel of foliage, he heard running feet behind him and turned just in time to be bowled over and off the road by two figures, one large, one small, who were obviously in a great hurry. Hermitage thought it odd that their hurry evaporated as he fell into a shaded area of woodland. They were probably going to help him up.

'All right, monk,' said the burlier of the two as he grabbed Hermitage by the habit and pulled him to his feet. He held on to the material tightly for just one or two moments as he pushed the monk against a tree. 'Oh my God, what have you got all over you?' He almost screamed as he stepped back smartly and looked in horror at his besmirched palms. They were very besmirched.

'Oh, I am sorry,' Hermitage began to explain, but the less burly man stepped up smartly, stood right in front of him and waved what could only be called a club in the monk's face. The man grinned and smacked the weapon into his hand a couple of times for emphasis. Hermitage felt himself go pale and he started to shake. He knew that he was not a brave man. Not in the common sense of the word. He was not prepared to throw himself into a fight or to challenge anyone who looked like they were prepared, if not positively willing, to do so. In Hermitage's book, that wasn't common sense at all. Give him a dubious proposition or some shoddy interpretation and he'd stand before a howling gale to defeat it. He couldn't do men with sticks.

He cowered and closed his eyes to wait for the blow. Somewhere inside him he knew the moment it would land. He subconsciously calculated the time to raise the club and lower it with speed and he tensed. When that instant passed, he opened one eye.

The man was having trouble holding his club aloft. It had become too heavy for him and it was clear he was about to topple over backwards with the weight of thing. Hermitage wondered at his remarkably poor club selection skills if he couldn't even hold the thing up. When the fellow did indeed fall over backwards, Hermitage saw there was another man behind. This was the one who had given him the directions and who had been fascinated by the ditch. At the highest point of the ruffian's swing this new arrival had simply taken hold of the club and pulled gently backwards. This was not a direction the attacker could sustain, and so down he went.

At this defeat the original miscreant stepped up. He had cleaned his hands on some leaves and approached the stranger as if he was not going to stop. He pushed his now relatively unsullied palm into the man's chest.

'Push off,' he said, 'and mind your own business.'

Hermitage's rescuer looked in considerable horror at the hand which had pressed into the middle of a very nice jerkin. He reached up, grabbed the fingers of his attacker and bent them backwards with such vigour that the burly man had to fall to his knees.

'If I break these,' the stranger said amicably, indicating the fingers, 'you do appreciate that the pain of getting them fixed will turn the pain of having them broken into one of your fondest memories?'

The man simply nodded, clearly in considerable pain already.

The man with the club had now recovered, got to his feet and was advancing to rescue his comrade. He whacked his club in his hand, obviously a favourite precursor, and stood, legs braced.

The stranger raised his eyebrows in some disdain, flicked his left leg out and smacked the man firmly between his braced legs with some highly polished and expensive boots. Club man was instantly in so much pain he couldn't even howl. The look on his face was all that was required to express his feelings fully – to anyone who cared to know. Hermitage's face metamorphosed into the 'ooohhh' look adopted by all men when they observe one of their ilk on the receiving end of such an injury. This one clutched both hands to his groin and slowly toppled sideways back to the ground.

Finger man was now released. He took several steps backwards, nursing his digits under his armpit.

The stranger turned to Hermitage. 'Are you all right?'

'I am indeed, sir, thanks entirely to you. Oh,' Hermitage called out as the one with the fingers had decided to have another go and was rushing up to the back of the stranger.

'Oh, really,' the stranger said, in irritation at bad form. Just at the last moment he reached out, pushed Hermitage to the left, stepped to the right and turned to assist his attacker in his headlong rush straight into the tree.

'Persistent, aren't they?' the stranger observed.

Hermitage didn't know what to say.

With one attacker dazed and bleeding at the bottom of a tree and the other balled up on the floor calling for his mother, the stranger shrugged.

'Better have their trousers then.'

'Er…' Hermitage didn't know whether he'd fallen in with a rescuer, a robber, a madman or one of Brother Findos's friends.

'We'll leave them naked. Much less likely to follow us if they don't have any clothes on,' the stranger explained. 'Tends to deter people from taking to the main highways.'

Hermitage felt guilty but relieved as they stepped from the woods back onto the main road, leaving the naked and groaning men behind them.

Once on the path, with other travellers passing by, Hermitage felt safe again. He stood and faced his new companion.

'Sir, I cannot thank you enough for your actions today. You have saved me from great harm, if not death indeed. I am Brother Hermitage.' He held out his hand.

'Odd name for a monk,' the man muttered. 'Wat,' he announced.

'Brother Hermitage,' Hermitage repeated, still holding out the hand.

'No, I'm Wat,' the man said, looking with some disdain at the hand. 'Wat the Weaver.'

'Oh, I see,' said Hermitage looking at his hand to see why the man wouldn't shake it. He saw straight away and put the hand sharply behind his back. 'Wat the Weaver, eh?'

Wat shrugged, 'It keeps me remembered.'

'I suppose it would.'

Now that Hermitage examined the man he could see that he was a weaver. Under a shock of unruly dark hair sat an open and friendly face, albeit one somehow worn by the cares of the world. There was a worried look behind the eyes. Trade was always hard and Hermitage imagined the slight furtive look in Wat's eyes was an indicator that the man was constantly on the lookout for his next opportunity. Simply putting food on the table was a constant challenge, and competition among weavers must be fierce.

Wat's clothes were very good, though. A striking red top was wrapped around by a thick cloak of the finest quality. His jerkin was decorated with the fruits of his art as tiny images of deer and trees paraded around his waist. His legs were clad in a material of such quality that it probably even kept the cold out. Finally his boots, which had done so much damage, were solid, well-fitting and looked new. Remarkable. He put Hermitage to shame.

Wat put his hands on his well-clothed hips and examined Hermitage with an increasing frown. 'Why were you attacked?'

'Who can say why the trials and tribulations of the world are visited upon us?' responded Hermitage helpfully. To him, being attacked was simply what happened when you ventured on to a road.

'No, I mean why were *you* attacked?' Wat repeated. 'It's very suspicious. Nobody in their right mind attacks a monk for profit, and they certainly weren't trying to steal your habit. What is it about you that they were after?'

Hermitage looked at Wat, expecting the weaver to have the answer to his own question.

Wat looked back at Hermitage, apparently expecting the same from the monk.

They both looked away into the trees, but there was no answer there. Perhaps the road ahead would explain everything to them. Hermitage could only hope it was better behaved than the road behind.

Day Three Sext

HY HE HAD BEEN ATTACKED was a fascinating question, Hermitage thought. When in doubt … He started warming up for an exploration of the nature of sin, the presence of evil and the consequences of the fall from grace in the Garden of Eden, but Wat interrupted.

'There's no sense in this particular attack. Monks don't have anything worth stealing. No point robbing a monk.'

Although this was sensible, it sounded rather heartless, even mundane. From his perspective, Hermitage thought the question why do people rob was far more interesting.

'Did you know them?'

'Certainly not.' Hermitage didn't know anyone like that. In fact he really knew very few people at all.

'So what's your business going to Lincoln?' Wat asked, carefully brushing the dirty palm print from the front of his chest.

Now here was an opportunity for a decent conversation. Hermitage leapt in.

'I have an important message for the Conclave there. Are you familiar with the Conclave? They are doing some magnificent work, you know. I am particularly interested in the notion of the expiation of sin through the prayers of others, but I have been engaged in a fascinating debate about the suffering of our Lord in the wilderness.'

Wat sighed, put his hand to his face, and shook his head as Hermitage rambled on. He gestured that they should walk, and together they resumed their journey. The day continued warm and comfortable, and their spirits rose like midges from a bog.

Which themselves rose in numbers, probably attracted by Hermitage's habit.

The next few hours were uneventful, as uneventful as any hours could be when Brother Hermitage had free reign and an audience. As scattered clouds departed from the country sky, the slopes of the Lincoln hill came into view and gave them pause. They gazed at what was surely the most magnificent sight in the realm. Probably the world. The towers of the Roman town still teetered here and there, with enough height to be seen from several miles. The raw outline of the church could be seen just topping the trees, albeit covered with the scaffolding that stopped it falling over.

Hermitage explained that Lincoln was so magnificent a place that it had more than one church. Old St Peter and Paul in Bailgate had been visited as a ruin for so long that many suspected it had been built as a ruin in the first place, simply to attract visitors. The new church, however – new because it had only been there for a couple of hundred years – had been doing its best to fall down ever since it had been put up.

'You haven't told me what takes you to the great city, my son,' Hermitage asked in a brief pause for breath.

'Erm, no.' Wat hesitated.

Hermitage waited.

'Just a sales trip. I weave tapestry mainly. Personal commissions, that sort of thing.' He was rather dismissive.

'Really?' Hermitage asked. His mind leapt back to the scary tapestry in the Abbot's chamber at De'Ath's Dingle. 'I saw a rather disturbing tapestry just yesterday, as it happens.'

'Oh?' Wat enquired rather nervously, his eyes darting back and forth, as if expecting the disturbing tapestry to have followed them.

'Yes, a very powerful image which my Abbot must use to concentrate his meditations on the potential of allowing the devil to take control of the world.'

'Oh, that one,' Wat muttered, but Hermitage missed it.

'Are you a master weaver, my son?'

'Not officially.' He showed some embarrassment at this.

Hermitage raised a monastic eyebrow.

'My guildsman did not make the necessary arrangements for recognition as a master, although I had completed all the necessary steps. The man was quite insistent on this.'

'I see,' Hermitage mused, not really understanding.

'Several times over.' There was a note of bitterness now.

'Ah.'

'To the very highest level.'

'Good, good.'

'Including dyeing and carding, cloth work, needle preparation, frames, hanging, horizontal and vertical, commissioning and stock control, sales and aftercare...' The sentence petered out rather than coming to an end, and even Hermitage could see that a change of topic was in order. Wat was getting over-excited and Hermitage did not like excitement in others.

There was a pause. Hermitage couldn't do pauses.

'Lincoln is a fine city, is it not?' he said.

'Profitable,' said Wat.

'I myself am travelling to the Conclave,' said Hermitage, 'or did I tell you that?'

'Yes,' said Wat as they began to move along the road again. 'Several times,' he added with a sigh.

'Ah,' said Hermitage, 'I have been told that I do that sometimes. You will stop me if I go on, won't you?'

'I'll try,' said Wat rather hopelessly. 'This Conclave certainly doesn't sound like motivation for an attack, though. What is this message you're taking?'

'One of the debates has not been concluded properly,' Hermitage said with great significance.

'Oh dear,' Wat responded, without any significance at all. 'I can't believe anyone would attack you over that.'

'Well, not physically,' Hermitage replied, slightly disappointed that Wat couldn't see the importance of debate. Theological importance obviously, but still, people should take an interest. 'Anyway,' he went on, 'although I am grateful for your concern the attack was just one of those things.'

'As I said, no one tries to rob a monk.'

'Maybe they were very stupid robbers?'

'Clever enough to follow you all the way from where we met.'

Hermitage looked at Wat as he absorbed this new information.

'They were probably waiting for their opportunity to get me. You know, no one watching.'

'They asked me if I'd seen you.'

'Did they?' Hermitage said slowly. He was starting to get his familiar worrying feeling again. He worried about most things most of the time, but every now and again something special would come along which demanded a little bit more effort. He started to concentrate quite hard on his worrying.

'Why would they do that?' Wat asked.

'They'd obviously decided I was their target and wanted to know where I was.' This was pure speculation, but it sounded convincing.

'I think that's true, but it makes robbery even less likely.'

'Why?'

'We've agreed that a robber would have to be a very stupid one to think about going after a monk?'

'Yes.' Hermitage's worry was dampened by a potentially enjoyable debate.

'So very stupid robbers, having lost sight of their monk, would simply rob the next thing that came along. They wouldn't ask for directions, follow the monk for a few miles and then rob him.'

Wat left a pause for Hermitage to think this through. 'Look at me,' he said, holding his arms out to show off his clothing.

'Yes?'

'I mean, I'm a better bet to rob, aren't I?'

'Of course. But then you seem very capable of taking care of yourself.' Hermitage nodded his head back to the woods in which naked and beaten robbers were probably still nursing damaged parts.

'They don't know that when they have a go. They could have robbed me when they asked directions. We were on our own then. They had their club, why didn't they?'

'Because a monk is less likely to put up a fight and even if they weren't stupid, they didn't seem very good.'

'That's another thing. Two men, one with a club? They should have had me easy. This clearly wasn't their normal line of work.'

'I still don't know what you're getting at?' Hermitage said, and he really didn't.

Wat sighed. 'Those two men were after you. Personally. Not just any monk – they followed you. And it wasn't to rob you.'

'What then?'

'That's what I don't get. This debate business can hardly be the stuff to motivate attacks in the woods.'

'Hardly.' Even though he was an enthusiast for argument, Hermitage had only ever seen one debate descend into physical violence. That was entirely justified as some fool had proposed that women could be priests.

After several moments thought Hermitage had an idea. He hesitated to mention it. This Mr Wat was obviously a worldly and clever fellow, and the pointless musing of a humble monk would be of no interest to him.

'Erm,' Hermitage found himself mumbling.

'Yes?'

'Well, I'm sure it's nothing really.'

'What is?' Wat was all encouragement.

'I just wondered.'

'Yes?' There was hint of impatience now.

46

'Whether it might be the, erm, death?'

'What death?' Wat almost shrieked.

'Well, Brother Ambrosius.'

'A monk is dead?'

'Didn't I mention that bit?'

'No, you did not mention that bit. How did he die?'

'He just died, that's why I didn't think anything of it. He was nearly fifty.'

'When did he die?'

'During the debate.'

'That must have put a dampener on things.'

'Oh yes, he was the speaker after all.'

'He died while he was speaking?' Wat was aghast and sounded it.

'No, he sat down first.'

'Brother Hermitage, this is very significant.'

'That's what Athan said.'

'Who the hell is Athan?' Mr Wat was getting terribly excited now, but there was no call for profanity.

'He's our Prior. He kept saying I had something to do with Ambrosius's death and wanted me punished. The Abbot insisted I come to Lincoln with the news though.'

'Why have I not heard of him before now?'

'I don't know. Do you move in ecclesiastical circles?'

'No, I do not move in lousy ecclesiastical circles.' Wat threw his hands in the air, apparently in frustration at something or other. 'Well, not unless they pay up front. I mean why, in all the telling of this tale of yours, have you made no mention of Athan? Or the death? Or the Abbot?'

'Well, I didn't think they were relevant.'

'Two men follow you for miles and attack you in the woods with no motive of robbery. All of this just after you have been engaged in a debate during which the main speaker died. The Prior wants you punished, but the Abbot sends you out on the road. No relevance?'

'Er…' Hermitage could only cope with the events of the world one at a time. He seldom saw they could be joined together, and it worried him if he did. 'Are you suggesting,' he began warily, not sure what was being suggested, 'that there might be some connection?'

'Doesn't it seem a bit of a coincidence?'

'Why would my Abbot send me out to be attacked?'

'Or murdered.'

'Or murdered. Thank you.'

'Well, I don't know him do I?'

'He's quite capable of attacking people himself if he thinks it needs doing.'

'Or murdering them?'

Hermitage could cope with no more of this outrageous fantasy. 'This really is ridiculous. I shall simply deliver my message to the Bishop and the whole matter will be closed.'

'Ah yes. Is the message written down?'

'Of course,' said Hermitage, patting his habit where the parchment lay nestled in a simple inner pocket.

'Let's have a look then.'

'Certainly not.' Hermitage was horrified.

'It might give us some clue about what's going on.'

'It is a communication from an Abbot to a Bishop. I can't possibly open it.' It was clear from Hermitage's tone that this question, rarely, was not up for debate.

'So what happens when you've delivered it?'

'The Bishop will consider the matter and take the appropriate action.'

'And what will you do?'

'As the Bishop directs me. If there is some function I can perform it will be an honour. If not, I will simply return to the monastery.'

'Yes,' Wat said in a very slow and deliberate way. 'If I were you

I'd think very carefully before doing that.'

'You are a very suspicious fellow, I must say.'

'Look, perhaps someone doesn't want word of this death taken to Lincoln and that's why you were attacked. They could have been after the message?'

'Wouldn't make much difference really.'

'Why not?'

'Well, I still know Ambrosius is dead. I can tell the Bishop that without having it on a piece of parchment.'

'Not if you're dead in a wood, you can't,' Wat concluded. 'Maybe they don't want news of the death to get out at all?'

'That would be a bit hard. Ambrosius was reasonably well known. He'd be missed when he didn't return to his home monastery.'

'But not for some time.'

'No, I suppose not.'

'Maybe just enough time.'

'Enough time for what?' Hermitage asked.

Wat looked at him seriously and intently. He frowned his usual frown and rubbed his chin. 'Not a clue,' he said brightly. 'You say the death was natural?'

'Oh yes. Poor Brother Ambrosius passed away just as he was completing his argument.'

Wat's frown returned. 'That sounds pretty unnatural to me,' he said.

'Really?' Hermitage replied airily, as if this sort of thing happened every day.

'Well, it seems a bit odd, doesn't it,' the weaver went on, 'dying in the middle of a debate?'

'That's what Brother Athan said. Sort of.' Hermitage did not want to lie, he wasn't capable of it, but nor did he want to lay all of the facts before this stranger.

'So he just finished talking, sat down and died?'

'That's about it,' the monk replied. 'He had finished his opening speech, but was quite exhausted. It was the fourth day.'

'Four days?' Wat exclaimed. 'For an opening speech? What was this debate about?'

Now Hermitage looked puzzled. Hadn't Wat been listening as they walked?

'Well, it was as I was saying,' he began, starting to go through the whole matter again.

'Never mind,' Wat said, interrupting, 'I'm sure after four days of debating anyone's entitled to drop dead.'

'Anyway, I've got to let the Conclave know so they can consider what to do about the question.'

'An important matter, I'm sure,' said Wat.

'It seems so to the Abbot and Athan.' Hermitage had doubt in his voice.

'You aren't so positive?' Wat was clearly engaged with the issue, which delighted Hermitage.

'Well, it is a rather esoteric matter. Of clear interest to the theological community, but to be honest...' He paused, wondering whether he should go on.

'Go on,' Wat prompted.

Hermitage hesitated, and then spoke with care.

'Neither the Abbot nor Athan have ever struck me as particularly engaged with the more philosophical aspects of the religious life.'

Wat paused now and seemed deep in thought

'Brother Hermitage,' he said seriously.

'Yes?'

'Bearing in mind what you said before.'

'Which bit?' Hermitage was enjoying himself.

'About your tendency to go on a bit?'

'Oh.' Hermitage stopped enjoying himself quite so much.

'Yes,' Wat said, 'bearing that in mind, can you tell me, in a very short time, say two sentences, what this debate was about?'

Hermitage looked very disappointed.

'Again,' Wat said brightly, 'by way of a summary.'

Hermitage frowned. He supposed that weavers shouldn't be expected to follow this anyway.

'Well, briefly,'

'Yes?'

'When our Lord spent the forty days and forty nights in the wilderness...'

'Yes?'

'Did he get sand in his shoes?'

'And?'

'That's it.' Hermitage couldn't see what else the weaver was expecting.

'Four days?' Wat was incredulous.

'Well, it's not as simple as you think.'

'It sounds pretty simple,' said Wat, 'in the wilderness, in sandals. I think the answer is yes.'

'So did Ambrosius.' Hermitage was enthusiastic again.

'Good.'

'So do I.'

'Not much to debate, then?' Wat shook his head seemingly in disbelief.

'Well as I say, it is fairly advanced.'

'It would have to be. And this is why it's odd that your Abbot and this Athan are interested?'

'Exactly,' said Hermitage, 'they'd be more concerned with, oh, I don't know, how many times you should beat an acolyte before sunrise.'

'Hmm, I had a weaving master like that,' Wat said with some feeling. 'And you think this Conclave of yours will kick the whole thing off again.'

'I don't know. It's up to the Bishop really.'

Wat shook his head in what seemed to be despair.

'Well, I can see it's a matter of the utmost importance.' It didn't sound like Wat thought this at all. 'The sooner we get to

Lincoln, the sooner you get your answer, the sooner we can all sleep safely in our beds knowing the great issues of the day are in safe hands.'

As they moved off Hermitage thought he heard Wat mutter an obscenity. Perhaps he'd trodden in something.

'Always assuming we don't get murdered before we get there, of course,' the weaver added with disturbing jollity.

For a moment Hermitage thought how annoying it would be to get murdered before all this was sorted out, but then he realised that he would be the murdered one. While he recognised this was the thought of an idiot, he was quite engaged by the idea of finding out what on earth was going on.

Caput V

Day Three Before Vespers

ROM THE SITE OF THE TUMBLING CHURCH of Lincoln, the whole of God's creation was laid out across the landscape. To the west the land dipped away quickly, the Lincoln edge sinking into the bogs and fields that made up the flood plain of the Rivers Trent and Witham. This was a fertile land, which had fed the inhabitants of the area for thousands of years. It was a treacherous one, too, as it had also drowned quite a lot of them.

Five hundred years after the Romans left the place to fall into wrack and ruin, if the phoenix wasn't actually rising from the ashes, at least it was twitching and coughing a bit. It had even coughed up the foundations of a new church.

It would be magnificent. It would be given a new tower, and this tower would tower over the surrounding land like a big building on top of a hill.

If the carpenter enjoying his afternoon beer while lounging on a foundation block for the statue of Saint Paul had had the eyes of a hawk, he would have seen Wat and Hermitage as they trudged along the Roman road towards the town. Unfortunately, the afternoon beer was only the most recent in an unbroken line that stretched back to the previous week. The carpenter wasn't sure he could even see his own hands any more. Nor was he sure why he seemed to have so many of them.

◆   ◆   ◆

Hermitage and Wat's journey proceeded without unusual incident. Some small boys threw manure at the monk on several occasions, but that was to be expected. At one point a very fur-tive man approached Wat, and an exchange of some money and a very carefully wrapped small package took place.

'Ah, for the life of the honest wandering merchant,' Hermit-age sighed.

'Yes.' Wat sighed rather as well.

At one point the thoroughfare of Ermine Street disap-peared completely. All of the stone had been removed and there was nothing left but a large pit, full of disturbingly green, deep-looking water. A fairly substantial dwelling stood off to the right just here, down a track of its own. The track was very well maintained and, upon close examination, the dwell-ing looked rather like a Roman road, only stacked up with windows in it.

The land to the left was heavily wooded, so the only option appeared to be past the house and down the side of the hill. An old drovers' track of some sort provided a usable path, but it did lead them almost straight down the hill. This they would, at some point, have to climb back up again.

Several minutes later they stood firmly at the bottom of the hill, gazing up at the city above them. Hermitage marvelled at the sight while Wat mumbled some very rude comments about drovers.

They joined the main road from the west which climbed out of the wetlands and headed straight up the hill. Hermitage thought the Romans had not got everything right after all. Any sensible builder, faced with an almost vertical slope, would have put some corners in to help loads zigzag their way upward. Not the Romans. They were obsessed with going straight on, come hell, high water or sheer cliffs. If you couldn't walk straight up a hill, you weren't welcome on their road.

'Well, my son,' Hermitage said as they arrived, panting, at the top of the hill, 'I think the time has come for us to part, for I must to the Bishop's house with tidings.'

'Yes, and I must about my business. It's been nice meeting you. Cheerio.' And Wat scuttled away without a backward glance.

Hermitage thought the departure was a bit brusque.

◆　　◆　　◆

The great city of Lincoln spread itself before Hermitage's eyes. Quite a lot spread itself before his nose as well, but he imagined town dwellers must find it difficult to manage the transport and disposal of waste.

Mind you, he was a fine one to talk. People bustled around, intent on their own business, or intent on avoiding whatever business the smelly monk had brought to their midst.

There were a number of substantial buildings gathered together at this entrance to the old Roman town, and much of the activity seemed focused on these. Hand carts came and went either loaded with produce for the kitchens or heading back somewhere for more. Craftsmen worked on roofs and walls, although whether they were being put up or taken down was hard to tell. Pedlars cried their wares and services, the competition seeming to be the louder you cried, the more likely people were to use you.

All of this life and activity could distract a young monk, sent from a rural outpost with a task not to his liking. It could whisk him away from his chosen path, with its flamboyance and promises of adventure.

Hermitage wished they would all go away so he could find the Bishop and deliver his message.

Scanning the seemingly disordered chaos before him, from the poorly organised arrangements for the movement of carts to the random shouts of people who ought to have better things to do with their time, he looked for any sign of civilisation.

To his left the walls of the old town stretched off along the edge of the hill, through the mud and filth of the town. To his right, with a sigh of relief, he saw the entrance to the church building site.

The way was plastered with litter, mud and half-finished bits of woodwork. A stack of completed gargoyles, the very latest thing in architecture, sat on a pallet to one side waiting their elevation on to the extension roof, from which they could hurl the rain away from the building and on to the peasants below.

Even Hermitage, who had no knowledge of building practices, thought this was a bit odd. It looked like the roof was still years away. It was an indication that this job was going to be as successful as old Canute's strategy for sea defences.

To the right again of the main site entrance lay a beautiful lawn and path – a manicured anomaly in the surrounding chaos. The lawn was semi-circular, edged with dozens of identically shaped and painted white stones. It obviously took a lot of effort to keep up.

Wondering what such a pleasant vista could be part of, Hermitage went in search of the Bishop's house which he reasoned must be somewhere in the vicinity.

A considerable time later, in complete darkness, he knocked with due deference on the door which had been on the other side of the lawn. The intervening time had been spent following directions from several local folk of varying accuracy and, Hermitage suspected in one instance, some deliberate devilment. After a further wait the door was opened by a very surly-looking fellow who occupied most of the space.

'What?' It was a simple enquiry and all that was needed really, but Hermitage felt it was delivered with a less than reverential tone. It did not help his state of mind which, despite himself, was showing signs of the onset of encroaching testiness.

'I have come with a message for the Bishop,' he said blankly.

'What?' Again it was sufficient to the situation, but could have been more engaging.

'I am Brother Hermitage from the Monastery at De'Ath's

Dingle and I have a message for the Bishop's ears from my Abbot.' Hermitage waved his parchment in the man's face. He thought that this got the point of the visit across, and also made clear that he was not some urchin or chance traveller.

He felt a pang of guilt, as the trials of his journey seemed to have wrought a change in his thinking. Calm deliberation was being elbowed aside by an unnatural impatience. Pride had reared its shameful head, and anger made him want to put this common little turd in his place.

'Oh, right.' The figure in the door relaxed, seemingly relieved that the odd, dirty, smelly individual was just another churchman returning from some ungodly activity in town, and not a beggar or a lunatic.

He opened the door cautiously, glaring all the while at the waiting gargoyles as if expecting them to make a sudden move.

The imposing hallway of the building did its job and imposed itself on Hermitage. He gaped at such a space existing in a private house, lit, as it was, by a candelabrum of three relatively new candles. The ornate carving on the panelled walls, the expensive tapestry cast on the floor of all places and the sheer scale of the place were awe-inspiring. The reception hall must have been at least ten feet long and six feet wide. It was so high that Hermitage, a tall monk at five foot seven, hardly had to duck at all. It was simply magnificent. It even had some glass above the door to let the light in.

Whatever man was graced by God to live in such spacious luxury was clearly of great moment, and Hermitage must behave accordingly. He stood stock still.

'Wait here,' said the gruff fellow. 'I'll fetch Nicodemus.'

If this was supposed to mean something to Hermitage, it passed him by. Left on his own in this great building, he stood even more still.

Several minutes passed, during which Hermitage considered the detail of some of the carvings. He was alarmed and impressed at the same time, and occasionally by the same image. Before he could examine further, a tall man in clerical garb stooped into the room from behind a wall tapestry that obviously hid the entrance to another room.

'Brother Hermitage, I understand. You have a message for the Bishop?' the new arrival said in well-rounded and educated tones. Here was someone Hermitage could relate to.

'Indeed I do, Father.' Hermitage responded with a short bow.

'Oh, I am no Father. I am merely Nicodemus, the most humble servant of my Lord the Bishop, and the formalities of my position call upon this dress.'

With this Nicodemus bowed to Hermitage, but somehow without bowing. He managed to incline his head and body in the monk's direction while facing forward, giving the impression that it was Hermitage who had the honour of meeting Nicodemus, not the other way round.

'Ah, I see,' said Hermitage, not really seeing at all.

There was a long pause, which did nothing but get longer. The look on Nicodemus's face got more and more expectant, while the look on Hermitage's face got older.

'Perhaps,' Nicodemus seemed to burst into speech, 'you might let me know the content of the message?'

'Ah,' said Hermitage realising he should have spoken some time ago. 'It is for the Bishop,' he explained.

'Indeed,' said Nicodemus. He didn't seem pleased with this answer. 'And I have the ears of the Bishop.'

Hermitage caught himself looking for them, somewhere on the man's person.

'I am sure you do, my son, but my Abbot was most specific on the matter.' Once again Hermitage wanted to put someone in his place. The sensation was uncomfortable and satisfying at the same time.

Nicodemus didn't seem to know his place.

'Perhaps you'll follow me?' He gestured through the tapestry into a room even more magnificent than the hall, if that were possible. This room was dominated by a huge desk, which took up most of the floor. Behind the desk a large, ornately carved and extravagantly cushioned chair sat with its back to the fireplace, in which a couple of the most enormous logs gently burned away, filling the space with glorious warmth. Two similar but smaller chairs sat on this side of the desk with their backs to the door. Hermitage's muscles complained as they saw the comfort of the Bishop's throne.

'So,' said Nicodemus, as he walked around the desk and sat comfortably. Hermitage was rather shocked.

'Do take a seat,' Nicodemus gestured Hermitage to sit before him. For a humble servant he wasn't being very humble.

Hermitage sat and looked expectantly at the man opposite for some explanation.

'The message then,' said Nicodemus, explaining nothing.

'Is for the Bishop's ears, sir. My Abbot was most clear on that point.' Although this was compounding a small lie into a medium one, Hermitage felt it was justified, it was reasonable and it was all this stuck-up servant was going to get.

Nicodemus's expression of disdain didn't change; there just seemed to be more of it.

'As I said, I am the Bishop's ears in all matters, Brother. Unfortunately he is unable to attend himself, and so as asked me to receive you in his place. The business of the Conclave, you understand.'

'It is a matter of some delicacy, I'm afraid, and I am sure that having waited thus far I can attend further upon my Lord the Bishop.'

Nicodemus peered at Hermitage, having trouble comprehending what he was being told.

'Does it concern the unfortunate demise of Brother Ambrosius during the debate?' Nicodemus suggested.

How did you know about that? Hermitage thought.

THE HERETICS OF DE'ATH

'How did you know about that?' he inquired.

'Ah, Brother, the Bishop has knowledge which surpasses us all, I fear.' Nicodemus laid the humility on with great pride.

With his diversions around the walls of De'Ath's Dingle and up and down the hills of Lincoln, Hermitage thought it possible for rumour to have reached the Bishop before he did. In which case the last two days had been a complete waste of time.

'It is indeed to do with Brother Ambrosius's death during the debate,' Hermitage said with some assurance and irritation.

'What is it exactly then?'

'That Brother Ambrosius died during the debate on the question of sand in our Lord's shoes during his time in the wilderness.' And with this Hermitage made great play of handing the parchment over to Nicodemus.

The man unsealed the roll, opened it, read it and rolled it up again without giving Hermitage any indication of what it contained. Hermitage had no entitlement to know, but he still felt aggrieved.

'Yes.' This was a long, drawn out yes from Nicodemus. 'It seems the debate was not concluded. There were no counter-arguments?'

'I was engaged in the debate myself,' said Hermitage with pride. He neglected the fact that he had been the only one engaged in the debate, although he suspected that Nicodemus probably knew that as well.

'So I understand,' Nicodemus confirmed.

He did.

'Well, my Lord the Bishop's view on this sort of thing is very clear,' Nicodemus smarmed.

This sort of thing? thought Hermitage. How often did 'this sort of thing' happen?

'There will have to be an investigation,' Nicodemus announced.

A what? Investigation? Hermitage's learning woke up. What

an interesting word. Must come from the Latin, vestigo, vestig-are, to track. Why would there need to be some tracking? Her-mitage knew perfectly well where Ambrosius was. He was hard-ly likely to have left De'Ath's Dingle, if he wasn't already in the ground. He certainly didn't need tracking.

'I'm not sure I understand.'

'Very likely,' Nicodemus sympathised.

With a start Hermitage achieved a new understanding. This man was being contemptuous towards him, and he had recog-nised it at the time rather than two days later. He marvelled at his appreciation of a rather subtle feature of human behaviour. The punishment for this gift arrived at the same instant. He felt an overwhelming urge to be contemptuous in return.

'In cases such as this the Bishop requires us to ascertain the reason for the demise,' Nicodemus was explaining in simple words.

'Brother Ambrosius was nearly fifty.'

'We need to look into events and see if there is any cause for concern,' Nicodemus emphasised the last word.

'And he was exerting himself in the debate.' Hermitage was on a track of his own until he came to the end of Nicodemus's. 'Concern? What concern could there be?'

'If the outcome of the debate was close, and was terminated for some unnatural reason? We live in an evil world in evil times amongst evil, with evil all around us.'

There was no arguing with that.

'And the Bishop simply wants to be assured that none of that evil fell upon the departed.'

'Well, what evil could there possibly be? I was there and I didn't see any evil.' Hermitage couldn't follow this line of argu-ment.

Nicodemus's eyebrows rose halfway up his head, and he in-clined his head in a very knowing sort of way.

'Indeed you were.'

A sinking feeling told Hermitage that he shouldn't be emphasising his involvement.

Nicodemus rose from his chair, or rather the Bishop's chair, and began to slowly to pace up and down the little unoccupied space in the room.

'We are fortunate that we have some expertise in this area with us at present in the shape of the King's own investigator.' He took a short pause as he said this, emphasising its utmost significance. 'He has a particular interest in the Conclave, and the Bishop has asked that he return with you to the monastery in order to fully explore all the circumstances surrounding the death. He will provide a comprehensive report, or take whatever action he sees fit.'

'Really?' Hermitage saw that this was getting rather serious. He suspected that he might be heading for even deeper trouble. Not the sort of trouble Athan usually provided, which concluded with a swift blow.

'Really.' Nicodemus now stepped over to the tapestry guarding the door and held it open for Hermitage to leave. Not really knowing why he did so, the young monk complied. 'If you return to your lodgings, the Investigator will meet you here at Prime.'

'Ah, yes,' said Hermitage, standing on the step of the door again as it closed in his face. Soon after that he remembered he didn't have any lodgings. After standing still and wondering what to do for so long that people started to stare at him, he wandered off into the city.

◆　　◆　　◆

In the house, the humble servant sat behind his humble desk in thought. Probably humble as well. Eventually he reached over and rang a small bell that was perched on the edge of the desk. After a few moments the gruff servant appeared and waited for Nicodemus's instructions.

'Find Brother Simon,' Nicodemus instructed.

'What?' the servant said in a tone of disbelief.

'Find Brother Simon,' Nicodemus repeated, with more instruction in his voice.

'Are you sure?' the servant questioned an unbelievable order.

'I've said so, haven't I?' Nicodemus' impatience was clear.

'Please yourself,' the servant shrugged, and shambled off to do his master's bidding.

As the servant left the house a curtain at the back of Nicodemus twitched, and a darkly dressed shadow cast a gloom across the room.

'Interesting.' The new figure spoke without removing the well-tailored cowl which obscured his features.

'It was to be expected,' Nicodemus responded.

'I suppose so. This Abbot?'

'A lunatic fellow, nothing to worry about. He's been off throwing dirt over himself somewhere or other and Rome have put him here out of the way.'

'Rome?' There was concern under the cowl.

'Happens all the time. They get someone to do a really nasty piece of work for them and the reward is a non-job where you can be left to die in peace.'

'Charming. And this Hermitage? Odd name for a monk.'

'Don't know him. Clearly several sorts of idiot without a clue what's going on.'

'And Brother Simon,' the cowled figure sounded as surprised as the servant. 'Are you sure about that?'

'Oh, he will serve our purposes admirably.'

'If you say so.' The cowl did not sound sure.

'You have heard about the legacy murder, have you?'

'Not one that I know of. Him?'

'Not directly, of course, but he was boring the teeth off Father Das, an old boy who insisted on giving all his possessions to the poor and tending the sick without being asked.'

'Revolting.'

'There was a fight involving a young man visiting Das to do with a legacy.'

'Surprised he had one if he gave everything away.' The cowl clearly found such an approach to life very hard to believe.

'Well he did, although Simon assumed the same as you and told the young man.'

'Who wasn't happy.'

'Exactly. The young man gets terribly upset at this and starts brandishing a knife. Or he doesn't get excited at all and the knife is simply to peel an apple, depending whose story you believe. When Das turns up there's a big bust up, some sort of scuffle and the knife in the young man's hand ends up in the priest's stomach.'

'Nasty.'

'Turns out the young man is the priest's son as well.'

'Oh, right,' said the cowl as if killing your own father was much more acceptable. 'How do you know all this?'

'How else? Simon gave the key evidence at the trial, even volunteered to be an official witness at the execution.'

'Handy he was there then.'

'Except, of course, the son and the rest of the family deny all this; they say it was an accident caused when Simon tried to run away and pushed the old boy over on to the knife.'

'So the reputation of Brother Simon is well earned.'

'Absolutely. Which makes him just the man for us.'

'But this Hermitage might know him as well.'

'Him?' Nicodemus released one short laugh from his very short supply. 'He couldn't follow the bent end of a Bishop's crook. I've met his sort before, all brains and no sense.'

'The schedule mustn't be interrupted.'

'It won't be.' Nicodemus turned to warm his face at the fire. 'This is just a minor diversion. Might even prove useful. Occupy the minds of those who do have some sort of attention span.' He turned again, but the curtain had twitched. The figure was gone.

Caput VI

Day Three Compline

ERMITAGE'S WANDERING WAS NOT EXTENSIVE. Within a few yards of the Bishop's house he found a collection of wooden trusses, lying on the ground waiting to take up their tasks above. He spent a fascinating time working out which one joined to which and how the final shape would look.

As he realised that this was a largely pointless activity – only after twenty minutes or so – he saw a figure approaching him in the dark. Clearly a drunk, it meandered around and he was just preparing to step out of its way, or shrink into the shadows, when he saw it was a monk.

'Brother,' Hermitage acknowledged with a short bow. He was not inclined to start conversations with monks who swayed about in the dark.

'Ah, some assistance,' the figure called, holding out an arm.

Hermitage stepped up smartly at this, and saw that the fellow was grasping the top of his head with one hand. Even in the dim moonlight Hermitage could see a dark liquid, staining the fingers and running down the side of the face.

'Brother,' Hermitage cried in alarm, 'have you been attacked?' He took hold of the other man and supported his weight.

'An accident, they said,' the injured man responded. 'They shall not hear the last of it though.'

'Sit down, Brother, sit,' said Hermitage, guiding him to a corner of the path.

As the man sat, Hermitage took advantage of the moment to examine the wound. He was not an apothecary, but had dealt with many injuries and illnesses, being the only Brother who could read the medical texts.

The top of the man's head had a distinct, single wound in it, from which the blood had nearly ceased to flow. It wasn't too deep and would probably recover with a simple bandage. Hermitage considered tearing off a piece of his own habit for the purpose. He then remembered the state of his habit and decided this was probably a bad idea. He knew dirt in a wound helped ground out evil humours, but there was dirt and then there was dirt.

'What happened?' Hermitage asked.

'Idiots,' the monk replied.

'Rather particular ones,' Hermitage said, glancing at the neat edges of the wound, which was right on the crown of the head.

'I was in the site tavern,' the monk began.

'Ah,' said Hermitage knowingly.

'I was instructing some master carpenters on the selection of wood and care of tools,' the other insisted. 'I had just embarked on a critique of the modern apprenticing system, when one of the craftsmen carelessly got a chisel from his tool bag and dropped it on my head.'

'Outrageous,' Hermitage said. 'What was he doing getting dangerous tools out in the tavern?'

'Exactly my point. And one which his superiors shall hear of.' The man lifted his hands and gazed at the congealing blood.

'The gathered tradesmen expressed great concern and hurried me off to seek aid.'

'None of them accompanied you?'

'They had an urgent guild meeting to attend, apparently.'

Hermitage frowned. 'The wound does not seem too serious, but we should get it dressed.'

'If we cross the site, Brother, there is an aid tent. See,' the man pointed across the dark, 'a candle still burns.'

Hermitage looked. He saw a dim glow, softened by a canvas

screen, from somewhere closer to the church itself.

'Hembert the Physick will still be there,' the man explained.'I have given him much guidance in the more learned aspects of his trade. He will sort this out.'

Hermitage helped the Brother to his feet, and they stepped slowly across the site towards the tent.

Stumbling through the darkness, they made quite a noise which caused a face to appear between the flaps of the tent. Obviously Hembert the Physick.

Hembert, if it was he, squinted in recognition at the injured monk and a very few moments later was seen leaving the tent in the opposite direction. At high speed. Perhaps news of some emergency had been brought to him.

Never mind, Hermitage thought. If there were supplies in the tent, he would bind the wound himself.

'Ah, Mistress Hembert,' the wounded monk croaked, as they pushed through the canvas,'I have received a wound from a careless carpenter, who will be hearing more about it, of course, and it needs attending.'

Hermitage looked at Mistress Hembert, doubtless the physick's wife, who struck him immediately as a caring and friendly woman. She had an expression of lightness and sympathy and, although her hair was covered in a close bound scarf, he could see that she was young and beautiful. She looked up with concern as soon as the tent was opened, clearly prepared to offer any aid that was required. Anyone with an illness or injury would be pleased to be tended by this angel of mercy.

For some reason her charming face dropped several degrees of sympathy when she saw who the injured party was.

The damaged head was thrust at Mistress Hembert and the man pointed unnecessarily at a chisel-shaped hole in his skull.

'Do you know,' the monk said to Hermitage, 'for several months Magda Hembert here was profoundly deaf.'

'Really?' Hermitage looked at the woman as if there would

be some physical sign of this. Mistress Hembert glanced back at Hermitage with a guilty look. She shrugged.

'Absolutely. Whenever I engaged with her, she could not hear a word I said.'

'Remarkable,' Hermitage commented. Magda Hembert refused to catch his eye.

'And then one day I found that she was able to answer her husband back. To this day, I do not understand why no one takes note of the miracle of Magda's ear as the first indication of the sanctity of the church site.'

'I see,' said Hermitage, trying to sound as noncommittal as possible.

Magda grunted in disappointment at the trivial nature of the damage. Perhaps she preferred more challenging work. Amputations and the like. She slapped an old bandage on the wound, tied it firmly to the head with a length of cord around the chin, and told the monk he mustn't speak for a week, preferably a month. Then she rushed out of the tent on some muffled errand.

'Well, Brother,' the patient tested the bandage, only now appraising Hermitage. He frowned deeply at the state of the man.

Hermitage acknowledged the mess with a reluctant shrug.

'It seems I owe you considerable thanks,' the monk said. 'I,' he paused as if for effect, 'am Brother Simon.'

'Pleased to meet you, Brother,' Hermitage responded politely. 'I am Brother Hermitage.'

'Really?' Simon frowned. 'Odd name for a monk.'

He rose, trying out what might be shaky legs.

As he did so Hermitage considered him more clearly in the candlelight. The man appeared to be all points. His nose was needle-like, drawing attention like a screaming baby at a funeral. A baby with a massive nose. The rest of the features of his face crowded round this protuberance like an audience. The eyes, brown and muddy, looked as if they were constantly trying to catch a glimpse of the end of the nose, but the cheeks had given up the unequal struggle. By sinking into concave insignificance in the shadow of the mighty nasal mountain, they merely emphasised the point. The whole of the monk's head had been created to give prominence to his single defining feature. It wasn't the Roman nose sported by so many of the population. It had no crook, or bend in its profile. It simply sprang from the head and went straight on.

Once able to drag his eyes away from this, Hermitage saw the rest of the man followed its model. He was as thin as a week-old corpse. Even beneath his well-cared for habit, Hermitage could tell that his legs wouldn't hold muster against some rather poor kindling. His age didn't help the overall impression: he must have been well over forty. If he had one foot in the grave, it was because he was just climbing out of one.

Before any general conversation could be started, the tent flap was flung aside and the bulk of Nicodemus's servant filled the space. He looked from one monk to the other, and was confused.

'Nicodemus wants you,' he said to Simon. He frowned at Hermitage, clearly unable to understand why he was seeing this monk again.

'Excellent,' Simon said. 'I have a particular issue I wish to raise with him. This is most opportune. Brother Hermitage here can accompany me as a witness.'

The servant shrugged in comprehensive disinterest. Hermitage and Simon followed him out of the tent.

'I shall give him all the details of the carpenter's poor performance, and press for a fine or a reprimand for the man,' Simon said as they walked back towards the house. 'I have an excellent record of reporting to Nicodemus. He relies on me quite heavily, you know. I monitor everyone from peasant cleaners to members of the priesthood. Almost all of them have been remarkably careless of their duties in one way or another. It's a good job I'm here, even if it does mean I have to be on the receiving end of their incompetence.'

This time the door was opened by the humble servant himself.

'Ah,' he said, looking out at the arrivals. 'Fortuitous you should both be here.' He stepped aside and gestured them in.

This gave Hermitage some trepidation. His previous dealings with this fellow had been peremptory at best and the man had seemed only too anxious to see him on his way. To be invited back in by Nicodemus, with what appeared to be a smile, was an unnerving experience. What could have happened in such a short time that meant Hermitage was now wanted? Had the Bishop returned and countermanded his servant's orders? Had more news arrived from De'Ath's Dingle? And where did Nicodemus get a smile like that? Hermitage found it rather disturbing.

Simon seemed to have no qualms about any of this at all and strode into the building as if he owned it. Hermitage crept back over the threshold, keeping a lookout for the alarming doorman, who might take exception to a return visit. Hermitage had made the connection from the man to the fellow's fear of the gargoyles; he looked like one.

❖   ❖   ❖

As Nicodemus led them to the inner room, which had a lingering whiff of Hermitage about it, he walked around the desk and sat. Simon took a seat on the other side without question and so Hermitage followed suit.

'I'm glad you're in, Nicodemus,' Simon began, without any niceties, 'because I have a number of issues I would like to discuss concerning the performance of the labour.' He was prepared for a long session.

Nicodemus looked down at the desk and raised a hand to stop the flow.

'I'm sure you do, Brother, but a matter of utmost import has come to the Bishop's attention, helped on its way by Brother Hermitage here.' He nodded an inconsequential acknowledgement to Hermitage, who was just pleased that his name had been remembered.

'And in the Bishop's mind your name sprang to the fore.' Nicodemus laid special emphasis on 'the bishop' and 'your name'.

Simon's pose acquired a rather haughty pride.

'Indeed?' he said slowly, intrigued.

'The word our Brother has bought is of an incident during one of the debates of Conclave,' Nicodemus poured into Simon's ear.

'I am sorry to hear that. How may I be of assistance?'

'You may be aware that the issue of sand in the shoes of our Lord was being resolved at a monastery some distance away?'

'By Brother Ambrosius, I understand. I hope it went well. I did give such guidance as I could in the construction of his arguments.'

A frown crossed Nicodemus's face. 'Really?' he asked, finding that very hard to believe. He even shook his head slightly in some amusement. Hermitage didn't think this was funny.

Nicodemus went on. 'It is sad to report that Brother Ambrosius has been taken from us. Before the conclusion of the debate I might add.'

'I see.' Simon's tone said he knew exactly what the situation was, had pierced to the central issue immediately, and was of a mind with Nicodemus.

'And so naturally the Bishop is concerned.'

'I imagine he would be,' Simon said, sagely.

'He is concerned that the questions surrounding this matter have not yet been resolved and he would like someone of integrity to look into things.' Nicodemus looked straight into Simon's eyes.

'Ah, I think the debate can be concluded with some minor

attention to the salient points,' Simon nodded, quite capable of dealing with this.

Hermitage felt a pang of disappointment. It felt unjust that the debate should be taken away from him like this.

'No, no, Brother, you misunderstand,' Nicodemus said, with some pleasure at the observation.

'The Bishop wants the matter of Ambrosius's death looked into. It is feared that there may have been foul play.' He let the concept sink in.

Hermitage frowned now. Foul play? No one had suggested any foul play. He assumed it was foul and not fowl. He cast his mind back and could not recall that the debate had been disturbed by any hens. In fact he'd only ever seen one hen walking about De'Ath's Dingle. And that hadn't lived long. Dragging his mind back to the matter in hand he reminded himself that there wasn't anything sinister at all. Ambrosius simply died. As he kept telling Athan.

All of Nicodemus's attention was on Simon, 'If there is a danger to the Bishop's flock, he wants it rooted out.'

'Danger?' Simon was a little put out. Nicodemus smiled.

'And the Bishop thinks that I would be a suitable person?' There was a real question in the voice. 'Perhaps one of the Sheriff's men might be better for such a task while I consider the theological issues?' Simon wriggled in his chair.

'A very apposite suggestion, Brother, but the Bishop sees this as a purely monastic matter and is looking for a resolution in the shortest possible time. It is a minor journey to De'Ath's Dingle and you can leave in the morning. Brother Hermitage here will accompany you.'

Oh, will he? thought Hermitage. This was a very presumptuous humble servant.

'Oh.' Simon was put out by this. Nicodemus was enjoying every minute.

'The Bishop's view is that there may have been some...' Nicodemus paused for the most suitable word and tapped his lip with one conspiring finger. 'Some interference with Brother Ambrosius, bearing in mind the significance of the Conclave.'

'Interference?' Simon was panicking now. 'Monks being interfered with?' It didn't sound like he wanted this job at all.

'Interference?' Hermitage mouthed to himself. He was very puzzled indeed. It would be a bit of a coincidence if there was another dead Ambrosius. Perhaps Nicodemus had got them muddled up, and the one at Peterborough had passed on as well. No, couldn't be. He wasn't engaged in the Conclave. There was certainly no other monastery called De'Ath's Dingle. There wasn't another one even remotely like De'Ath's Dingle, in any way whatsoever.

'What significance?' Simon blurted out, 'Surely Brother Ambrosius's case was a rather esoteric point of interpretation? Who would, erm, interfere with him over that?' Simon took a long, hard swallow.

'The ways of sin are a mystery to many of us, Brother. If the devil is at work in the Bishop's demesne, he must be exposed.'

'The Devil?' Simon's voice broke into a squeak.

Hermitage had to speak. 'I don't think it was anything like that, sir,' he said to Nicodemus.

The man glared at him.

'If the Bishop is anxious that the matter be resolved,' Nicodemus went on, ignoring the interruption, 'and he wants it done quietly and quickly, then that is what will happen. The evil of De'Ath's Dingle needs to be eradicated. That can only be achieved by a monk of some considerable insight, ability and courage.'

Simon rallied a bit at this. Only a bit, though. He was lost in his thoughts. From the look on his face they weren't very encouraging ones.

Hermitage thought that this was all getting out of hand. Foul play, evil, the devil. All patently ridiculous. After all, he had been there at the time.

'You may also need to know that the Abbot of De'Ath's Dingle is a remarkable man.' Nicodemus chose his word carefully.

'That's true,' Hermitage mumbled, before he realised it had been out loud and clapped a hand to his mouth.

'He may take some persuasion that there is indeed evil afoot in his monastery. Once you have uncovered the evidence you may feel that the best course of action is to bring it back to the Bishop's attention, and let him deal with it as he sees fit.'

Simon looked like he didn't know whether to sigh or be sick. His strength of purpose had withered and dropped off.

'Perhaps, Nicodemus, there is a monk who is more adept at this work than I?' he suggested hopefully. 'Brother Wulfan has always taken a keen interest in the works of the devil, and how they may be countered.'

'Yes,' said Nicodemus, 'And we all know what form the "interest" has taken. And why Brother Wulfan has to be restricted to the confines of the church during the hours of darkness. The Bishop is quite clear: you are the man for the task, Brother. He has even gone so far, for the purposes of this matter, to nominate you as the King's Investigator.'

Calculation crossed Simon's face. The previous panic subsided, his chest swelled.

'The King's Investigator.' Simon spoke as if he had asked for a glass of ale and been handed the Holy Grail.

'Absolutely.' Nicodemus let the title and the moment sink in.

Hermitage was puzzled once again. He half-raised a hand to ask a question, but realised that whatever the answer was, it would put either Simon or Nicodemus in an awkward position. Hadn't Nicodemus indicated, in his conversation with Hermitage, that the King's Investigator had expertise? Yet here he was, appointing the Investigator for the first time. And he wasn't even close to the king.

Nicodemus rose, keen to see both men gone.

'So, Master Investigator,' the tall man said, helping Simon towards the door, 'perhaps if you arrange to meet at Prime you can make the short journey to De'Ath's Dingle in the company of Brother Hermitage.'

'Hermitage,' said Simon, as if trying to remember who that was. 'Very well.' He assumed his most self-important look. 'Perhaps I had better be about my preparations and let one or two key people know of my appointment.'

Nicodemus pressed a firm hand on Simon's back to help him out of the main door. He gestured at Hermitage and waved him away.

Outside it was almost dark. 'Well, Brother,' Simon said, in a rather ungrateful and remote tone, 'I have some business to be about. Return here at Prime and you may accompany me.'

With that he was gone.

'Well, really,' said Hermitage crossly. He spoke loudly, half hoping that it would be heard.

✦   ✦   ✦

He turned away from the church compound, intending to find the monastic house where he could arrange his lodgings. The evening town had come to life. Lights were lit, taverns were full and bustling. People were wandering up the hill from the town below, keen for some sort of treat after the labours of the day. Hermitage could imagine that he was back in ancient times, and any moment a column of Roman soldiers would appear.

Directly opposite were the remains of the Roman Fortress and the young monk found himself drawn to them. As he wandered across the large square between the two buildings, sacred and profane, he noticed a group of men gathered in a rather large huddle. Hermitage lingered, puzzling over what was going on.

There was a major piece of drainage work in hand. Two large trenches were dug in the slope of the square, presumably to di-

75

vert all the filth of the nearby housing over the edge of the hill. From there it could safely be deposited on the poor people who lived below.

The group of men must have been working on this, as a pile of tools mirrored the huddle. What was it, he wondered, that had drawn them away from their task? Perhaps there had been an injury. Could he render some assistance?

As Hermitage approached, an urgent whisper ran round, followed by much nudging and turning of backs. Had he been remotely worldly-wise, Hermitage would have seen a number of articles being hastily held behind backs and thrust up tunics. Rather like a wave breaking against rocks, the band of misbehaving workmen scattered in the face of the tide of a religious do-gooder.

In the centre of the rapidly dispersing men, who seemed to have found a sudden interest in their discarded tools, was a single figure, bent double, rapidly packing a roll and binding it with rope. It was a figure Hermitage recognised.

'Ah, Master Weaver,' said Hermitage, 'good evening to you.'

'Oh,' said Wat as he watched the workmen scatter, 'it's you.'

'We seem fated to meet,' Hermitage said.

'Yes, we do, don't we?' said Wat, not happy with the Fates.

'Is your business done for the day?'

'Looks like it now.' Wat scanned the square, but everyone looked the other way.

With Wat's roll of tapestry safely stored in a bag, the pair wandered up the Bailgate. Hermitage expanded at length about the investigation and the need to return to the monastery in the morning. Wat, however, seemed distracted and looked around constantly.

At one point a rather large fellow approached from an alleyway and took steps towards them. He seemed intent on discussing an issue with Wat, but somehow shied away when he saw Hermitage. Despite the smell, Wat moved closer to the monk and was suddenly interested in the conversation. The large man followed at a not very discrete distance.

'So you say there's to be some examination of events?'

'That's right,' Hermitage replied. 'Absolutely fascinating. I've never been engaged in one myself, but I will be most interested to see the King's man in action, as it were. To be appointed King's Investigator must mean he has the most impressive intellect.' Hermitage was trying to convince himself as much as Wat.

'But what's he going to be examining?' Wat raised pertinent questions, while still looking everywhere but at Hermitage.

'The circumstances of Ambrosius's death,' Hermitage was positively excited.

'Good idea.'

'There might be evil.'

'What? About sand in shoes?'

'Well, I don't know exactly. I expect the King's Investigator will unearth all the details. I must say, I hadn't realised that this debate was of such importance.'

'Great importance to someone,' Wat said lightly, although his brow had creased. 'So what are your plans now, Brother?'

'Oh, I must return to the Bishop's house at Prime and attend upon the Investigator. It will be an honour to accompany him back to the monastery.' He wasn't really sure about this, but Simon had been appointed by a figure of authority and that was that. Even if the figure of authority was casting shadows of doubt across Hermitage's normally crystal clear view of the world. A view entirely black and white, but nonetheless crystal clear.

'I see. And where do you stay until then?'

'Oh, I shall find the monastic lodgings. They must be around here somewhere.' Hermitage cast his gaze up and down the street as if there would be a sign.

'I shan't hear of such a thing.' Wat said, in a rather loud and declamatory style. 'I too will be leaving Lincoln at dawn, and as we travelled here together we could leave together. You must share my lodgings, and then I can accompany you part way in the morning.'

'My son, my son, you shame me with your generosity and you restore my faith in the fundamental goodness of the human spirit,' Hermitage beamed.

Wat rolled his eyes.

The large fellow, who was still close by harrumphed. Hermitage thought it most rude, listening to other peoples' conversations.

'But, my son, why would you want to return with me? You have only just arrived in the city yourself? Is your business done so quickly?'

'It usually is,' Wat was much quieter now. 'I find that it's in my best interests to move on to the next opportunity as quickly as possible.'

'In fact,' Wat continued, 'it is a religious establishment that I am seeking next as I have heard that major building work is taking place.'

'Really?' Hermitage was always interested to talk of the religious world.

'Yes.' Wat went on. 'The last group I was speaking to said that a search had gone out for craftsmen of the highest standard to make themselves known for a significant body of work. Doubtless some noble wanting the world turned around because it faces the wrong way.'

'Weren't they going themselves?'

'Them?' Wat said with some shock in his voice. 'No, no. They're more journeymen than craftsmen. The new place sounds interesting, though. Wherever there are craftsmen, working folk and nobles gathered together I find commissions for new works. If I take orders early, then by the time the building is complete I can deliver tapestries to personal designs to add that individual finishing touch.' Wat sounded like he was trying to sell Hermit-

78

age some tapestry.

'Well, of course I am most gratified that we shall share company a little longer. What is the establishment you seek?'

'It's a monastery,' said Wat, 'in a place called De'Ath's Dingle, do you know it?'

Hermitage was knocked back.

'I do, my son, I do. And I can go further than give you excellent directions to it as I am travelling there myself.'

'Oh, marvellous,' said Wat, although he didn't sound like it was marvellous.

'But I am afraid you have been misinformed.'

'Oh?' said Wat in clear disappointment. 'What makes you say that?'

'De'Ath's Dingle is the very monastery I have come from. The place of the debate and poor Ambrosius's death. I have been there for some months and can assure you that there is no development taking place. Indeed, the monastery is one of the most austere I have ever visited. Its Abbot is one of the most austere parts of it and he wouldn't sanction improvements of any sort. He's more likely to have any comfortable parts knocked down.'

'That's very odd. The workmen were clear about the name. It's not the sort of thing you get wrong, not in my line.'

Hermitage raised an eyebrow.

'It's always important to keep the clients in the right order,' Wat explained with a wink. 'Doesn't do to turn up at the door of the nobleman with a tapestry showing scenes of our Lord curing the blind. Or at the monastery step with a, erm, hunting scene, shall we say.'

'I can see that,' Hermitage said, nodding. He took the point.

'Perhaps there is somewhere else in the vicinity that goes by the same name, a chapel or a church perhaps?'

Hermitage thought hard.

'It is possible, I suppose, I haven't travelled outside the walls of the monastery until now.'

'That could be it then,' said Wat. 'I shall confirm the place later. In the meantime my business is done and we can retire to my lodgings for some food and a good night's rest.'

'Perhaps I might even press upon your hospitality for some fresh clean water. Just between you and I,' at this point Hermitage leant conspiratorially towards Wat, who shied away, 'I do believe my habit is becoming unsavoury.'

✦   ✦   ✦

When Hermitage saw Wat's lodgings, he began to suspect that he was more than a simple and humble weaver. The man had said they could share, which usually meant a portion of floor, or at very best a corner of a straw pallet.

When Wat led him into the large building, for building it was, Hermitage thought that they must have more business to conduct before moving on to the lodgings in the shacks beyond the Newport Arch. They were greeted as if Wat was a long-lost member of the family.

'Ah, how wonderful to see you again, sir,' said a well-dressed man who greeted Wat with a handshake and immediately took his bag. He handed this to a small boy, who, to Hermitage's mind, could not possibly afford the clothes he stood up in if he were a working child. 'I trust you had a good journey.'

The man led them through an entrance hall which made the Bishop's House look like a woodshed, and into a room which had tables and chairs and even books just lying about with no sign of the librarian to guard them.

'Oh good enough, Barns, good enough, thank you.'

Hermitage was perplexed by both the place and what was going on around him.

'This is Brother Hermitage,' said Wat to the man called Barns, who acted as if having a dirty, smelly monk in his nice house was the most normal thing in the world. 'He'll need a room with facilities, and I think we'd be ready to eat.'

'Of course, sir. I'll put him in the Augustus room and send a boy straight up. Welcome to The Hill Top Lincoln, Brother Hermitage.'

Hermitage gaped.

'The very best lodgings in the country, sir, and every one on top of a hill. Away from all the filth and the people who wallow in it.'

It sounded like some sort of slogan. Hermitage didn't think much of it.

'And I think he'll need a new habit, this one has suffered some misfortune along the way.'

'Indeed, sir,' said Barns in clear agreement. 'I shall send a boy out immediately.'

How many boys did this man have?

Wat made to move off. 'I'm in the usual room?'

'All ready for you, just as you like it.'

'Excellent, oh, and Barns?'

'Sir?'

'I'm not available should there be any, erm, visitors.'

'Of course, sir.'

'Right Hermitage, see you back here in about an hour then. Make yourself at home.'

As they were parting for the night, after a long dinner of fine lamb, followed by many strong drinks, Wat came close to Hermitage and spoke in a low voice. 'You are sure that going back is a good idea? Can't the Investi-what not deal with it?'

'Of course I must go back. It is at the Bishop's command. Well, his man's command. I must render what assistance I can to the investigation.'

'Even though this Athan was making accusations against you?'

'A natural reaction.'

'And your Abbot sent you out on the road?'

'Quite understandable.'

THE HERETICS OF DE'ATH

'Where you were attacked?'

'A coincidence.'

'And there's already one dead monk.'

'These things happen.'

'Please yourself, but on your own head be it.' Wat said in a very serious tone with an unnecessary emphasis on 'head'.

As Hermitage settled down for sleep in a bed far more comfortable than he deserved, his stomach began a long, one-sided conversation, enumerating all its complaints. First, King Harold was now involved in this business, whatever it was, and his Investigator would be dealing with it. This was bound to put Hermitage in just the sort of situation his stomach hated most; people be accusing him of things, asking him questions and generally getting very excited. Second, he was out of his routine: he hadn't followed the daily orders for some time now and that was always unsettling. Finally he had eaten and drunk too much. His stomach made it quite clear this was going to be a long night, so Hermitage had better stay awake and pay attention.

Caput VII

Day Four Prime

HE NEXT DAWN WAS COLD AND REFRESHING. After the warmth and comfort of the Hill Top, Hermitage felt he had fallen through the ice of a lake. This new habit was a garment of marvellous quality, far better than his old one, which the Hill Top had burned for some reason. It still did little to keep out the freeze.

Wat waited while Hermitage fetched the King's Investigator. De'Ath's Dingle was on the way back to the tapestry workshop, so the journey would not be wasted when he found no building work and no craftsmen.

At the Bishop's House Hermitage found Simon pacing up and down in a very impatient manner.

'Greetings, Brother,' the young monk said and offered a bow.

'Where have you been?' was the irritated reply. 'It is long past dawn and the King's Investigator is a busy man.'

Hermitage thought this was a bit rich after he'd helped the man last night. 'Ah,' was all he could say. The man had only been appointed last night – how could he be busy already? His short days away from the monastic discipline, combined with the luxury of the Hill Top, had affected Hermitage. The behaviour of this churchman of new-found importance somehow rankled with him.

'Well, come, come, let us be off. I must attend to this matter at De'Ath's Dingle and return to the Bishop's service forthwith.' Brother Simon's fussiness was tangible.

After a short walk they drew up to the end of Bailgate. Hermitage peeled off and made for the door of the Hill Top.

'Where are you going?' the King's Investigator barked.

Hermitage paused. 'We are fortunate to have a travelling companion with us for our journey and he is staying here,' he explained, gesturing a hand towards the lodgings.

'I don't think we can have anything to do with anyone staying there, Brother.' Simon was shocked. He fidgeted on the spot and wrung his hands.

'Oh, it's not too bad,' Hermitage responded. 'I stayed there myself last night. I'm ashamed to say it was very comfortable.'

'Good Lord,' Brother Simon said, put out by this piece of news.

Hermitage frowned. He had probably come across as terribly ostentatious.

'It's actually quite pleasant,' he tried to sound humble. 'Far too good for a man of devotion, of course, but Mr Wat...'

Simon didn't seem to be listening. 'Quite pleasant?' he said, rather nonplussed. He looked Hermitage up and down, took a step forward and ran a fold of Hermitage's brand new habit between thumb and finger.

'Good Lord,' he said again.

Hermitage was embarrassed by his raiment. It was better than any habit he'd ever seen before. Better than most clothes he'd ever seen before.

'Oh, this old thing,' he said dismissively.

Simon's eyebrows shot into his hairline and his whole demeanour underwent a miraculous change. He grinned widely, which Hermitage found rather disturbing.

'Of course, we must wait for your friend,' Simon said, whining now with sycophancy, 'absolutely no trouble at all.'

Hermitage thought Simon gave him a short bow. He skipped across to the building and returned with Wat in his wake.

'Wat, this is the King's Investigator, Brother Simon,' Hermitage said brightly.

Wat frowned and grimaced at the rising sun, holding his

head in some pain. 'This is very early. Brother Simon? The King's Investigator, eh?' He stumbled over the title.

'It's fascinating, isn't it?' said Hermitage. 'Brother Simon is to look into the death of Brother Ambrosius.'

'Really,' said Wat, in rather over-done interest.

'Yes. I can tell him all about it as we travel.'

For the next two hours, which took the party well beyond the bounds of the town, down the hill and a good way along their journey, Hermitage explained the circumstances of the death of Brother Ambrosius. He described the background to the Conclave, the nature of the proposition Ambrosius had been supporting and, in a considerable amount of almost entirely unnecessary detail, the points where the argument had failed on both theological and linguistic grounds.

Brother Simon seemed a bit distracted – rather odd given that he was the Investigator. He was probably taking it all in and would have some piercing questions later. The shadow of doubt waved at Hermitage again, but he never really knew what to do with doubt, so it soon wandered off.

✦   ✦   ✦

At the monastery in De'Ath's Dingle, preparations fit for the passage of Brother Ambrosius into the hands of the Lord were made. He was put in the meat store.

Some Brothers expressed genuine concern over this, for well-argued reasons.

Firstly it did not seem sensible to mix the monastery victuals with the decaying dead. Some ill humour might leap from the one to the other, and there would be plague or ague.

Secondly, it was not a fitting end for one of Ambrosius's erudition and learning. He should be buried with all due ceremony and respect. Yes, the Lord would be waiting to take him – but He could hardly be expected to do so if the dear departed were accompanied by departed deer.

Thirdly, it was pointed out that Brother Jeremy, the monastery's butcher, was a fellow of remarkable speed in his work but of equally remarkable poor sight. It was some time since he had lost a finger, but there was no guarantee he would differentiate a Brother from a boar. He might serve something wholly unsuitable, not to say sinful.

Athan listened to the case carefully and then told the complaining Brothers to shut up and get out. A couple of the less cowed took it upon themselves to sneak into the store and lay a cover over the corpse, weighed down with large stones. By this means they felt that they could at least have some confidence in their dinner.

◆　　◆　　◆

The undisturbed rest of Brother Ambrosius was short lived. Hardly had his corpse had time to settle before its cover was removed. A cowled head peered over the face, and at least had the decency to cough a bit at the smell. Moving down the old man's body, poking here and there for some hideously personal reason, the cowl tutted and hummed as it considered.

By the time it reached the feet it seemed either satisfied or frustrated. The cover was thrown over once more. With further grumbling noises at the inconsiderate nature of the dead, the cowl made to leave the meat store.

'Who the hell are you?' Brother Jeremy demanded, detecting a shape move about in a room where there should be no movement. He had only come to get a haunch of something for tomorrow's lunch. The haunches didn't generally try to get away.

'Just checking something,' the cowl answered.

'It's a meat store. What is there to check?'

'I needed to find something out.'

'By sneaking around in a meat store? There's nothing to find out in here you don't know already.'

Brother Jeremy was a large man. Whenever he served a meal,

the chances were he'd made two and eaten one himself. Anyone who knew Jeremy reasonably well also grew large on his benefi-cence, the butcher considering the meat store to be his own per-sonal larder. He was a generous man, but he didn't like people creeping about his larder, taking the food out of his mouth. He also carried a wide selection of knives, one of which he now drew from his belt.

'Now, now,' the cowl said, 'no need for any trouble. I was just checking on Brother Ambrosius.'

'Well, he's not in here.'

'He is.'

'No, he isn't.'

'Yes, he is.'

'Where is he then?'

'Over there.'

Jeremy squinted hard in the direction of the talking shape.

'Here, let me show you.' The cowled figure stepped forward and took Jeremy carefully by the knife hand. He led him over to the covered corpse and revealed it once more.

Jeremy squinted again.

'Bloody hell. Who put that there? Was it that Brother Snod? I tell you, one more of his so-called jokes and I'll cut the other one off.'

'Nothing like that. It seems Brother Ambrosius has died.'

'I should think so, looking like that. What did they bring him in here for? I can't serve that, it's not allowed. Well, not un-less there's exceptional circumstances. The guild would have my badge.'

At the word 'guild' the cowl looked up and took a step for-ward, holding out its hand for shaking.

Jeremy peered hard and considered carefully before holding out his hand in response.

The shake was considered and careful.

'Ah,' Jeremy nodded.

'Indeed,' the cowl responded.

'So what do you want to know, Brother?' Jeremy asked.

'I think I've got all I need.'

'You don't want much from this place, I tell you.'

'Really?'

'Oh God, yes. They're all nuts as squirrels as far as I can tell.'

'But you're part of the community.'

'Certainly not.' Jeremy was clearly offended. 'I only come here to do the butchering.'

'You are dressed as a monk.'

'I know. They call me Brother Jeremy, make me wear this thing and know perfectly well I'm not a monk.'

'Why would they do that?'

''Cos they're stupid. And mad.'

'How strange.'

'Yeah, and strange.'

'Perhaps they're very devout and don't want to deal with any outsiders. I have heard of establishments like that.'

'Devout?' Jeremy found this extremely funny, 'This lot, devout? You make me laugh, you do. You should see what they get up to when the sun goes down.'

'Should I?'

'No, you shouldn't. It's horrible. It's every sort of horrible you can think of. And in a monastery. That's why I always serve cold dinner in the winter. I'm not staying here after dark.'

'So you think if the church authorities knew what they were up to there might be trouble?'

'I doubt it.'

'But you said?'

'Of course. But church authorities are even worse, aren't they? Everyone knows that.'

The cowled head nodded in reluctant agreement.

'What is it you want to know about Ambrosius, anyway? Good chap that. He knew how to eat.'

'Just wanted to check he's dead.'

'Well, he's not moving much, is he? How did he die?'

'That was what I wanted to find out.'

'And?'

'Nothing obvious.'

'Mind you, he was fifty or so. And he could eat.'

'I suppose so.'

'What they bring him in here for?' Jeremy repeated, clearly flustered by the slab of monk. 'It's not decent.'

'I think they want to find out what happened. He was in the middle of a debate when he died.'

'Oh yes, I'd heard about that. Better ask Hermitage then.'

'Really?' The cowl was very interested in this.

'Yeah, he's the one who does debates. And reading and writing and stuff.'

'Another suspicious character, eh?'

'Mad as March that one. Nice enough bloke, but off with the clouds most of the time.'

'And the Abbot and Prior.'

Despite his disconnection from the religious community Jeremy crossed himself vigorously. He became very serious.

'Never seen the Abbot. Heard about him though. Put the fear of God up God he could. Monks called to see him tend not to get seen again.'

'I see. And the Prior.'

'Shit.'

'What?' The cowl thought Jeremy had dropped his knife or something.

'That's what he is, pure and simple. Don't touch it, smell it or take it home. It'll get all over you and you'll never get the smell out. Best to leave it where it is and walk away.'

'Nasty piece.'

'I've seen nastier, but I am a butcher. He's even after a monastery of his own I hear. God knows who he'd get to join that one.

He'd have 'em all flogged to death within a week.'

'So if there were to be some changes here?'

'They'd only be for the better. You'd have to get rid of those two though. Probably permanently. I don't think they'd even die like normal people.'

'Get them out of the way then.'

'It would have to be something pretty damn impressive.'

'You give me plenty to think about, Brother.' The cowled figure nodded appreciatively and shook the hand again. 'It is time I was about my business.'

Brother Jeremy nodded in return and returned the shake. 'And, of course, if you have any butchering needs.'

'You shall be the first,' the figure responded with the correct form of words and was gone.

◆   ◆   ◆

The examination of events leading up to Ambrosius's arrival in the meat store was continuous on the road from Lincoln and Hermitage was having a marvellous time with a captive audience. This audience was now as responsive as Ambrosius's corpse, having stopped paying attention several miles ago.

At the start there was the occasional 'ah, yes' and 'I see', which only encouraged Hermitage to expound whatever topic he was on at even more length. After a while these changed to 'yes, I know' and 'yes, you already said that'. As such comments didn't really take the argument in any direction, Hermitage ignored them.

The responses came exclusively from Wat. Brother Simon, the King's Investigator, maintained a masterful silence. Hermitage reasoned that King's Investigators were very important people and listening to his ramblings was the sort of thing they probably had people for. Nicodemus must know how clever Simon was. Surely.

There were occasions, early in their journey, when Simon

made some observations on Hermitage's biblical interpretations. The young monk was puzzled as these were wildly inaccurate, if not actually blasphemous. He soon realised he was being tested. He responded with the accurate doctrine and Simon was satisfied. He simply harrumphed and said no more.

'So, Brother,' Simon butted in at one point, as if he hadn't been listening to a word Hermitage was saying. 'This, erm, death then?'

'Yes, Brother?'

'A straightforward enough event, I imagine.'

'I believe so. As I was saying some time ago, Ambrosius simply sat down and the next I knew he was dead.'

'No, erm, evil then?'

'Not that I saw. I did wonder at Nicodemus's conclusions.'

'Excellent. Excellent.'

Wat was frowning heavily at him, but no one noticed.

'Mind you,' Hermitage added.

'Mind you what?' Simon said rather quickly.

'There are few who know the workings of evil.'

'Apart from Father Elick,' Simon responded.

'Oh yes,' Hermitage said, crossing himself, 'apart from Father Elick, of course.'

Even in a place as severe as De'Ath's Dingle the name of Father Elick, the Pope's Inquisitor of Demons, was used to frighten the novices.

'But you will be investigating the death, so we'll find out,' Hermitage went on, anxious to change the subject.

'I'll be what?' Simon snapped.

'Investigating.'

'Oh, that. Yes. I will, won't I?'

There was a long pause.

'Investigating,' the Investigator said, as if trying out the word.

'Isn't it fascinating?' Hermitage said, fascinated.

'Aha, yes, it is indeed.' Simon thought deeply. 'I will consider what my first step shall be.' He looked sideways at Hermitage.

'Well, I hope you'll forgive my presumption, Brother, but I think the examination of the body itself will be most illuminating.'

'The what?' Simon looked horrified.

Hermitage had obviously chosen the wrong step. He knew nothing of investigation and would have to leave it to the expert. He was Hermitage, though, and he couldn't leave anything alone.

'Well,' he said. 'If any evil was done it would have left its mark somewhere on poor Ambrosius. In my fleeting sight of him I could see no indication of foul play.'

'Foul play.' Simon contemplated the expression. 'Such as?'

Hermitage considered this a very pertinent question.

'There were certainly no visible injuries, no wounds, no sign of a struggle of any sort. In fact the elderly man was simply resting in his seat. As we left he fell from the chair, but that was all.'

'Fell from the chair, eh?' Simon nodded knowingly.

'But he was already dead,' Hermitage reassured him.

'Interesting.'

Hermitage found that this train of thought, about who did what to whom and when was rather satisfying. 'Brother, your experience far exceeds that of any and so I would consider it a great honour if I could observe you in your work?'

'I shall consider it. Examine the body, eh?'

'I am sorry, Brother,' Hermitage said, 'I know nothing of investigation or the techniques used, so you must forgive my presumption.'

'No, no,' Simon said brightly, 'you carry on, Brother. It will be illuminating to hear your thoughts on the matter. Unencumbered as they are by my extensive experience. Perhaps the ideas of the innocent will unearth some feature which the expert would take for granted. I may be able to offer you some instruction and guidance as well.'

Wat succumbed to a fit of coughing at this point and Brother Simon ignored him, quite hard.

'It would be an honour.' Hermitage was as happy as a Cardinal in a convent. 'As I say, I would examine the body. There are usually signs of an unnatural death, missing limbs, parts of heads damaged, that sort of thing. If there really is nothing like that, as I suspect, then we might conclude that the death was natural.'

'You may proceed,' said Simon.

'Next I would look at the place of the death and anyone who might have been there at the time.'

'Yes, good.'

'But that of course was mainly me. Apparently.' This did give Hermitage some pause for thought. 'Although I maintain that Brothers James and Francis were there with me throughout.'

'Aha,' Simon said with great interest.

Wat coughed again.

'And what would the place of the death tell you, Brother?'

Hermitage thought this was marvellous. It was the most fun he'd had since he'd cared for Brother Mark in the infirmary. That poor man suffered an accident in the kitchen and had been laid up, unable to speak or move for weeks. Hermitage kept him company every single day and covered a wide variety of topics. Nobody had seen Brother Mark after he recovered the use of his legs.

'Well,' Hermitage went on, 'if there was any evil, there might be some trace of it left.'

'Such as?' Simon really was giving Hermitage the opportunity to test himself.

'Perhaps a weapon, or even an indication that there had been something there. Footprints, disturbed furniture. All very routine to you, I imagine.'

'Absolutely.'

Wat really seemed to be suffering from some sort of coughing disorder. It was all he could do to stay upright. His face was flushed and he had both hands over his face.

'Are you all right, my son?' Hermitage asked.

'Oh, yes,' Wat said through gasps of breath. 'Er, this is where we turn off.'

A further short walk in relative silence as Hermitage considered his return brought them to the very gates of De'Ath's Dingle. As usual, they were firmly shut. Off to the right, on a piece of clear ground, a number of tents had been erected which Hermitage stared at. They had not been there when he left.

'Ah,' said Wat, 'builders.'

'Really?' Hermitage asked. 'How can you tell?'

'Prime customers,' Wat whispered. 'There are encampments like this all over the country. Wherever there's work to be done and money to be made. Those doing the work live in virtual squalor in the mud. Those doing the money making are miles away, paying as little as they can get away with to keep their workforce alive. For as long as is necessary anyway.'

The secular world was another country to Hermitage and he was always interested to hear how it worked. Another country, possibly on the moon. His 'most interested' expression took camp on his face – the one that opened his eyes, moved his face forward and demanded further discussion.

Wat took a step backwards. 'They're usually in the middle of nowhere. With nothing to do but work and nothing to entertain one another but one another, they sometimes treat themselves to a bit of, erm, decoration,' Wat explained. 'Mind you, this one should be above average, being next to a monastery and all.'

'I don't know where it's come from or what it's doing.' Hermitage said. 'I didn't believe you when you mentioned De'Ath's Dingle, but you were obviously right.' Hermitage desperately wanted to know more about working men and their habits.

'I shouldn't worry about it,' Wat said. 'It's clearly a very new camp. There's hardly any filth yet and not a single whore.' He shrugged at Hermitage's offended look.

Wat slung his pack from his shoulder and headed off for the tents.

'I'll catch you up,' he waved to Hermitage, who was disappointed to see him go. This weaver didn't wince whenever Hermitage opened his mouth and on occasion seemed positively interested. That was a very rare experience. Wat also had knowledge which Hermitage craved. He craved knowledge about everything, but if it was a new area for him he got positively frisky.

Hermitage reluctantly turned away to see Simon rapping firmly on the gate of the monastery.

'Admit the King's Investigator,' the man boomed as if the fabric of the wood would give way before his eminence.

The young and the old monk waited a reasonable time to allow someone to reach the door from his distant cell, but it remained closed.

Simon looked unhappy at this and scanned about for a solution.

'You there,' he called to Hermitage, waving a hand in his direction.

Hermitage looked around and confirmed the call was aimed at him. He wondered why Simon had not used his name.

'Find a piece of wood or something to knock on the door.'

Hermitage was too busy considering the rather rude manner in which he was being addressed to hunt for timber.

'Oh, for goodness sake,' Simon huffed in frustration and looked around. Finding a fallen tree limb some few steps away, the investigator made an attempt to lift it but gave up after one desultory heave. Moving down the scale he eventually lighted upon a stout stick which he could manage. It was still fairly substantial and should make an impact on the door. He made his way to the gate, staggering slightly under the modest weight of his door knocker. Steadying himself on spread legs he hoisted the wood to shoulder height then swung it forward to strike a mighty and noisy blow against the timber.

Just as he did so, the doorman, having limped to his post following Athan's recent review of his poor door opening performance, finally got the gate open. He was greeted by the rapidly advancing end of a piece of tree.

Given his dysfunctional legs, moving out of the way was never going to be an option. The poor man received Simon's knock on the door full in the temple and dropped to the ground like a pigeon under a peasant's pile driver.

'Oh, Lord,' said Hermitage and ran forward to help the fallen man.

'Idiot,' said Simon, and it wasn't quite clear who he was talking to. In any event it didn't matter as the King's Investigator simply threw his log away, stepped over the prone man and entered the monastery of De'Ath's Dingle. He looked around for someone of a suitable rank to receive him.

The only person who could be wandering the enclosure with anything like liberty was Athan. Sure enough, a few moments later he imposed himself upon the situation.

'What?' he barked at the sight of a well battered and prostrate doorkeeper being tended by the idiot Hermitage.

'Ah,' a voice called to his right and he turned to see the weedlike figure of Simon looking around.

'I am the King's Investigator,' the newly arrived authority announced. He had his nose in the air, but seemed to be watching Athan rather warily.

Athan was not accustomed to people speaking to him in that manner. He frowned at the title.

'I am Brother Athan. The Prior,' he said bluntly.

'Excellent,' said Simon, trying to hide a slight intake of breath at the mention of the name, 'take me to your Abbot.'

'Really?' Athan enquired in genuine surprise.

'Of course. I am on the Bishop's business.'

Recognition crossed Athan's face. He muttered a curse under his breath.

The fallen gatekeeper was being helped back to his feet by Hermitage although he was bleeding profusely and staggering in a daze. His unfocused eyes latched on to the figure of Simon and he took a deep, if stuttering breath.

He addressed the King's Investigator with what dignity he had left. 'You stupid bastard,' he said, before he collapsed again into Hermitage's arms.

Simon shook his head in puzzlement at this man's strange behaviour, but his unconscious form was of no interest. He turned back to Athan.

'Your Abbot, Brother?' he asked pointedly.

'Indeed, Brother,' Athan said in his wheedling tone, which didn't wheedle much. 'I imagine you are here to consider the matter of Brother Ambrosius?'

'I think that is a matter for my determination.'

'Of course, of course, I have received word from Lincoln to expect a senior figure for just this purpose. Do I have the honour of addressing him?' Athan even bowed his head slightly which made Hermitage gape. The man was unrecognisable. And what did he mean he'd received word? Hermitage was bringing the word. He'd come straight back this time as well.

Simon's questing nose rose even higher.

'You do,' he said with a rising tone of majesty, which sounded as if he was about to sneeze.

'Then I am charged to give all assistance necessary. Our Abbot is, erm, in retreat at present. He is of a reclusive persuasion and so perhaps we will meet him at a later stage. In any event I am his authority in this place and so I am at your disposal.' Athan gave the overwhelming impression this was very hard work. He would probably take it out on someone later.

'If I could show you to the Bishop's quarters?' Athan offered with an obsequious gesture.

Simon condescended magnificently.

'Oh, and Hermitage,' Athan called out to the young man who was staunching the gatekeeper's bleeding with the hem of his nice new habit, 'I want to see you.'

The nervous feeling which lived in Hermitage's stomach whenever he was near Athan, but which had been entirely dissipated by the necessity of action, now returned with a vengeance and headed straight for his bowels.

◆　　◆　　◆

In many monasteries the accommodations of the Bishop's quarters were places of luxury. Enormous luxury when compared to the accommodations of many monasteries. In the case of De'Ath's Dingle, of course, all was not as other monasteries. In fact, pretty much nothing about it was as other monasteries.

The only reason the Bishop's quarters were so named was you could probably only get a quarter of a Bishop into them. Simon was clearly disappointed at the appointments, but as he was the physical antithesis of a Bishop, being three stone underweight rather than ten over, at least he could get in the room.

'I will leave you here to make yourself comfortable, Brother,' the word soured in Athan's mouth, 'while I attend to Brother Hermitage. I shall return momentarily.' He left before Simon could ask for anything.

Outside the room Brother Hermitage was properly waiting. He knew that keeping his head down and hoping Athan would go away was as pointless as putting wheels on a chicken, as brother Yewo always said. Not that it stopped him trying. Better to get it over with straight away, whatever 'it' might be. He still had some fresh blood on the bottom of his habit and was feeling nervous and expectant. Athan looked at him as if he might be infectious.

'I've made Thomas as comfortable as possible although I do think he needs to rest,' the young monk said.

'Who?'

'Brother Thomas? The gatekeeper?'

'Oh him.' Athan shook his head in puzzlement at why they were talking about the gatekeeper. He stepped forward, put an arm around Hermitage's shoulder and steered him away from the door to Simon's chamber.

Hermitage prepared himself for the punch on the head for which arm holding was the usual precursor, but it didn't come. This made him even more nervous.

'You took your time getting to Lincoln, Brother,' Athan said as he escorted Hermitage through the pointlessly winding corridors of the monastery.

'Yes, I, er, had some difficulty locating the right road.' He didn't want to mention the attack even though Wat thought it significant. He also wanted to keep the existence of Wat a secret from Athan. He couldn't think why, it just seemed prudent. Perhaps being late was the only reason for whatever punishment was on its way, in which case why make things worse by confusing Athan with information or facts. They always made him cross.

'But you made it eventually.'

This was strangely idle conversation for Athan: he must be brewing up to something.

'And you passed the message to the Bishop?' Athan was as amiable as he could be. Which wasn't very amiable at all.

'Well,' Hermitage feared that this was the point for some physical interaction with the elder Brother, 'to the Bishop's man actually, Nicodemus, he seemed most insistent. He reported that the Bishop had instructed him directly to take the information which I was...'

'Yes, yes, I'm sure.' Athan seemed entirely disinterested in this point. Which was odd considering it was he who sent the message with Hermitage in the first place.

'And you brought back the King's – what did he say?' Athan asked.

'Investigator.'

'Yes. Investigator, an important position,' Athan commented although it was clear he was unfamiliar with the term.

It didn't do to correct or inform Athan. Not unless invited and only then from a distance.

'I imagine so, although I must confess I didn't know the King had one.' Hermitage was genuinely interested. He wanted to know more about this investigation business. It sounded just the sort of thing for him.

'Oh, yes,' said Athan as if this were common knowledge among more senior members of the Church.

Hermitage was puzzled again. If Athan didn't know what the word was, how did he know whether it was a real position or not? He chastised himself for this thinking. Quibbling like this was what kept getting him into trouble.

By this time they were in the lower parts of the monastery, passing along corridors seldom trod. Hermitage examined the walls, noticing they appeared older than the main buildings. Most unusually the stones were tightly laid with neat and even mortar. Perhaps the monastery had been put on top of some proper building.

He pondered this, only coming back to himself when he realised they had stopped walking and Athan had stopped talking. They were standing outside a lone and unused cell which still had its solid oak door in place. The Abbot had all cell doors removed as they were encouragements to privacy. Everyone knew what went on when there was privacy.

'Well, Hermitage,' said Athan with some finality.

'Brother?' Hermitage asked, not knowing what was expected of him.

He had no more clue after Athan had pushed him hard in the back and sent him sprawling into the dark and dank cell, ventilated only by a small outlet high in the wall.

Nor did enlightenment come as Athan slammed the door

closed as he left.

'Brother?' Hermitage's plaintive tones muffled their way out.

In the top of the oak a small opening appeared and Athan's face poked into the gloom. Hermitage rose to face it.

'What?' Athan snapped.

'What's happening?'

'What's happening?'

'Yes, what's happening?' Hermitage couldn't have missed something so obvious that would lead to him being locked in an unused cell surely. He knew he could be pretty oblivious to normal human behaviour a lot of the time, but this seemed extreme.

'Oh, I see the problem,' said Athan, as if some realisation had suddenly come upon him.

'You do?'

'Yes, of course,' Athan replied, 'I can see where you've gone wrong.' The tone was so friendly that for a moment Hermitage believed that this was all going to be explained away in a trice.

'Really?'

'Absolutely,' Athan said in a friendly tone. 'You're an idiot.'

Hermitage's heart sank back to where it had come from. 'So you tell me, Brother.'

'I tell you because it's true. You had your chance to escape yet you came back. I've helped you as much as I can, Hermitage, but now that the King's Unvestingbator is here I can do no more.'

So Athan really didn't know what an Investigator was.

'I don't understand,' Hermitage said, not understanding.

'Of course you don't. You wouldn't understand a rock. How you managed to murder Ambrosius is beyond me.'

To say Hermitage was shocked at this would be inadequate in every conceivable way. All thoughts that had been in his head rapidly left for somewhere safer. His stomach leapt up his windpipe and tried to get out through his nose. Meanwhile his legs simply refused to hold him up. From the ground where he now lay he discovered that his voice had also taken flight to some place where it could hide until things got better.

'I killed Ambrosius?' he croaked.

'Save your confession for the King's thingy,' Athan said, slammed the little opening shut, locked the door and walked noisily away although his voice drifted back.

'Once we've got that out of the way, we can have the execution and get things back to normal.'

Hermitage's stomach did now find its exit and his expensive habit began its long journey back to normal.

✦ ✦ ✦

Outside the monastery, a furtive figure poked tentatively at the gate, which swung gently open before him. The figure was dressed for furtive. Dark cloak and leggings, dark boots and even a monk-like cowl shielding most of his face. A real monk's cowl would have been far cheaper and more tatty than this piece of bespoke head wear.

The figure looked backwards over both his shoulders and then leaned cautiously into the monastery proper. If he was trying to look furtive, he was having a very good day.

'Oh, what do you want?' the gatekeeper wailed at an unwelcome visitor.

The figure looked with surprise at the gatekeeper who was lying on the ground outside his hovel of a gatehouse. He looked about a few more times and scampered over to the man. He squatted and whispered into the bandaged head.

'Really?' the gatekeeper responded. 'Help yourself.'

Maintaining his style, the figure slipped over the ground until he was standing against the wall of the main monastery block. From here he seemed to sidle his way along, all the while looking about to make sure he wasn't followed.

'Idiot,' the gatekeeper commented.

✦ ✦ ✦

The figure continued his passage round the building. As he came to the first open space he stopped at the edge of it, looking carefully about once more. This time he seemed to be taking in his surroundings. He examined the buildings and the spaces. He looked to the north, south, east and west. Once satisfied with his examination he moved on. This process was repeated for each building and space in the place. He was probably one of the only people to take any interest in the monastery of De'Ath's Dingle since it had been built. Considerably more interest than those who had done the building, for sure.

It took quite a time, but eventually he returned to the gatekeeper, giving the man a simple nod before slipping out of the gate again.

'Bloody idiot.'

Day Four After Compline

T THE BISHOP'S HOUSE IN LINCOLN, the latest arrival was not being made to wait in the hall. So welcome was this fellow, Nicodemus himself opened the door. He led his visitor straight through the inner sanctum and on into the Bishop's own chamber, where he poured wine into the largest goblet before the guest had even sat down. Coats and baggage had been dumped on the servant without a word, and humble Nicodemus stood waiting, so that he was not the first to sit.

'Bollocking awful journey,' the visitor said. He was a very large man and had squeezed himself into the Bishop's favourite chair despite several cracking noises. He belched as he took the wine without acknowledgement. 'What you're doing in this Godforsaken hole is beyond me.' The man sneezed into his hand and carefully examined the resulting mess before wiping it nonchalantly on the fine wool of the chair. Nicodemus winced.

'The new Church is our motivation, my Lord,' Nicodemus said.

'Of course, of course,' the fat man said, patently not listening.

'And the distance from other centres does have its advantages.' Nicodemus left the comment hanging in the air.

The Lord raised an eyebrow. 'Indeed it does, ha ha.' He quaffed the wine and held the goblet out with the simple expectation that it would be refilled. It was.

'Still a bloody awful journey. Do you know the road stops at Newark?' The man was surprised that the road had not been laid out before him.

'Some repairs are in order,' Nicodemus admitted.

'Repairs?' the man boomed into the room, 'it's beyond repair, man. The whole bloody country needs taking in by at least fifty miles. Bring everywhere closer together.' Travel was clearly a travail.

'If the journey to get here is a trial, then the journey to return is as difficult,' Nicodemus said, heavy with meaning.

'There is that, I suppose.' The large man seemed to ponder this point. He took a deep sigh as if his next statement would expand upon it.

It didn't. 'When do we eat?'

'Any time of your choosing, my Lord, unless you wish to dispense with business beforehand?' Nicodemus was hopeful.

'Never think well when I'm hungry,' the man said, patting his enormous stomach as if it were a dog. For one fleeting moment Nicodemus wondered if he did in fact have a dog in there. There was certainly room for quite a large one.

The Bishop's humble servant had intelligence on the new Earl of Northumbria, which for God's sake wasn't that far away. The man hadn't come from somewhere truly at the other end of the world, like Cornwall. He knew the Earl's eating habits were regular – he ate all the time – and so a huge feast had been prepared. He had been told that once the Earl sat down, he didn't move. For anything. The food would have to be brought to him, along with everything else he required. A lot of stuff would have to be taken away as well.

Special staff had been hired in for this visit. Staff with a single, very special property: a complete lack of pride.

One very relevant piece of information about the Earl was very hard to believe, looking at the lump which brolloped before him. The idea that this revolting heap could have fathered quite so many children was, quite frankly, revolting. Obviously the Earl had not been in this condition all his life, but he must have been working his way towards it for some considerable time.

You didn't end up like that overnight: it took years of dedication. What must the mothers of those children have been thinking? Presumably something along the lines of 'If I want to be still alive in the morning, I had better get on with this.'

The food now arrived, ferried in by a raft of servants – not all of whom had benefited from the same warnings as their master. One or two of them gagged as they entered the room, and coughed their way in and out. One young girl actually screamed when she saw what was in the chair.

'Aha,' laughed the Earl, 'you can send me that one later.'

Nicodemus knew that his standards were low, but even he drew the line somewhere. Mind you, with the girth of the Earl to be considered, any line would have to be pretty damn long.

The Earl's mind seemed suitably distracted by the display of food before him, enough to feed the entire workforce of the Church for a week. He began to tuck into joints of meat, bread, pickles and sauces, more wine, eggs, cheeses and fish, fine stews and soups, delicate sweetmeats and exotic fancies, stodgy puddings, fruit, nuts and creams – most of it pretty much at random, but all of it at great speed.

Nicodemus sat observing the nobleman before him for some time, until he judged that the rate of intake had slowed ever so slightly. The eggs were going down less rapidly. There was even an occasional pause for breath between fish and game. When the Earl finally let his hands rest on the arms of the chair, each one clutching a chicken leg, Nicodemus suspected this was because of simple exhaustion rather than the inability to consume more. It seemed the moment to discuss business.

'I believe we may be of service to your family then, my Lord,' Nicodemus proposed.

'Indeed,' the Earl said, simply continuing the conversation of an hour ago. 'Sons, eh? What can you do with them?'

Nicodemus didn't answer this. Neither desire nor opportunity for procreation ever bothered him.

'Got one obviously, the next Earl, he's all sorted, and got a few others who don't matter, but you never know how long you're going to live these days.'

Nicodemus's judgement was that it wouldn't be too long. His eldest son must be counting the days.

'Troublesome times we live in,' the Earl went on, 'the young Earl might come a cropper any day now.'

'Yes,' thought Nicodemus, 'you might fall on him.'

'And we've got to keep the family going, so younger ones need managing as well eh, eh?' The Earl spoke as if they were livestock.

'Of course,' Nicodemus agreed. He'd agree with anything.

'Got the youngest in the diplomatic service. Probably get killed somewhere or other, but hopefully not until the inheritance is safe. It's the middle one who's trouble.'

'Ah,' Nicodemus said in encouragement, 'this is where we come in.'

'That's it. This proposal of yours seems to fit the bill. Bishop of Peterborough told me about it.'

The Bishop of Peterborough and this man – now that was a pairing to creep into nightmares.

'Got to keep the young whelp in functioning order in case his brother pops it, but want him out of the way naturally.' The Earl said this as if death might be going just a bit too far. Only a bit, mind.

'Naturally,' Nicodemus nodded.

'Joining the Church the obvious choice, but not a very attractive proposition for young people these days. Even offered to buy him a Bishopric, but he wasn't having it. "Memorising Mass", he said. Wasn't having it.'

'Ah, the young,' Nicodemus commented sympathetically. It seemed something to say.

'Of course, if a son had said that to the old Earl he'd have flogged him to death. Lost two children that way. We've gone soft, that's the trouble these days. No discipline.' The Earl seemed in danger of wandering into some hideous reverie.

'So, our proposition?' Nicodemus pulled him back.

'Well, the young colt seemed to find some favour in it. I suppose I blame myself. The earlier generation was harsh but fair. I've gone the other way.'

Tales of the old Earl of Northumbria's 'harshness' were still used to frighten children. It was only a flamboyant festival of truly horrific discipline that had led to the old Earl being deposed and this lump installed in his place.

'And this is a real monastery, is it?' the Earl enquired, some doubt in his voice.

'Oh entirely, it's a whole new area of theological thinking.'

The Earl considered this for a moment. 'I should think it is. The size of the endowment required to secure a place.'

'A family place, of course. You will be free to avail yourself of the facilities for quiet prayer and contemplation.' Nicodemus managed to keep a straight face while saying this. If the Earl ever did anything quiet, Nicodemus didn't want to know about it.

'Yes.' The Earl lingered over the word and seemed to take considerable pleasure from it. 'And the premises?'

'One of our more remote communities, well off the beaten track.'

'Not the sort of place people are likely to pop out of, then.'

'Oh no, and of course extra arrangements can be made for special residents to ensure that they maintain their vigils within the bounds.'

'Excellent. At extra cost I presume.'

'Well, there would be...'

'Yes, I rather thought there would be.'

The Earl and Nicodemus fell into a contemplative silence for a few moments until Nicodemus started to get a bit twitchy that he still hadn't got a firm commitment.

'So your son will join us?'

'That's the expectation. He's been touring my southern estates, so he tells me. Getting drunk and fornicating away from home is more like it. All the people of Northumbria know him well and tend to close the doors when they see him coming.'

'A great character, I hear.'

'He certainly has, and he puts it about far too much. We've arranged to meet here. I'm on my way to a council in Warwick and he's on his way home. We'll examine this monastery of yours and if we like what we see then we can proceed.'

'You do understand that the site itself is still at the development stage?' Nicodemus didn't want to raise expectations too high.

'I understand that you can't steal all the stone from the Church at once, of course.' The Earl eyed a small bread roll that was within reach.

'My Lord!' Nicodemus expressed shock at the suggestion.

The Earl laughed with vigour and rocked backwards and forwards in his chair spraying crumbs and spittle from his gaping maw.

'I know it's not built yet and hopefully we won't need it for a year or two. I also know that you need my money to get on with it and I'm buying ... what did you call it?' The Earl actually looked at Nicodemus.

'An investment, my Lord.'

'Yes, investment. Bizarre idea if you ask me. I give you a considerable sum of money for something you haven't done yet. You then use the fact that I have given you money for nothing, for this investment, to persuade others that it must be a good idea. They give you their money for nothing as well. Meantime you still haven't actually done anything. When you get enough money for nothing you get some builders involved and actually get on with it.'

'I think that's a slightly harsh summary of the arrangement, my Lord,' Nicodemus protested, thinking it was actually quite accurate.

'But a true one, eh? And it's bloody genius. If I'd have thought of it myself I could be getting all the money for nothing instead of you.' The Earl laughed. At least Nicodemus hoped it was a laugh.

'But I will have to deliver, my Lord. Those like yourself who may be investing are people of high standing and worth. Should the time come for them to take possession of their property and I did not have it ready...' Nicodemus held his arms out. Further explanation was unnecessary.

'They would take possession of your body and divide it up between them, ha, ha, ha.' Another food distributing laugh erupted, and it was all Nicodemus could do to avoid being coated in breadcrumbs.

He contemplated this possible outcome and his mind wandered off again to ensure that all his escape routes were open and available. This moment of reverie distracted him from his surroundings and when he looked around, he saw that the Earl was sound asleep. Or dead. He checked: no, he wasn't dead. He couldn't die yet. All the plans would come to nothing. He could die later. Nicodemus crept from the room. All he now had to do was await the arrival of the son of Northumbria, who no doubt would be as awful as his father.

◆　　◆　　◆

In the far more humble surroundings of the De'Ath's Dingle building site, Wat was displaying his special wares to a gaggle of workmen. Their jaws were so slack they could have chewed the grass at their own feet.

'Bloody hell,' said one, 'how did you get her to do that?'

'What?' Wat was puzzled.

'That.' The builder pointed a stubby finger at one of the more fanciful images.

'What do you mean, get her to do it?'

The builder struggled to express the concept.

'It's a picture, right?'

'Right.'

'So it's a picture of these people doing that. And them animals, and all that equipment.'

'Berber, you idiot, it's not real.' A more sophisticated member of the audience slapped the man around the head. 'You don't think people stand there doing this while the man makes a tapestry of them. Ha ha, they'd get cramp.'

Wat now understood what he had been asked and simply shook his head in disbelief.

'You'll have to excuse Berber, he's an idiot.'

'A difficult birth,' Wat commented with some sympathy.

'No, no, it's nothing physical, he's just stupid.'

The man slapped Berber again, who seemed used to it. 'The man probably does a quick sketch first, before they all fall over, and then does the tapestry from the sketch.'

There was no point in engaging these people. They were obviously the advanced guard of the building team, sent ahead just to get the site ready and the tents up. Have to take what money they had and find out if it was worth waiting or not.

'So, anything of interest?' Wat asked. He was starting to doubt that these people would be able to afford him.

'I like that one,' said a large man from the back, reaching over to stab a finger on to a work which portrayed one of the ladies of the current court. A lady renowned for her beauty and refinement. In this depiction she was doing something very unrefined indeed.

'Excellent. Would you like to order one?'

The man studied the numbers Wat had chalked up on his slate. He was clearly getting nowhere, so Wat held up fingers.

'Can I have the four by nine,' the man said, after muttering numbers to himself.

'Certainly can. Framed?' Wat asked, hopefully.

'No, just roll it up.'

Damn, thought Wat, he made as much profit per frame as he did from the tapestries. He shrugged. It was clear the financial resources of this particular market would be very limited.

A couple of other men gave orders as well, so the trip was at least paying for itself.

'Here you are, Hodric, there's one for you.'

The mature man held up one tapestry from the bottom of the heap, which portrayed several figures engaged in what could only be described as debauchery. It was one of those special works that Wat kept in an inner bag in his sample case, and which he would always claim was a special commission. It had a huge mark up, though, so he usually put it in the sales pitch somewhere.

'Oh, nice,' said Hodric as he took the work and examined it carefully. 'I'll take one. Lovely to see something honest like this for a change, something without any bloody women in it.'

His orders totted up and the men wandering off, some of them clutching samples which they promised to return in a few minutes. Wat thought he would approach the apparent leader of the men to see what prospect there was of more business turning up.

'So,' he said.

'So,' said the chosen man.

'Wat.' He held out his hand.

'What what?' said the man, clearly not as bright as Wat had hoped.

'No, no, the name's Wat, Wat the Weaver.'

'Brough.' The man held out his hand to be shaken.

'Nice to meet you, Brough.'

'It's not weaving, though, is it?'

'What isn't?'

'What you do. I mean, Wat the Weaver sounds good and all,

that but weaving is cloth and stuff, it's not, erm,' he searched for a word which summed up Wat's product but couldn't come up with one. 'It's not cloth. What you do. You don't make cloth.'

'No. I don't make cloth, but weaving covers a multitude of sins.'

'And you make pictures of most of them.' The man laughed hard at his own joke. He laughed as if he was trying to cough up his toes, while Wat watched in some despair. When the man had recovered, he tried to get the conversation on track.

'So what's going on here then?' he asked. 'A repair job?'

'No, no,' said Brough, 'this is major work, this is. We're setting up camp, but there's dozens coming. Virtually taking the place down to the ground and re-building it as far as I can tell.'

That sounded hopeful.

'I was coming along with a monk from here who didn't seem to know anything about it?'

'Typical innit. Bloody Church. They never tell anyone what's going on, least of all the people who are going to be affected. I was there when they started to lay the foundations for the new Church extension. We all turned up right as rain, but no one had bothered to tell the priest who was living there at the time, had they?'

'Hadn't they?' Wat knew that engaging in conversations like this, mind-numbing though they were, often paid dividends in the long run.

'Course they hadn't. He was just planning a small lych-gate and we come along with the encampment for a hundred-foot high church tower, driving a cart and horses through his house and most of his neighbours as well. It's no good going on to him about the advantages of development is it? It's his living we're ploughing into the ground.'

'I can see that,' said Wat, running on automatic now.

'Not in my back yard,' he said.

'Did he?'

'Yep. And we said it's all right, mate, it won't be in your back yard. It'll be in the front as well and we're taking down your privy. Some people just don't want to move with the times.'

'Talking of moving, how many do you think you've got coming and when? Only I need to get back to the workshop to start replacing this lot, but it might be worth my while to wait.'

'Oh, probably will be. As I say it's dozens all told, but there should be about five or six here next week.' Brough paused at that moment, even though he appeared to be in mid-sentence. He took hold of Wat's elbow and moved him about six inches to one side. As he did so he looked around, obviously making sure that no one was within listening distance. He leant forward conspiratorially.

'I, er, might be able to do you a favour or two.' He held out his hand to be shaken again. Wat held back, he had been caught out by deals made on the shake of a hand. There was always some argument afterwards about who had shaken on what exactly. It was never what Wat delivered or at the price that had been agreed.

'No go on, shake,' Brough raised his eyebrows and nodded.

There was clearly more to this shake of the hand than Wat appreciated. Clarity flashed into his mind at once. Curse his bloody business. While it was good for the money, he was really not interested what people got up to in the privacy of their own hovel. Why did they all assume that he was as up for it as they were?

He did one of a mistress and her husband after the man had been dead for three years. Nice and nostalgic, Wat thought, until the commission became clear. That was exactly how she wanted him shown, worms and all. Not at all Wat's cup of mead. She thought he'd be as excited by it as she was. He was a simple businessman who happened to operate in the more disreputable districts of society.

He cautiously held his hand out and Brough immediately

grasped it. As far as he could tell it was a normal shake, but then Brough seemed to start stroking his knuckles. He withdrew quickly.

'Oh, right,' said Brough in disappointment.

'No, no, really.' Wat tried to recover the situation and some potential income. 'It's just that I'm not, erm.'

'Not one of us, then.'

Wat had never heard it called that before.

'Er, no,' he said with some finality.

'Shame.'

Wat just nodded in as noncommittal a manner as he could muster.

'Got a lot of contacts.' Brough clearly wasn't giving up.

'I'm sure.'

'You, erm, ever thought of joining?'

'No.' Wat realised that had come out a bit too quickly and sharply.

'Only it's a good thing to be in.'

Now Wat was confused, this wasn't sounding like what he thought it had been.

'Really?'

'Oh yes. Mind you I'm probably saying too much already. It's supposed to be secret, but you know, how are we going to attract new members? Apparently I'm supposed to look out for anyone suitable and then approach them without approaching them.'

'I see.' In situations like this Wat always found it most effective to pretend to understand perfectly what it was the other person was talking about. Until the opportunity presented itself to run away.

'I've not been in it long myself.'

Now Wat really was adrift and he didn't know whether he wanted to come ashore or not. The prospect of the contacts sounded interesting, but on the other hand Brough was clearly as mad as the moon.

'I'd have thought a well-travelled businessman like yourself would be in the thick of it, you know?'

'Never really occurred to me, to be honest.' Wat fished for the slightest clue of what was going on.

'Oh, you should think about it. Very influential people, the Masons – could put a lot of business your way.'

The masons? thought Wat. What, all of them?

'You're a mason then?'

'Oh yes.' Brough's chest swelled with pride.

Wat wanted to know how this man could possibly be a mason. He had met lots of them, many as customers. Well paid men with time on their hands, ideal, but Brough simply wasn't one. He didn't display any of the signs. He wasn't so begrimed with stone dust that his skin had turned white. He appeared to have all his fingers, not having absent-mindedly chiselled off a couple. He didn't walk with a limp, so hadn't dropped large pieces of masonry on his feet. Anyway, if he was a mason he wouldn't be here putting up the tents.

'So how does your being a mason work around here, then?' said Wat, implying that he knew perfectly well how it worked around his way.

'Oh well, same as everywhere I expect. You pay your dues, you attend the meetings and get the secrets and the contacts.'

Light started to dawn. Most of the masons Wat knew were crafty at getting and keeping their money. If they spotted a dupe, it wouldn't be long before what had been in his pockets was in theirs.

'Pay your dues, eh?'

'Yes, but it's well worth it. Our lodge has got a hundred members.'

'Any masons?'

'Ha, ha.' Brough thought this was enormously funny. 'Yes, we have got a few, but mostly not. Lot of businessmen like yourself, needing to keep in contact with the market, know what's going on and where there might be an opportunity.'

'Of course.'

'Again I shouldn't say so, but I got the contract for all the building camps in the county because the major contractor was a member. He put my name around his own contacts. In turn I put a bit of work his way when I got asked about a camp over Nottingham way.'

Whatever this thing was, Wat liked the sound of it more and more. Perhaps he should join. If there were some of these Masons coming to the camp, it would be well worth his while to stay on.

'And of course they make sure that any works which are needed are passed among one another,' Wat suggested, seeing a tapestry factory in his near future.

'Absolutely.' Brough was clearly very proud of this blatant and criminal corruption.

Wat wanted some.

'In fact...' Brough sounded even more conspiratorial. Wat began to doubt that this man would be given the innermost secrets of the organisation if he went around telling total strangers on first meeting. Total strangers in Wat's line of business at that. He was seldom welcomed at guild gatherings or companies. 'I hear tell that some of works going on in these parts wouldn't be happening at all if it wasn't for the lodge.'

'Really?' Wat was intrigued.

'Yep. You know the old mill at the top of Spring Hill?'

Wat tried to nod as if he knew the place while being able to explain later that he didn't, if that became necessary.

'Well, they was going to knock it down seeing as it was so old and rotten and wasn't really needed any more. Suddenly the elders have a change of heart and order a brand new mill, state of the art and everything. Bevelled gears, round shafted driving gear, auto wind adjustment, water back up, the lot. Even had a bloody dome on top, can you believe. Cost an absolute fortune, and then it turned out there wasn't any flour to mill anyway, it was all being done at the bottom of the hill to save carrying it up.'

'But everyone got paid?'

'Of course, and all of them members.'

Typical, thought Wat. Mind you, a stroke of genius to set up the secrecy bit and make people pay to join. Corruption was perfectly normal, but with this arrangement it could go on and on for years before anyone got exiled. Or even found out at all. Wat made a connection in his head.

'So what about this place?' he gestured up to the walls of the monastery.

'What?' Brough had not made the same connection.

'Do you think it could be another dome?'

'This? Don't know.' The man thought for a while. 'Unlikely.'

'Really?'

'Church innit.'

Wat accepted the response. If there was any organisation guaranteed to out-corrupt an honest crook, it would be the Church. Wat had been stung too often himself. An awful lot of his work hung in the private chambers of senior churchmen, but little of their money hung at his belt. Orders were placed and occasionally a small deposit paid, but it didn't matter what happened when Wat's payday came. Blackmail, threats, physical violence, even bringing in the law. The Church would do anything to avoid paying a bill. And they wanted all the really filthy stuff as well, the ones that cost the earth in pink dye.

Of course, the works planned for this monastery might be above board, but with the Church involved it was highly unlikely.

'Unless, of course, some of the Church have joined the Masons?' Wat suggested.

'God spare us,' Brough said, in heartfelt horror. Having the Church interested in your business was like a Viking asking after your wife and daughters. Someone was going to end up shafted.

Wat thought this explained why Hermitage knew nothing about it. He was certainly of too humble a rank to be brought into anything like this. And too honest to know what to do in any case.

'So you're off when this place is set up then?' Wat asked Brough.

'Oh yes, any minute in fact, got a major erection over Nettleham way.'

'I think I will hang around then. Perhaps I could use one of the tents until the crew arrive?' At least that would save Wat having to get his own kit out.

'Sure, help yourself. First lot should be turning up in a day or so. Give you a chance to set up your stand.'

Wat nodded and expected Brough to move off, but he didn't. There was obviously something more.

'So,' said Brough.

'So,' said Wat.

'Good bit of info for you, then?'

'Oh yes.'

'Very profitable, I expect.'

'Could be, you never know.' Wat wondered where this was going.

'And my lads bought a couple.'

'They did.'

'Including Hodric's little extravagance.'

'Yes.'

'Must have spent a week's wages on that thing.'

'Could be.'

'So I expect you'll come out all right.'

'I should hope so.'

'Did you a favour then.'

A hugely pregnant pause followed, which eventually delivered.

'So how about a free sample?'

✦   ✦   ✦

Clutching a very small but very explicit sample, made by Wat's apprentices for just such a purpose, Brough scurried off towards his own tent. Before he could enter, a part of the canvas peeled itself into the evening and a figure stood in his path.

The cowl over the head revealed nothing, but the figure held its right hand out to be shaken. Brough stepped forward, took the hand and shook it significantly.

'Welcome, Brother,' Brough said.

'Your preparations are going well?'

'Indeed they are, all set up as you see.'

'That fellow.' The cowl nodded slightly in the direction Brough had come from.

'A weaver, here looking for work. Not one of the Order and so I sent him on his way.'

'Without revealing anything?'

'Of course not, Brother,' Brough did shocked outrage very well. 'There are already enough weavers within the lodge. He might be a prospective member, though.'

'No, Brother.'

'No?'

'No. He is unsuitable.'

'Really?'

'I know to my certain knowledge that he has had dealing with...'

'Yes?' Brough was all expectancy.

'...the Bishop.'

Brough simply crossed himself in defence of his soul.

'Of Lincoln?' he asked with a trembling tone.

The cowl simply nodded

'Bloody hell.'

'Absolutely. In fact my information is that he has come here as part of specific warrant from the Bishop to look into a death at the monastery.'

'But he said he'd come here to sell tapestry. Rather particular tapestry, if you get my drift.'

'He's hardly likely to tell his true mission, is he? Especially if the Bishop has instructed him not to. This tapestry is probably a cover for his true intentions.'

'They were very unique tapestries.'

'Perhaps he really is a weaver. Perhaps that's part of his usefulness to the Bishop. He doubtless reports all his encounters to his master.'

Brough swallowed hard.

'Have nothing to do with him, Brother.'

'No. No indeed.'

Brough turned back to the tent that Wat was now emerging from, with a worried look in his eye. He turned to raise another question with his Brother, but the figure had gone.

'Mister Weaver,' Brough called, waving his free sample in a lively attempt to give it back.

Day Four Before Vigils

HE ROUTE TO HERMITAGE'S CELL was as long and tortuous as any path in the monastery of De'Ath's Dingle. It was impossibly long and unnecessarily tortuous. It was a good job that Athan was leading the way, as Simon would never have found it on his own. Athan thought the King's whatever-he-was would most likely never find his way out again if he was simply left down here. To rot. It was very tempting

✦ ✦ ✦

In his cell Hermitage had no idea he was about to receive visitors. Not that it would have made any difference as he couldn't see anything to tidy up anyway. He could have moved the vomit straw into one corner and the privy straw into the other, but the discerning guest wouldn't really have noticed much difference.

He had been fortunate to find any straw at all. Not that he had found it until after he had added to the contents of both piles. The new arrivals would have to tread very carefully indeed.

Hermitage had been racked by conflicting emotions during his short incarceration. Shock was soon replaced by anger – of such vehemence that it shocked him even more. He hadn't known he had the capacity to long to smash someone's head, face first, into the various piles that he had deposited on the floor. Let alone that he should have such feelings towards a Prior.

He was at such a fever pitch that if Athan had really been in the room, he would have seriously thought about considering having a strong talk with him.

Hard on the heels of rage had come despair. He simply wanted to curl up in the corner and die – before realising that if he did curl up in the corner with what was already there, he probably would die.

Just recently fear had moved in for its very own Conclave. Fear of the dark spoke first, followed by fear of the scrabbling in the corner where surely no creature of God would willingly scrabble. Then there was fear of what was going to happen to him in the long term and fear of what was going to happen to him in the next few minutes. Then there was a bit of a queue. Fear of what would happen if he went to sleep jostled with fear of staying awake. Also in contention were the fear of lying down in something and fear of standing in something. Not to forget the fear of being punished by God for whatever sins it was that he had committed and fear of being punished by the devil, the Abbot, Athan and his Father – all of whom melded into one. Then there was fear of someone suddenly opening the door, and fear of someone never opening it again.

These, and many other terrors, became so confused in Hermitage's mind that it was hard to differentiate them. They became a general alarm about almost everything, which now manifested itself in a helpless whimper. This seemed to have a life of its own as it escaped Hermitage's mouth and fluttered briefly around the cell. The ambience of the room killed it dead, but another followed like a bleating lamb to the slaughter.

As a desperate measure to get some sense that there was a world outside the walls of his cell, Hermitage got as close as he could to the small opening high in the wall and let out some more whimpers for a bit of a wander. Some of them made their way through the opening and escaped into the night air. It would have been clean night air, but for the fact that Wat had chosen just this moment, and just this place, to take his evening evacuation, well away from the tent he was going to sleep in. Very sophisticated, Wat.

Thinking that there was some wild animal in distress nearby and, judging from the noise that it was quite a small one, he wondered if his evening meal was close at hand. He scrabbled about in the brush against the monastery wall until the whimper came again. He saw that it originated from a small opening at the base of the stone. A rabbit or something had obviously climbed down there and couldn't get out again.

Reluctant to poke his hand in, as even a small rabbit could give you a nasty scratch, he searched quickly for a stout stick. Finding a suitable weapon he braced himself for the attack. If he could kill the thing in the hole, so much the better; if all he did was lever it out, it would probably escape. He raised the stick high and plunged it into the hole, expecting to hear a squeak or at least a scrabble.

'Ow!' Hermitage leaped backwards as a large stick appeared from the opening and caught him right in the eye.

There was noise outside as whoever had thrust the stick moved about.

'Hello?' A voice came down the hole now. A familiar one.

'Who's that?' Hermitage asked with desperate hope.

'Who am I? Who the hell are you and what are you doing down that hole?'

'Is that Mr Wat?'

There was more rapid noise from outside.

'How do you know my name?' the hole said. It sounded worried.

'It's me, Hermitage,' the monk bleated.

'Hermitage?' Wat's voice was having trouble believing this. 'What are you doing in this hole?'

'I'm not in a hole.'

'You are from where I'm standing.'

'I'm in a cell.' Hermitage looked around as if checking this was still correct.

'My God, it must be a small one,' Wat marvelled. 'Ah,' the

truth dawned with little illumination. 'I didn't know monks' cells were underground.'

'They aren't,' Hermitage replied with a little more clarity now as he got his mouth a bit closer to the hole.

'Then?'

'Brother Athan put me in here.'

'So this was the worse that could happen, eh? Thrown in a cell underground. They're usually called dungeons, by the way.' Sounds of Wat settling himself down for a comfortable chat came through the hole.

'I know,' Hermitage wasn't happy. 'There's a door and everything. And he's locked it.'

'This is your fate, is it? Not too bad then.' Wat sounded cheerful.

'This is the least of it,' Hermitage swallowed hard. He had to tell Wat. He was getting nowhere trying to figure his situation out on his own. 'He's just gone off saying that I killed Brother Ambrosius and that I'll probably be executed.' Hermitage's voice broke a little at this point.

'What? You killed Ambrosius?'

'No, of course I didn't, but Athan says I did.'

'Bloody hell.' The shock in Wat's voice did nothing for Hermitage's mental state.

'I know.'

There was a long pause and Hermitage began to wonder if Wat had run away to leave him to his fate.

'Erm,' said Wat, hesitantly, 'you didn't, I suppose?'

'Didn't what?'

'Kill him?'

Hermitage was outraged. 'No, I did not.'

'No, I didn't think you would have done, but I thought I'd better check. I'm not very familiar with monks and what they get up to.'

'We don't get up to killing one another. Ambrosius died, he

simply died. He was an old man, he got very excited about his debate and he just … died. Why am I being blamed?'

'You were there at the time,' Wat said, matter of factly.

'Well, yes.'

'In fact, you were the only one there.'

'Well, I was at the end.'

'And Athan came in and found you with the dead monk and you were doing – what did you say?'

'Contemplating his argument.'

'Yes, contemplating his argument.' Wat paused again. He let out a deep sigh before speaking again. 'It's not exactly the usual form of behaviour for such situations, I would imagine. You know, dead body in room, just that moment died, and the only other person there is busy contemplating an argument rather than leaping up and down and doing something about it?'

'I was engrossed,' Hermitage said coldly, as if this was sufficient excuse for not noticing the apocalypse.

'I'm sure you were, but look at it from Athan's point of view,' Wat suggested.

That was an interesting approach, so Hermitage paused and did just that.

'I still don't see the problem,' he said to the hole, after he had rapidly considered the proposal. 'I know I can be a bit odd now and again, but I don't kill monks. I've never done it before, so why would I do it now? What did I have against Ambrosius? His argument? I'm hardly likely to fly into a murderous rage at the proposal that the forty days and forty nights must have started at midnight, am I? In any case I don't do murderous rages.'

'Needn't have been a rage, could have been carefully planned.'

'What? Do you think I did it then?' Hermitage felt a tear form at the back of his eye.

'No, no, I don't, calm down, I'm just trying to think through the situation and get you to do the same. That way we have chance of getting you out of this.'

The tear receded and Hermitage felt a surge of warmth and comfort flow through his stomach at this. Wat was a figure of the world, he knew his way around people and places, and the young monk felt that he had been snatched up in his mother's arms to save him from that old family dog that had tried to eat his foot one day. If anyone could help unravel this it would be him, and he appeared to be on Hermitage's side.

'Perhaps you've held a longstanding grudge against this old boy and have wreaked your revenge?' Wat's voice sounded light, even though the topic was deadly.

'I'd never met him before the Conclave,' Hermitage said reasonably.

'But you'd heard of him?'

'Only in passing, a rather esoteric chap, bit of a specialist.'

'On what subject?'

'Well, the days in the wilderness, of course.' Hermitage wondered why Wat was asking again. He had been over all of this in great detail on the journey.

'That's it? I thought that was just this debate.'

'Well, you can't debate without comprehensive knowledge.' Hermitage wasn't sure he understood the question.

'And that was his entire monastic life, specialising in the forty days and forty nights in the wilderness?'

'It's a very important topic. Pivotal.'

'I'm sure it is,' said Wat although his voice wasn't sure at all, 'and did you have any views on it? Before he arrived.'

'No, not really, wasn't my area. I was studying the lexicography of the post-Exodus Prophets.' Hermitage hoped that they could move on to his favourite topic.

'Right,' said Wat in the tone that most people used when Hermitage said this. He didn't want to explore the lexicography. Shame.

'So why were you at the debate at all?'

'Well, there were a number of us there to start with, but it was clear that Ambrosius was going to take some time. At the end there was just me, Francis and James. And I don't know where they went. Father Genly was supposed to be the debating opponent, but he left quite early. He said that if our Lord had had an hour of Ambrosius instead of forty days and forty nights of wilderness he would have taken Satan's offer. Which I thought was quite rude. If not blasphemous.'

'Back to the point in hand, Hermitage, please,' Wat insisted. 'You were in the room with a living monk and soon afterwards he was a dead monk. You were the only one there, what would you conclude?'

'That the old monk became a dead monk as a result of natural processes. Old monks do that sort of thing all the time. Why didn't Athan believe that Ambrosius had simply died?'

Wat paused for a long time which stretched on so long that Hermitage began to worry he had given up and gone away

'Yes,' he eventually said, 'that's what I'm wondering.'

'So you don't think I did it?' It was half statement, half question, as Hermitage begged for some support.

'No, of course I don't. You don't have it in you.'

Hermitage was hugely relieved at this. He knew it was what he wanted to hear, but it sounded like an insult. He was sure he could kill someone if he had to.

◆　　◆　　◆

That Athan and Simon made it to Hermitage's cell without another murder being committed was itself a bit of a miracle.

In the time it had taken to get even half way, the King's Investigator had lectured Athan on a number of religious topics. He had spoken with great authority on matters which caused even Athan to frown in doubt, and he was not renowned for his theological learning. Or rather he was, but it wasn't the good sort of renown.

Simon had said some truly ludicrous things about the virgin

daughters of Lot, had recited a huge list of animals for some reason or other and insisted that Noah's Ark had in fact come down in Suffolk. Which was odd considering most of that county was still under water.

A lot of the time was taken up by him speaking with great authority about his own great authority.

With Simon's talking, Athan almost missed the entrance to the cell and had to step quickly backwards a couple of paces. This brought him on to the King's Investigator's feet. The King's Investigator had much to say on the clumsiness of the servant classes. If Simon had been a perceptive fellow, he would have noticed that the fingernails on Athan's clenched fists had just drawn blood.

Hermitage heard the squeal and argument from outside the door.

'Quick,' he said to Wat, 'someone's coming.'

'Good.'

Hermitage didn't think it was good at all.

'Perhaps now we'll find out what's going on,' Wat whispered, 'I'll stay up here and listen. Try to get them to speak up a bit.'

Hermitage thought that speaking up was one thing Athan could do, and was about to say so, when the locking bar drew back and the door swung open.

The figures of Simon and Athan presented themselves to Hermitage. He felt some relief at the sight of Simon. The King's Investigator would be able to get straight to the heart of the matter. Perhaps his travelling companion had come to release him. He must share Wat's concern at this blatant miscarriage of justice.

'So you're Hermitage, are you?' said Simon.

Odd, thought Hermitage, perhaps it was dark and Simon couldn't see who it was. He stepped forward into what little light there was.

'Yes, Brother,' he said, in clear recognition of Simon. 'It's me,' he added, as Simon continued to look blank.

Even Athan was confused.

'The man you travelled from Lincoln with?' Athan barked.

'Yes, yes,' said Simon as if he were talking to an idiot child. 'I know perfectly well who he is. I am puzzled though.'

'Well, there's a thing.' Athan seemed confident that anything less than a direct insult would go over this man's head and sail off into the sunset.

He looked Hermitage up and down and appeared to be thinking very deeply. Hermitage knew that this had to be a good sign. After a very long pause the Investigator nodded to himself.

'You told us much about the death of this Ambrosius during our travel here, Brother.'

'I did,' Hermitage replied, wondering why he wasn't being let out straight away.

Simon pondered some more.

Surely he could remember it all, Hermitage thought.

'Indeed,' Simon said in a musing sort of tone to imply that he was thinking carefully about this reply.

A suspicious mind might have concluded that Simon didn't know what he was going to say next. Fortunately there were no suspicious minds in the room.

'As I said, Brother,' Athan interrupted, 'Brother Hermitage was there at the time. The only one there. Apart from the dead body of course.'

Hermitage didn't like the way he said that.

'Indeed,' said Simon again, this time using the tone that said, I know how significant this is so you'd better answer properly. 'And how do you explain that?'

'Erm,' Hermitage wondered why he was having to repeat everything already said on the road from Lincoln. The King's Investigator wouldn't forget things like that.

Realisation dawned. No, of course he hadn't forgotten. This was a brilliant piece of questioning. What technique. Hermitage was very impressed. Simon had obviously taken in everything that Hermitage had said during the journey. He had even done so in a remarkable manner, never asking any questions or probing any statements at all. The ignorant would be easily fooled into thinking that Simon wasn't interested and wasn't particularly paying attention. Now Hermitage was in front of a monastic witness, even if it was Brother Athan, he was being asked to repeat the tale again. By this means Simon would spot any inconsistencies in the two versions. He would soon pierce the case to the core.

Hermitage had the confidence of the honest, of course, but he was still slightly nervous in front of such a powerful, yet cleverly disguised intellect. Simon must be able to lull all sorts of miscreants into false senses of security by his outwardly disinterested and frankly ignorant manner. He would obviously pounce when it was least expected.

'Well, as I said, Brother...' and Hermitage proceeded to repeat many of the words said between Lincoln and De'Ath's Dingle with any bearing on the death. He also included many words that had nothing to do with the death whatsoever, as well as several which were of merely general interest.

Athan's irritation at this experience became more and more visible as it went on. He was clearly controlling the urge to do some physical damage to something.

Simon was doing a very good impression of someone who really couldn't care what was being said to him.

Eventually Athan could contain himself no longer.

'Shut up,' he ordered.

Almost simultaneously Simon said 'Yes, yes, Brother,' for about the seventeenth time.

Aha, thought Hermitage, the investigator was obviously satisfied that his re-telling of events was consistent with his original exposition.

'So, basically, what you're saying is...' Simon said, leaving the sentence unfinished.

'What I'm saying is,' said Hermitage, marvelling again at Simon's ability to make the accused repeat their tale over and over again until they made some mistake, 'that I didn't kill Ambrosius, that he simply died of being old.'

'And near death,' he added.

'Yeesssssss,' said Simon weighing up complex alternatives.

'Well, he was near death, wasn't he?' Athan spat. 'He was near you.'

'But, Brother,' Hermitage now felt a tremor of annoyance slip into his tone, 'I was contemplating. You saw me when you came in. I was carefully weighing up Ambrosius's argument from my place in the stalls. I had been there for hours.'

'How do we know that?' Athan retorted.

'Indeed,' said Simon, as if it was the only word in the Investigator's armoury.

Clever again, thought Hermitage, getting others to pose the questions. It was as if Athan was being allowed to play an aggressive part while the investigator himself took on a more sympathetic role. Sort of good monk, bad monk.

'How do we know that you didn't get up from your stall, do Ambrosius to death and then sit down again?' Athan was inspired by the topic.

'But why?' Hermitage asked, 'why would I want to kill Brother Ambrosius? I can't deny that I had the opportunity to do so, that much is clear, but why would I want to? I didn't have anything against him. I was simply interested in his proposal, ill-conceived though it was. Quite apart from that, how did I do it? We don't know that he didn't simply drop dead. What killed him, that's the question, not who?' Hermitage felt that he had made a very significant point, but it seemed to pass everyone by.

'Ill-conceived, eh?' said Simon, as if this was a point of some significance.

'Well, yes,' said Hermitage. He was clearly unable to keep up with the Investigator's thinking.

'Yes?' said Simon, probing again.

God be praised, this man was insightful.

'Yes, ill-conceived. It was clear that our Lord did suffer in the forty days and forty nights because does not caput four verse two of the book of Matthew say that "he was hungry"?'

'Yes?' said Simon clearly leading Hermitage on further.

'So if he was hungry, he suffered. Ambrosius's argument was that the Lord suffered because of his footwear. There's very little biblical support for that.'

'What?' Athan seemed shocked for some reason.

'I maintain that as the Bible says,' began Hermitage.

'Yes, I heard what you said. I thought Father Genly's case was that the Lord didn't suffer at all. That was what Ambrosius was against.'

'Oh no,' Hermitage was taken aback at this patently ludicrous step. 'No one would accept that.'

'I don't believe this.' Athan seemed lost, intellectually, theologically and personally.

'I'm not lying,' said Hermitage, quite offended.

'I'm sure you're not,' Athan went on. 'Are you seriously telling me that this monk spent four days arguing for the bleeding obvious?'

'I'm not sure I understand.' Hermitage was having trouble following people today.

'You say that our Lord suffered in the wilderness?' Athan enquired.

'Yes.' Hermitage was sure of this.

'And the Bible says that our Lord suffered in the wilderness?' Athan clearly knew this to be the case, but seemed anxious to check.

'Yes,' Hermitage said clearly.

'And Brother Ambrosius put together a debate that lasted more than half a week to say that our Lord suffered in the wilderness?' Athan's reasoning was struggling.

'Yes.' Hermitage was very impressed that Athan was reasoning at all.

'Did any one disagree?' Athan asked.

'Well, not really. As you say, Father Genly was to take the opposing position, but it was only really on the point about the sandals.'

'Unbelievable,' Athan exclaimed.

'I know,' said Hermitage with sincerity. 'Not only was there no case to make for the sandals, but one could argue that the whole question was futile.'

'Oh, could one?' Athan still seemed terribly excited about this issue. Perhaps Hermitage had misjudged him.

'And if Father Genly had argued his case, what would have happened?' Athan wanted to know.

Hermitage was more than happy to tell him. 'Well, the record of the debate would have gone to Conclave in Lincoln who would determine for one side or the other.'

'Sandals or not sandals.'

'Exactly.'

'The outcome of which would have made the slightest difference how exactly?'

'Again, that's an interesting point. It could have been a nullity.'

Athan simply looked puzzled.

'It would have no effect at all,' Hermitage explained.

'HA!' Athan threw his hands into the air. 'Why does that not surprise me?' He stalked away from Hermitage and stalked into something on the floor. He stalked back again.

Hermitage had thought some more and came up with one outcome. 'I suppose there was an outside chance that sandals would be declared anathema. That would obviously affect the shoe industry quite badly, but apart from that...' He shrugged and then realised where his own argument had taken him.

'Which proves I had no reason to kill him because it proves

there wasn't one. If his argument was going to have no effect on anyone at all in any way whatsoever, why would anyone want him dead?' Hermitage was quite triumphant about this. He imagined it was where the Investigator had been leading him.

'To spare the world half a week of life lost.' Athan stalked around some more, only this time in very small circles.

'Perhaps it was personal,' said Simon. 'Perhaps you had a longstanding grudge against this man and chose this insignificant moment as the perfect opportunity, precisely because no one was interested.' He seemed quite pleased with himself at this. But then he seemed pretty pleased with himself most of the time.

Hermitage almost said that he had already explained this to Wat. His secret, yet growing, reserve of discretion stepped up and kept him quiet. Instead he explained again that he wouldn't have known Ambrosius from a Druid.

'Perhaps,' said Athan slowly, thinking things through carefully, 'perhaps the debate simply drove you mad? One old monk arguing for four days about nothing at all would be enough to drive anyone to distraction. Perhaps you killed him in a moment of madness and don't even remember it.'

'Absolutely not,' Hermitage said with some surprise, 'the debate was fascinating.'

'What?' there went Athan again, getting all hot under the habit. 'How could it be fascinating? It was a load of rubbish.'

'Oh, not at all,' said Hermitage. There was a cough from Wat's hiding place.

'The argument itself was most illuminating. Ambrosius called on references from several different books of the Bible. He put together a very cogent and consistent line across different time scales and neatly combined some Old Testament prophets with the healthcare instructions from the Book of Leviticus. He even employed a new technique known as deduction. It was very exciting.'

135

'But you still disagreed with him, even if the result didn't matter?' Simon asked.

'Well, of course.'

'Violently,' Athan concluded, as if this was enough to start building the gallows.

'Even if I did,' Hermitage offered, realising that this was tantamount to a confession although no one else in the room seemed to spot it, 'what killed him? If I had done it, there would be marks of some kind surely. Strangulation, beating, stabbing, suffocation – they must all leave their tracks. Surely it is the job of the Investigator to follow such tracks?'

Hermitage seemed to think this was a rather clever remark, but it obviously meant nothing to the others. They'd probably heard it a million times.

'What are you saying, Brother?' Simon asked.

'That even if I did have the opportunity to commit the crime we've established that I had no motivation to do so. The argument was certainly not worth killing for and I didn't know Ambrosius anyway. The question we haven't established is how he was killed. Or even if he was killed at all and didn't just die as I maintain. We should examine the body of Brother Ambrosius.'

'All in good time, Brother,' said Simon, who appeared annoyed at Hermitage's presumption.

Despite the senior company Hermitage dropped on to his straw and sat cross-legged. He really couldn't see what else there was to say. Simon didn't have anything else to say either. Athan was still fuming.

'All in good time,' Hermitage muttered to himself, starting, for the first time in his life, to question his conclusions about people. At one moment Simon seemed brilliant and at the next stupid. It was of course unbelievable that someone of authority could be actually useless at what they were supposed to do. It must be a ruse.

'What if he's still alive?' Hermitage said, leaping to his feet again.

'Hardly likely, Brother,' Athan said, 'He's been lying in the meat store for several days. I think he'd have let us know if he wasn't really dead.'

'Perhaps he's stunned?'

'Stunned? He'd have to be pretty heavily stunned to lie still in a freezing room for days on end. Anyway, we saw him fall from his chair. Several Brothers carried him between them and covered him with a sheet. I think he'd have responded to some of that.'

'But he fell on his head, that could have stunned him more.'

'Oh, this is ridiculous.' Athan was nearing the end of his tether, which was never far away. 'Let's see the damn body. This is getting as stupid as the whole argument in the first place.'

Simon frowned at them both and Hermitage was ashamed at usurping the Investigator's position. The man put on his highest authority and gestured the others to get on with it.

Hermitage just assumed that he would be going with them and so followed the two monks to the door of his cell. Neither Simon nor Athan seemed to object so he stayed at the back and kept quiet, like a child hoping that he hasn't been noticed at bedtime.

Athan turned on the following Hermitage and glared at him.

Resigned to his fate, Hermitage's heart sank.

'In the morning,' Athan said simply.

Hermitage's heart rose again. Then it fell at the thought of spending the night in this place. Probably standing up.

Outside of the wall, Wat rose from his hiding place.

'Examine the body, eh?' he muttered to himself. 'Good idea Mister Investigator,' he added in a less than respectful tone. 'Still,' he shrugged, 'might provide a new work for the client in Worcester. He likes this sort of thing.'

Day Five Prime

A T THE FIRST SIGHT OF DAWN the following day, there were awakenings across the monastery. The lone and rather despondent bell, rung by a lone and very despondent monk, roused those who had indulged in the luxury of sleep.

The monks who had made the night-time observances were dozing in a variety of places, postures and company. They blinked with frank disbelief that the sun had the temerity to appear so early.

The Abbot looked out of his window in disgust at another bright and sunny day.

Athan leaped from his cot and reached instinctively for his largest stick. If he could beat the day into submission at its most vulnerable moment, he would.

Hermitage leaped from the floor, which he had sworn he would keep away from.

Wat stretched himself from another dream, the details of which he would note down quickly. As usual he shook his head in some disgust at the thoughts that came unbidden to his slumber.

The King's Investigator snored on.

Emerging from the tent, where the camp builders still lay, Wat gathered his wits and looked around. There was a good thickness of the walls of De'Ath's Dingle between him and the others. Including the corpse. He looked these ramparts up and down, but could see no obvious way in. Given the quality of their construction, the walls could easily have been dismantled, but the bigger problem was the King's Investigator – he might think it a bit odd if a weaver turned up wanting to have a look at the body.

Wat paced up and down a bit, then was struck by an idea.

'Of course, you fool,' he reprimanded himself. At some speed he made his way back to his tent to collect something from his pack and thence to the main door of the monastery.

Arriving at the huge edifice of wood and iron, he looked and started. How on earth he was going to get anyone's attention on the inside? He noticed a small door set into the main opening, and gave it as hard a thump as he could manage without damaging himself.

'What?' said the bandaged figure that opened the door before Wat could knock a second time.

'Er,' Wat was taken back by the sudden response and stumbled over his words, 'ah, erm, yes,' he thought as he spoke. 'Can I come in?' he asked bluntly.

'Do what you like,' said the door keeper stepping out of the way. 'Don't know why I don't just leave the bloody thing wide open anyway for all the thanks I get.' The strange figure mumbled to himself and shuffled off to a small lean-to shack next to the gate. He entered it and slammed the door behind him, rattling the whole structure so much Wat feared it would fall down.

Once inside the monastery he looked around to see if there was a clear way to go. Not knowing the place at all, the location of the meat store was a mystery. Reluctantly he went over to the shack and tapped lightly on the door.

'I don't have to open this one, you know,' the voice spat in response.

'I'm sure,' Wat said, seriously but with some hesitation.

'I only want to know where the meat store is,' he said, through the cracks in the door.

'You're all sick,' the voice replied for reasons which weren't clear at all. 'Follow the wall round to the left until the second square and it's at the back on the right.'

'Thanks,' Wat tried to sound cheerful.

'Oh, don't mention it, I'm sure,' said the voice in the shack, which clearly had significant problems of its own.

Hurrying along the directions, Wat followed the outer wall of the monastery. He passed through an open-topped corridor between the outer and inner walls, then came to the second space. Opposite this was a more carefully constructed square. It had two separate buildings in it, one of stone and one of wood. Walking towards the door of the former were Hermitage and another monk. Their journey must have been a quick one because Simon came running up behind, still pulling on his habit. As they went through the door and closed it behind them, Wat ran over.

He paused outside the door, girding his loins to enter when it was flung open and Brother Simon emerged at some pace. The monk stopped for a moment in front of Wat and gave him a most peculiar look. His eyes bulged and he turned rapidly to one side before vomiting loudly and comprehensively into the dust outside the building.

'He's definitely dead, then,' Wat commented.

He frowned in distaste at the sight and smell of the regurgitating Investigator, but the more revolting, sweet, sickly smell of death welcomed him as he pushed the door open and entered. Hermitage looked up and an expression of surprise and gratitude lit up his face. He immediately looked sideways at Athan, who hadn't noticed. He gave Wat a slow nod, which said that he was prepared to deceive his superior in any way Wat saw fit.

Hermitage knew the odour of decay as a background annoyance when a mouse or something had died in the furthermost reaches of the monastery stonework. Or when a rook had fallen down a chimney and died. Or vice versa. In such situations it was possible to imagine that there was nothing amiss until the faintest whiff brought the only possible conclusion.

Brother Ambrosius had brought the conclusion and all the arguments that went with it. The place stank, and it had taken Hermitage several moments to get used to it. How anyone could eat any food that came out of this place was beyond imagining. In learned circles of the time there was much theorising about the properties of evil humours. All the circles had to do was convene in the meat store of De'Ath's Dingle and they could ask them in person.

Hermitage returned to the task in hand. Athan was intently looking at every inch of Ambrosius. They had bared him by cutting away his habit and all question of survival had been quickly despatched. It was obvious from the perfume that the angel of death had passed this way. It was obvious from what was left on the slab that the angel had probably been accompanied by several cherubs of death, had stayed on for a day or two and then left, taking everything of value with them.

The flaccid and lifeless skin was more like parchment than livid flesh. The muscles, dropping towards the floor, were only restrained by the bag of water in which they hung. The fact of death was blatant, but somehow the sunken, sullen and concave cheeks of the man really brought it home.

Athan and Hermitage rolled Ambrosius on to his back and the face looked even worse. It appeared that the man's lips were trying to work their way back into his mouth and out the back of his throat.

'Who the devil are you and where did you come from?' Athan snapped, noticing the stranger in their midst.

Hermitage looked up again and tried to look neutral.

'Wat,' said the weaver, extending a hand but pulling it back again when he saw where Athan's hands were, 'weaver by trade, but the Investigator thought it would be useful if I took some sketches of events as they unfold.' He held out the slates and chalk he had brought from his tent and began to sketch the recumbent Ambrosius.

'Pervert,' said Athan, but he turned back to his examination.

Hermitage gave Wat a questioning look, but the weaver indicated that discussion now would not be wise.

'Investi-what-not my arse,' Athan grumbled. 'Man's a bloody idiot. Can't stand the sight of death, doesn't know his Bible from a brothel.'

'So,' said Wat trying to defuse the approaching tirade, 'anything I should be looking at particularly? Nasty blow on the head, I see.'

'That's where he fell,' said Hermitage, to a glaring look from Athan.

'Is that what killed him, then?' Wat asked.

'No, he was already dead.' Hermitage wanted to make sure that his point was made.

'And you haven't found anything else.'

'Not yet,' Athan snapped back.

'Looks a bit blue,' said Wat, 'like his blood ran out.'

'Have you got some blue chalk then?' said Athan in a threatening manner which, being Athan, came out as more threatening than manner. As he said this, he came to his senses.

'What's a bloody weaver doing out here?'

'I was travelling with the Investigator and, erm…'

Hermitage held his breath.

'What are you, his bloody personal record keeper?'

'No, no. Just good luck really. We met in Lincoln, his route was on my way and as he seems to be erm, indisposed.' Wat indicated towards the door.

'Indisposed,' Athan virtually exploded. 'I don't know what it is he supposed to do, but whatever it is he isn't doing it chucking his guts up out there.'

'Quite right,' Wat agreed.

'Useless prat.' Athan could have been talking about any of them.

Wat started making some chalk sketches of the face of Ambrosius with its large red mark.

'We still don't seem any the wiser as to what killed Brother Ambrosius,' Hermitage said to Athan in a loud clear voice.

'At least we know that he is dead though. We already know you were the only one there at the time, so there doesn't seem to be much left to sort out, does there.' It wasn't a question, and the certainty of Hermitage's guilt shone brightly in the grimace of Brother Athan.

'If we don't know what killed him, couldn't it simply have been natural causes? As this gentleman says he is very blue. I saw someone like that once after they were pulled out of the River Witham. Well, until they pulled a bit too hard and his arm came off, but that was very blue. Once you'd brushed the mould off.'

'Belt up, Hermitage,' Athan countered.

'A few people were sick then as well, come to think of it,' Hermitage said, his mind wandering in happy reminiscence.

'The Lord would not take a servant of Ambrosius's eminence in the middle of debate, would he?' Athan at last seemed prepared to discuss the proposition with Hermitage.

'Well, he did wait until the argument was concluded.'

'But not the debate.' Athan was insistent. 'Father Genly had not made the opposing view and so the debate itself was not concluded. This is God's business and He wouldn't allow it to stop halfway through like that. Therefore someone killed Ambrosius.'

Hermitage was somewhat surprised at Athan. He had to admit it was a pretty solid argument.

'Perhaps the Lord had his reasons. Perhaps He wanted the debate left inconclusive?'

'Hardly likely.' Athan seemed pretty sure. 'This Conclave has been in the planning for years. If God had wanted it stopped He would have rained a plague or something months ago. He wouldn't wait until the most inappropriate moment possible to knock off one of the minor protagonists.'

While Hermitage appreciated the case Athan was making,

he wondered why his elder and better was making quite such a fuss about it. Athan was excitable, of course. If anything out of the ordinary crossed his path, he would be the first to beat it to death. He was getting completely carried away by all of this though. He held the debate in the very deepest contempt, and this can't have been the first dead monk he'd ever come across.

'Or it was just bad luck?' Hermitage was not going to give up, but he felt that he was on slippery ground.

'Bad luck?' Athan was rightly contemptuous. 'What on earth has bad luck got to do with the debates of the Lord? You should know better than that. No, it's quite clear that these natural causes of yours are completely out of the question. Ambrosius was done to death, and you were the only one there who could have done him.'

That seemed to be pretty much that, and Hermitage simply looked over at Wat and shrugged his shoulders. Wat raised his eyes to the ceiling and shook his head. Hermitage couldn't tell whether this was because he too saw the infallibility of Athan's argument, or had seen a loophole in it that Hermitage had failed to spot. He would have to ask him when they had a moment.

'Just because we can't find anything on the body which shows how you killed him doesn't mean it wasn't done,' Athan went on. 'You'd have to be pretty stupid just to go up and stick a knife in him. While I know that you are pretty stupid, you obviously didn't do that on this occasion.'

'This occasion?' Hermitage didn't know what was going on now.

'Well, we don't know that this is your first time, do we? How many other Brothers have met the Lord before their time because of you?'

'This is ridiculous,' Hermitage squeaked. 'I didn't kill this monk,' he gestured at Ambrosius, 'let alone any others.'

'Pah,' said Athan, as he went round to the far side of the room to gather up the sheet which had covered the deceased.

Wat approached Hermitage and whispered sharply. 'This really is mad,' he said. 'If this is the standard of debate in the modern Church then God help us all. With a couple of cuckoos like you determining the fate of mankind we might as well all go and jump in the burning fiery furnace straight away, and to hell with paradise.'

Hermitage was taken aback.

'I'm about done here,' Wat said more brightly, holding his slate out for them to see the very good rendition of Ambrosius's decay. 'What do we do next?'

'God knows,' Athan almost spat. 'Presumably we wait for that dung heap out there,' he gestured in the direction of the dung heap in question which was still retching loudly, 'and see what he has to say. We're just humble servants.'

Athan strode to the door and flung it open, almost shoving Hermitage in front of him, allowing Wat to follow them both.

Brother Simon was sitting on the chopping block outside the meat store trying to brush his stomach contents off his shoes with some old straw. He looked up,

'So,' he said, 'what are your conclusions?' He looked at them and frowned at Wat as if trying to understand why he was there. Another bilious attack took the questioning from him.

This was odd, thought Hermitage, the man was behaving as if they were acting on his instructions and that he hadn't just thrown up at the first sight of the dead body at all.

'My conclusion is that Ambrosius is dead because I examined the body carefully.' Athan laced his sentence with enough contempt and sarcasm to tie the boots of every monk in the place together. It still wasn't enough to register on Simon's understanding.

'I concur,' Simon said, and Athan did nothing but let his jaw drop. If this had been any other monk he would have been picked up bodily and locked in the meat store with Ambrosius for a week. Being the King's something or other though made

Athan bite his tongue. The taste of blood always calmed him.

'Are we also concluding that this monk did it?' Simon asked.

'Brother!' Hermitage exclaimed. How could he have concluded this as well? He hadn't looked at the body or made any argument of his own. Granted Athan's exposition was very solid, and if Hermitage didn't actually know from first-hand experience that he hadn't killed Ambrosius, he would be convinced as well.

'We are.' Again Athan gave his words enough weight to sink a small Abbey.

'Then we must see your Abbot and conclude this business.'

Athan smiled his smile, and Hermitage shivered.

'Of course,' Athan said and gestured the direction they should take.

Taking the situation to the Abbot was another chance, but Hermitage was not comforted. There was no telling whether such an audience would make things better or worse. Not that he could imagine what worse would look like.

Wat was smiling and nodding slightly. 'Excellent idea,' he said. 'Bound to be a sensible, down to earth, well-adjusted sort of chap.'

◆　　◆　　◆

At that moment, the sensible chap was very down to earth. He was down on the earth, cursing it for holding him up and preventing the descent into hell, which was all that he deserved. He had wallowed in some filth for a while, spent a good long time thumping one of the open wounds on his leg, and then had a spell of pulling his hair out by the roots. Even by the extremely dubious standards of the day, there was something very wrong with the Abbot.

His abiding desire to keep himself to himself suited everyone eminently, and so he carried on unobserved. Occasionally there was discussion amongst the Brotherhood about how exactly this man had got to be an Abbot in the first place and, more interestingly, how he managed to remain one. He didn't seem to do any of the Abbot-like things that others did. He never visited anyone, from the Bishop to the local poor.

It had been suggested once that he should visit the local poor, but there had been such strong objections from the poor that the event had been cancelled.

Some speculated this was one of those ancient positions where the Abbot was appointed in perpetuity and couldn't be removed, even by the Pope. Others opined that he had performed some great and terrible service for the Church so all his odd behaviour was excused. Most prevalent was the idea that he had something on the Bishop and so could pretty much do what he liked. In any event, what he liked doing wasn't very nice at all and so people kept their distance.

Athan knocked again at the Abbot's study and this time he was answered quickly. He pushed the door gently open and peered around the corner. It seemed that the light of day was as reluctant to enter as any penitent. It was so dark that he had to step inside to find the Abbot and gestured Hermitage to follow.

The young monk had seen the Abbot three times now and the occasions were getting progressively worse. The Abbot had surpassed himself. The wizened old man was sitting on the floor of his cell and had clearly been punishing himself comprehensively for some considerable time. Obviously he hadn't eaten or drunk anything, but that hadn't stopped the rest of his bodily functions continuing as normal.

His drool was of a particularly gelatinous consistency and his incoherent mumbling was positively disturbing. As Hermitage beheld the scene before him, his hopes dipped. He wanted the Abbot to be coherent and decisive, not gibbering and offensive. There was little hope of help from this quarter. Still, better get the man to put some clothes on.

Athan stepped back and pushed Hermitage into the doorway, blocking the entrance of the others. He closed the door, glaring and hissing instructions to Hermitage.

After a few moments the door was opened and Athan beckoned the others in. The Abbot was now in his habit and on his stool. It was as much as anyone could hope for.

Simon was lucky that he had spent a good long time at the meat store emptying the contents of his stomach. As the smell of the Abbot's chamber hit his nostrils, the retching was simply magnificent.

The small party gathered in the most squalid conditions ever seen in a religious house. Simon and Wat scanned the room for some sign of the leader of the community. They glanced at a piled up habit sitting on a stool and raised questioning eyebrows. Simon tutted like a man of great influence.

'What do you want?' the habit said and they jumped back, horrified. There was someone in there. It couldn't be a child as the voice was too deep. Deep and somehow unsettling at a very basic level.

'This is the King's, erm, man,' Athan announced and it sounded like he had glee in his voice. 'He has been looking into the events of Brother Ambrosius's passing.' Athan turned to the King's, erm, man. 'And this is our Abbot.'

Athan even managed a bow towards the huddled and stinking pile and gave the clear indication that the same was expected of an Investigator, King's or otherwise.

'I must say,' Simon began, and he clearly had a long diatribe prepared that was going to be withering. Unfortunately, he never even got started.

The shape on the stool threw back its cowl and glared at the Investigator before him. Hermitage had heard about the Abbot's glares. Even the mild ones were enough to reduce grown men to tears, but he had never seen anything like them in real life. Without knowing he had done so, he found that he had taken a step back, moving out of the firing line.

'You,' the Abbot spat and most of the spit found its target on Simon's already disgusting shoes.

This was not the reaction Hermitage expected. It didn't seem unhelpful though.

It was even more clearly not the reaction the King's Investigator expected. For a moment he was taken aback by the vehemence of his welcome, as anyone would be. He stared at the Abbot with a mix of shock and outrage. He was on his back foot, but preparing for a step forward. The step never came as the shock was followed by a moment's puzzlement and then recognition. With this came a remarkable transformation.

To begin with, the Investigator simply went very pale. He had been pretty pasty looking since forcibly parting company with his previous meal, but this was an altogether whiter shade. His mouth dropped open in a caricature of surprise, while his eyes widened to make room for the enormity of the sight that was trying to get into his head.

'The Turd,' the Abbot announced, giving the word an additional level of disdain, which made its use to describe bodily waste positively fragrant.

The Investigator was incapable of saying anything.

'Have you met?' Wat put in helpfully, enjoying the moment enormously.

'Oh yes, we've met.' These few, harmless words, issued from the mouth of the Abbot, stained and shamed the very letters from which they were made. They drew on all the filth and foulness that surrounded him, all the physical repulsiveness that made up his presence and were combined with the foetid torment that permeated his soul. They were words that would never show themselves in company again.

Simon looked like he was about to wet himself.

Athan's eyebrows rose in fascination.

Hermitage looked quickly backwards and forwards from one man to the other. What was going on now?

'The King's Investigator,' Athan said, inspired to get the title right at last.

'Investigator my arse,' the Abbot interrupted without taking his eyes off Simon for one moment. 'This isn't the King's anything. This is the Transubstantiated Turd, as he is widely known. And reviled, I might add. This,' and here the Abbot paused for effect, 'is Brother please-spare-us Simon.'

In Hermitage's rapid, flickering looks, trying to catch some event that would explain all this, he noticed Athan's mouth, open and fish-like. The man looked shocked and not in control. Not like Athan at all.

'Simon,' Athan said, very quietly and very carefully.

'So you and Brother Simon have worked together in the past, Father?' Hermitage spoke up now. Perhaps in this bizarre behaviour there was a vague opportunity to better his own situation.

'Worked? Ha!' the Abbot was almost human in his animation. 'This man is a blot on Christendom itself. He has all the intelligence and ability of a turd, and that is why he is so named. He combines this with a fawning self-importance and arrogance, and so some of the equally stupid people who run our Church are taken in by him. Not me though, and not the like-minded who had to put up with his preening ignorance. We see straight through him to the hollow, self-centred core which is his soul. King's Investigator? What the hell does that mean anyway? I shouldn't think he knows. Do you?'

The question was directed at Simon, but it clearly wasn't going to get an answer.

'It means to track, you moron. You couldn't track the tracks of your own piss if you'd done it on your shoes. Which it looks like you have. Sucking up, though? Oh, he's a master of that. Jump sir? How high sir? Bend over sir? How low sir? I dread to think how many truly useful people have had their progress halted by this useless pile of privy plop. Whose backside did you kiss to get this one, then?'

The Abbot seemed to have finished his extraordinary rant and left a pause that he demanded be filled by Simon's response. The others looked to Simon as well.

The King's Investigator seemed to have recovered, although his usual confident and patronising look was a bit shaky.

'I can see that this gentleman's ravings have not diminished over the years.'

What an insult, calling the Abbot a gentleman instead of giving him his proper title.

'It is true that I have encountered him before, but I will confess that I never for one moment assumed he would rise to his current exalted position. The sympathy of those in authority is to be admired when they take such as he to their bosom and give him what succour they can.'

The sympathy in Simon's voice was so patently false that even Hermitage spotted the insincerity.

'I myself have done my humble best to control his restless and disturbed mind, but I fear it cannot be done.' Simon shook his head in sadness. 'My appointment by the Bishop to the position of the King's own personal Investigator clearly rankles with him. It would be unkind to prolong the agony of so pitiful a figure. Perhaps we should leave and I can make my report to the Bishop himself. I think I may have one or two recommendations concerning the future organisation of this place.'

'Oh, give it a rest, Simon.' The Abbot didn't seem put out by this tirade against his sanity at all. Well, no more put out than he was already.

'You're still as pompous and stupid as you were thirty years ago. It sounds to me like you've been set up again. You never see it do you? Those wonderful people in authority, the ones with titles and land, and what you call respect, are only where they are because they trample on people like you. No one with any sense respects them. They're tolerated and placated and then talked about behind their backs.' It was the Abbot's turn to shake his head.

'You're not one of them and no amount of sucking up will make you one of them. You're being used, you're going to be a sacrificial lamb. Of every offering in the Book of Leviticus, you are the all dead ones. I've never heard of a King's Investigator, and I've been around longer than you have. I'm pretty damn sure there never was one until you turned up. Whoever it was gave you the title did so in the precise knowledge that it was just the sort of thing that would swell your empty pride to bursting point. It's Warwick all over again, isn't it? You took the fall then and you'll take it again now. Trouble is, you're so stupid you won't even know when it's happened.'

Simon turned to Athan who was staring at him in a most peculiar and disrespectful manner, so he moved on to Hermitage.

'Your Abbot is clearly most disturbed today and so I think we had better leave. I will escort you back to your detention.' He took Hermitage by the arm.

'Back to his what?' the Abbot snapped.

Athan was still incapacitated by something and to Hermitage's eye it was looking more and more like that old familiar blind rage. It was Wat who spoke.

'Back to the dungeon, Father. You see the King's Investigator has concluded that Brother Hermitage killed Brother Ambrosius.'

'Then he definitely didn't do it,' the Abbot responded without a blink. 'If this man concluded that arrows were sharp I'd stick one in my eye. Athan.'

The Abbot's command shook Athan back into the room.

'Father?' said Athan, although he seemed to have his teeth firmly stuck together.

'What's this about Hermitage?' the Abbot demanded.

'We did discuss this, Father. Brother Hermitage was there when Ambrosius died.'

'So were you for that matter,' the Abbot said, quite simply.

'I arrived after the event.'

'Yes, so you say. In any case, anything that this sheep's buttock has to say on the matter is, by definition, rubbish. Let Hermitage go.'

'I am the King's Investigator.' Simon tried to take command of the situation.

'Let him go, you dick,' the Abbot snapped back, 'or I shall put you in the dungeon and tell the Bishop you were an impostor. I've had no notification of an Investigator: you could be a pervert of some sort. Just get out.'

Wat seized this opportunity, while the Investigator was distracted. He took Hermitage by the arm and turned him sharply towards the door so that they could leave. It was only then that he came face to face with the tapestry that hung on the door.

'Yes, that's it,' he muttered to himself, noting the subtle 'W' stitched into the border. 'Come on, Hermitage, you're free to go.'

Hermitage stepped gladly from the room before anyone had a chance to change their mind.

Simon was stepping backwards as well, but spoke to the Abbot. 'You are clearly in no condition to deal rationally with events, sir, and so I shall leave to continue my duties. If I determine that this Brother is guilty, then that shall be that.' He turned on his heels and left as quickly as he could, giving the Abbot no opportunity to respond. He slammed the door behind him.

'Bollocks!' the leader of the community yelled in what sounded almost like good humour.

Athan remained in the Abbot's chamber.

'Father, this Brother Simon and Warwick,' he said, and knelt in the muck for a conversation.

✦　　✦　　✦

Outside the door Simon's usual condescending whine was fully restored.

'Well,' he said, assuming that they all agreed that the Abbot was mad.

'He seems a bit, erm, excitable,' said Wat, choosing his words carefully.

'Oh, undoubtedly,' said Simon, 'and while I could exert my authority over him I think in his condition it is best to humour him.'

Wat nodded sagely at this magnanimous gesture.

'However, young Hermitage, you are not to leave the monastery. It seems that I had best look into matters further. I shall be in my chamber.'

With this he left them and strode off. Hermitage and Wat exchanged looks.

'Right,' said Wat, 'I think that all seems pretty clear then. We'd better have a look at the scene of the crime.'

'Who, what, where?' Hermitage had so many questions they couldn't all get out at the same time. 'What's pretty clear?'

'That the Investigator is an idiot. I've had my doubts about him since Lincoln and I think I know him from somewhere. Warwick, that rings a bell,' he shrugged. 'It'll come.'

'What do you mean, he's an idiot?'

'You saw him. I think the Abbot has him pretty well summed up. Smart guy that, I like him. They obviously go back a bit and it's not a happy history.'

'How could the King's Investigator be an idiot?' This really wasn't making any sort of sense to Hermitage.

'Just as the Abbot said, I imagine. Someone on high is up to something unsavoury and they need a scapegoat.'

'This is shocking. He's in the King's name.' The concept was not making it through to Hermitage's thinking.

'There's your guarantee, then. I mean Harold is a reasonable sort, but you don't get to be King and stay there without a few wiles in your quiver. He wouldn't appoint a berk like Simon.'

'You mean the King is involved?'

'No no, don't be ridiculous, this is small beer. Whatever it is that's going on. Local stuff, wouldn't interest the court. Anyway, Harold's too busy fighting off the Danes to worry about one little monastery. At least with Mister King's Investigator out of our hair we can try and find out what really happened.'

'But he died. Ambrosius just died.'

'Quite possibly, but with the Abbot's information it is perfectly possible that there really is some skulduggery going on.'

'Oh, lord,' Hermitage quaked.

'Indeed. So, we've had a look at the dead, let's go and see the place of death.' Wat gestured Hermitage to lead the way which the young monk did, shaking his head slowly for so many reasons. Disbelief at the evils of man, shock that they could be played out within a religious community, horror that those in positions of authority might be abusing their position. Not to mention frank amazement that the Abbot might not be as mad as a whooping frog after all.

Day Five   Prime

ICODEMUS WAS A MAN of infinite patience. He had developed it over many years of working under the yoke of individuals who would not just try the patience of a saint – they would find it guilty and go straight to the lynching. He was a man hardened to the foibles of the high born, the well-connected and the just plain obnoxious, frequently in the same person.

Now he was wondering whether he had met his match. Was the Earl of Northumbria the epitome of ghastly and unbearable appallingness? Nicodemus wasn't even sure that there was such a word, but it fitted like a glove on the hand of a decaying corpse.

During a rare moment of reverie, away from the Earl who was slumped unconscious from a surfeit of surfeits, he was interrupted by one of the staff.

'We think the Earl of Northumbria's done a poo,' the man said.

'So?' was all Nicodemus's weary irritation could manage.

'What should we do? We don't think we can lift him, there are only six of us.'

'Then leave him,' Nicodemus shrugged.

'It's not very nice in there,' the servant pleaded.

'I'm sorry?' Nicodemus felt his old self again. 'It's not very nice? Am I paying you to have a nice time?'

'No, you're not paying us at all,' the impudent fellow retorted. 'You said that if we didn't serve tonight we would all go to hell on the Bishop's personal order.'

'It's probably just a fart,' said Nicodemus. 'He's hardly likely to go in his chair, is he?' Nicodemus didn't believe this for a moment, but he hoped for the best.

Reluctantly returning to the Bishop's chamber, he instantly realised that if this was a fart it was a remarkably solid one. God's holy teeth, the nobility were a disgusting lot. The church hierarchy were disgusting too, most of his fellow servants of God were disgusting and the staff were disgusting as well. The sooner he could get away from all of them the better.

'Where are his personal staff?' Nicodemus demanded.

'They ran away,' the impudent one answered.

'Well, go and find them and tell them to come back here now or they'll all be accompanying you on your journey to hell. They're probably in the tavern on Steep Hill.'

This was one errand the servant was keen on, and so he sped off.

Despite the smell Nicodemus sat opposite the snoring, stinking Earl and gazed at him with a mixture of contempt and pure disbelief. Once again his mind whirled at the thought of this lump of poo with a man on top siring children.

After only a few moments there was a loud rap on the door.

'Oh, for God's sake, you can let yourselves in,' Nicodemus muttered. He stood to go to the door thinking that tearing a strip off a bunch of peasants might lift his mood.

Throwing the door open he saw another bloody noble. Discretion and guile immediately got the better of his instincts, so he refrained from slapping this one in the face as a proxy for the Earl.

The new man was clearly a noble for so many reasons. His clothes were clean for a start, nor was he carrying anything, although he had obviously had a long journey to get here. Everyone had a long journey to get here. Over the man's shoulder Nicodemus saw a large retinue of men who toiled out on the road with carts, cases and horses. Most strikingly of all, the visitor looked Nicodemus up and down as if he were an extension of the door frame. Only someone of true class could display such natural contempt.

'You must be Master Nicodemus,' the new arrival said. 'I must say it's gratifying to see a man of the Church with the humility to open his own door.'

Nicodemus looked blank.

'Ah, forgive me, my dear fellow, I haven't introduced myself.' The man at the door removed one large black leather riding gauntlet and held out his hand. 'Toksvar. I think you're expecting me?'

The visitor took a step forward and Nicodemus thought that he was about to walk into the house uninvited. Instead he stood at the door and took a cautious sniff of the air.

'I'm...' Nicodemus was about to apologise for a problem with the garderobe.

'Oh God,' Toksvar said, 'has my disgusting father disgraced himself again? I'm most terribly sorry.' He gestured in a particular way to a part of his retinue who began unpacking towels and packages as a well-oiled team. 'Let's get the revolting reprobate sorted out and then perhaps we can get on with business and out of your hair.' He made to enter the house and Nicodemus willingly stood to one side. 'He really is the most hideous, stinking, shameful excuse of a man, and I hope you've told him so.'

Nicodemus was taking to Toksvar.

They entered the room and Nicodemus politely held a hand to his nose. Toksvar was more direct – he simply lifted a boot and kicked his august father on the shoulder.

'Oy,' he yelled, 'you foul stinking dung wagon. Stir yourself before I block your arse up permanently with my boot.'

The Earl did stir himself with surprising speed and rounded on his attacker.

'You,' he spat, 'I might have known.' He did have the decency to squirm in his seat rather as he discovered that what he thought had been a most unusual dream had very tangible results.

'The sooner we get this business completed and you out of my life the better,' the Earl snarled.

'Better for us all if you simply died here and now,' the young man replied, 'that way we could pick you out of the chair and drop you straight in a hole.'

'Your brother would have something to say about that, you little runt.'

'Not if I got him first,' Toksvar said with a very serious and anticipatory smile on his face.

Nicodemus was not a great believer in the more supernatural elements of his own religion. He had no truck with tales of witchcraft or spirits and he had other radical views, which he naturally kept to himself. These concerned the causes of right and wrong and the nature of good. His philosophy was thrown into turmoil by the grin on Toksvar's face, which could only be described as pure evil.

'Family,' Toksvar grinned a more earthy grin to Nicodemus. 'Who'd have 'em eh?'

It took some considerable time and not a small amount of inconvenience and to-ing and fro-ing to sort out the Earl. A number of men who seemed used to this sort of thing appeared and carried him bodily from the room. They were directed by Nicodemus to a place of privacy where they could do whatever you did to a leaky Earl. Another two men appeared and took the chair away, moving it outside to their carts and horses, which as far as Nicodemus was concerned was the best place for it. Apart from perhaps a bonfire.

Next a team of about four appeared with fresh clothes for the Earl. Two more men left the building carrying a sack, the contents of which Nicodemus could only speculate about, and shudder. When the hubbub died down the Earl emerged and took Nicodemus by the shoulder as if nothing untoward had happened at all.

Nicodemus led the way back into the chamber where the two chair carriers returned the furniture. This was completely un-blemished and looked like new. In fact it looked better than new, as a small tear the Bishop himself had made had been expertly repaired. Nicodemus marvelled at what was possible when you had serious money. He was grateful to notice that the Earl did not return to his seat. With Toksvar out of the room the Earl talked conspiratorially with Nicodemus.

'Now that I have experienced the presence of my son again, I am more anxious than ever that we proceed with our develop-ment as quickly as possible.' There were still a few crumbs in the Earl's mouth which splattered Nicodemus's shoulder.

'Of course, of course,' Nicodemus grimaced. Maybe some-thing good was coming out of all of this after all.

'Today?' While the Earl placed a question mark at the end of the sentence it was clear from his demeanour and tone that it was a rhetorical question mark. An Earl's rhetorical question mark: this was not a matter for any debate.

Nicodemus nodded and hurried to call for another messen-ger to take this news ahead. He was starting to run out of mes-sengers.

◆　　◆　　◆

In the monastery itself, Wat and Hermitage arrived at the refec-tory to examine the place of Ambrosius's death – only to find it locked.

'Why's it locked?' Wat asked. 'Who's going to steal anything from here?'

It was clear that any passing thief would have to be pretty desperate to believe there was anything inside this ghastly place worth stealing. Indeed, it would be a rather disturbed individual who considered the inside of this place worth entering at all. For a place of refreshment and revitalisation, it was remarkably grim and foreboding.

'It's part of the order.' Hermitage shrugged; it was a part he wasn't too keen on.

'To lock the refectory?'

'Yes. You see the Abbot believes that we all eat too much and too often. Just because we're hungry doesn't mean we should get a meal.'

'So how do we get in?'

'We could ask Athan for the key?' Hermitage made the suggestion although there was an alternative in his mind.

'Or?'

'There is another way,' Hermitage said, nodding slowly.

'Brother Hermitage, you surprise me,' said Wat with some admiration.

Hermitage shrugged in embarrassment.

'I've never really seen why it matters whether we're in here or not because this isn't where the food is. The locks and bars on the granary and the meat store I can understand. Perhaps it's because the refectory is so comfortable.'

Wat looked around the outside of the building, finding this very hard to believe.

'Compared to anywhere else, I mean,' Hermitage added.

He led the weaver around to the right of the building to an alleyway, squeezed between the outer wall of the refectory and an apparently pointless piece of high stonework, which jutted out from the adjacent building. They passed along the outer walls of both buildings and then turned left to arrive at the back of the refectory.

If the face of the refectory was so grim as to cast a pall over the happy proceedings of repast, the back of the place would have sucked the soul from a kitten.

It was a triangular area of bare ground walled on each side by buildings which took this open space as a personal insult. They glowered down on it with every intent of hurling themselves forward at any minute. This made it as disturbing a place as the kennel of a mad dog that's just been roundly taunted by a soulless kitten. The buildings were bullying the space mercilessly. They had already cast several pieces of their loosest masonry at it, so that the floor was a jumble of broken stone and mortar.

Hermitage led the way through this mess to a spectacularly thrown gargoyle, which had finished up feet first in the ground right up against the refectory wall. It looked like nothing other than a demon-headed dog that had not got out of the way fast enough when the refectory landed. The look on its face said the building had hit it somewhere extremely sensitive. Wat winced in sympathy at the creature's tortured expression.

'Here,' said Hermitage, and behind the emasculated mongrel was a small door set into the stone.

'We don't think the Abbot or Athan know about this, so we use it when the weather is extreme.'

'Ah,' said Wat. 'You get in out of the cold, eh?'

Hermitage looked puzzled. 'Oh no,' he said, 'we come in here when it's too hot outside. The inside of the refectory is always colder than outside. If you entered in midwinter, you probably wouldn't come out again.'

Hermitage pushed at the door. It swung open with little resistance.

'We're not even sure why it's here,' the young monk went on. 'Must have been a builder's thing, I suppose.'

'It is,' Wat said, 'it's the escape hatch.'

'Escape from what?'

'I know my fellow tradesmen very well,' Wat explained. 'Putting up a place like this refectory would take years. The men on the job certainly wouldn't want to devote their entire lives to it. Whatever the designers' plans, one of the first things the builders would put in would be the escape hatch.'

Hermitage looked puzzled.

Wat continued as they knelt and went through the door on

hands and knees. He seemed relaxed and comfortable in Hermitage's company and the young monk was gratified and hugely enjoyed this general conversation. It was nice to talk about something that wasn't his own execution.

'A secret door which allowed them to get in and out of the site,' Wat sprinkled trade secrets. 'They could be signed in in the morning, go straight out through the hatch to another job and then come back in again in the evening to collect their pay. With construction being such a naturally slow process, no one would notice if one of the trades hadn't actually done anything at all one day.'

'That's disgraceful,' Hermitage commented.

They now stood in the refectory, having passed through a convoluted passageway that emerged between two pillars at the very back of the room.

'Right,' said Wat, rubbing his palms and gazing around the large space. It echoed and amplified the nastiness of the outside to a peak of architectural malice. Malice towards everything. Life, love, food, good company, contentment and comfort. None of them were on the guest list.

'Where was Ambrosius?' Wat asked, once he had got his bearings.

'Er, just here.' Hermitage took three steps forward to the lectern at the head of the chamber from which Ambrosius had delivered his oration.

Wat came and stood at it and looked all around.

'And this was the chair he was found in?'

'Yes, that's it.' Hermitage stood respectfully back from the plain wooden backed chair which had held the corpse.

Wat prowled around it and the space. He looked at the chair in some detail, getting down on his hands and knees. He looked up at the windows and paced out distances from places of concealment to the Ambrosius memorial chair. He walked over to the main entrance door and also to the far end of the building.

'Where were you?' he asked.

'I was just here.' Hermitage indicated his seat, on the end of one of the long refectory benches.

'Sit there, would you?'

Hermitage sat.

'I'll be Ambrosius.' Wat took up position at the lectern. 'And you were the only one here?'

'Well, I was when Athan arrived. During the debate Brother James was over there by the fire.'

'There was a fire?' Wat was surprised. He was getting used to the place.

'Special dispensation for the Conclave.'

'Anyone else?'

'Brother Francis moved about a bit. Sometimes he was in a seat and at others he was on the floor over there.' Hermitage indicated a space between the benches.

'What was he doing on the floor?'

'Oh well, Brother Francis is a bit, erm...' Hermitage found it hard to explain. 'Well, he's not quite as other Brothers.'

'Probably the only normal one here then,' Wat concluded callously. 'And Athan didn't think it of any significance that there were two others here as well?'

'They'd both gone by the time Athan arrived. They had stayed longer than everyone else. People didn't loiter once Ambrosius got going. I suspect those two were using the debate as an excuse to avoid their daily toil.'

'That's disgraceful,' Wat said. Hermitage did not miss the dig. 'All right. So. If I was standing here giving my all to the debate, you were contemplating and not seeing anything, what were Francis and James doing? And where were they when the death actually occurred, as opposed to when it was discovered?'

'Well, when I looked round they'd gone.' Hermitage didn't see how this was going to help.

'Yes, but you only looked up when Athan shouted at you.'

'Yes.'

'So if Ambrosius had been dead for some time, James or Francis could have done it and then left without you noticing.'

'Oh, they wouldn't have done that.'

'Why not exactly?'

'Well, they just wouldn't. They were monks who, well, just wouldn't.'

'And you would?'

'No, no, that's not what I mean. Ambrosius just died, you've seen the body. I don't know how many times I have to keep saying this. There was no murder. There was a death and you can have one without the other.' There was irritation in Hermitage's voice.

'The body with a big red mark on its head?'

'But it got that after death.' Hermitage was feeling uncomfortable again.

'So you say, but if someone had hit him there and caused the death, the fact that he fell off his chair would disguise the fact.'

'But we would have noticed when Athan arrived. And I'm sure I'd have stopped contemplating if someone had come up to Ambrosius and hit him on the head.'

'Hmm.' Wat seemed reluctantly convinced by this. Hermitage started to worry again that the weaver might think that he had done it after all.

Wat returned to the lectern.

'There doesn't seem to be any evidence of a struggle.'

'How do you know?' Hermitage was intrigued.

'Well, there's very little disturbance in the dust – no broken furniture or windows. If he was done in, he didn't put up much of a fight.'

'I don't think he was in the physical condition to get involved in a fight. If anyone had tried to kill him his best response would have been a robust telling off. I'm positive I would have noticed that.'

'Yes, probably.' Wat paused to look about the place once

more. 'It would have been difficult to shoot him because the lectern would shield him from any outside view. And you probably would have noticed the swish and thud of an arrow followed by that little gurgle people do. Not that we found any holes in him that shouldn't have been there anyway.'

'This hasn't been much help, has it?' Hermitage was finding the constant leaping from the heights of optimism to the depths of despair and back again a bit wearing.

'Not at all. We've ruled out all sorts of possibilities. No fight, no scuffle, no shooting, not a violent death in fact.'

'Which leaves an old monk just dying in the natural course of things.' Up went Hermitage.

'Not necessarily.'

Down came Hermitage again.

'What we have come up with,' Wat explained, 'is a number of other names. While you might have been the only person in the place at the moment Athan found you, you clearly weren't the only one here at all. We've got these Brothers James and Francis, and who did you say was arguing against?'

'Father Genly.'

'Yes, I think we need to see these people.'

'But Father Genly wasn't here. In fact, he was hardly here at all.'

'No, but he had an interest in Ambrosius. Perhaps he was so angered by the argument…'

'That he did what? We know Ambrosius wasn't beaten, he wasn't hit, he wasn't shot. How else do you die apart from old age?' Hermitage knew he hadn't committed a murder and doubted anyone else had. He didn't want there to have been a murder at all. Just to prove all these accusers wrong.

'Oh my dear fellow, there are so many ways,' Wat explained with some relish. 'Suffocation, poisoning, strangulation, drowning…'

'Drowning?'

'All right, not drowning. This time. But just because there isn't a fatal wound in him doesn't mean he wasn't killed. First step is to find Genly, James and Francis; they've got some explaining to do.'

'I don't think Brother Francis is up to explaining things. He's been touched. I'm not sure I've heard him utter a complete sentence at all.'

'Then we can talk to Genly and James, and after that a really tricky one.'

'Who's that?'

'We need to question the one who discovered the body. Athan.'

'Oh dear.'

'Yes, I think we need to consider how to tackle that one. Meanwhile let's start at the top and do the priest first. Where will we find Father Genly?'

'He seems to spend rather a lot of time with the younger Brothers. Giving them special instruction apparently.'

'I can imagine,' said Wat shaking his head as if to remove images from it that refused to leave.

Hermitage led the way out of the refectory again. Back in the relative warmth of an autumnal day, he was thoughtful as they walked.

'I've been thinking about this investigation business,' he announced.

'Oh yes?'

'Yes. All those things we were talking about. Questioning people, getting them to explain, visiting the scene of death. I think all of that is investigation. Tracking the events that led up to the death.'

'Really?' Wat didn't seem to think this was adding anything to their progress.

'In which case shouldn't the King's Investigator be doing them?'

'Could be,' Wat shrugged. He paused and added, ' All I know is that if this Brother Simon is a true King's Investigator, come to solve a mysterious death with his skill and intelligence, then I'm a monk.'

Caput XII

Day Five   Ladye Mass

INDING FATHER GENLY TURNED OUT to be more of a challenge than Hermitage expected. There were all sorts of very strange conversations with Brothers, none of which led to the Priest's whereabouts.

'Ah, Brother,' he called to young Primbard as he was coming out of the privy. 'We're looking for Father Genly.'

The slim young man looked them up and down in a most impudent manner.

'Really?' he said in some surprise, which Hermitage couldn't understand.

'Yes, have you seen him?'

'Might have done.'

'Well, where is he?'

Primbard glanced over his shoulder at the privy and simply shrugged. Hermitage put this down to bad manners or ill breeding, and so they moved on.

Things didn't get any better. Brother Siward claimed never to have heard of a Father Genly, which Hermitage knew was ridiculous because he had seen them together, examining the quality of cloth in one another's habits.

Brother Barnard was positively offended by the question and refused to give information like that to anyone. And Brother Clement offered to sell them the answer for a loaf of bread. Remarkable.

'We're not getting very far, Hermitage, are we?' Wat asked with a wry smile on his face

'I don't understand it. The Father has been constant presence about the place since the Conclave began. Why can't we find him now?'

'Are you sure you don't know where his cell is?'

'Well, that's another odd thing. His cell was the place we went first, I was sure it was his, but it seems not. At least there's no sign of him having slept there.'

Wat chuckled and smiled benignly at Hermitage.

'I don't see what's so amusing. We need to find the man.'

'We certainly do. Let me talk to the next one you line up.'

Hermitage accepted that Wat knew more about the ways of the world, but he was a touch arrogant if he thought he was better at finding a priest in a monastery. After more moments of desultory wandering about, Hermitage spotted Brother Armand coming round a corner. As soon as he spotted them, the monk turned completely on his heels and headed in the other direction.

'Word travels fast,' Wat said, and ran after the retreating habit.

Hermitage stood where he was and waited for the outcome of events. He was confident the weaver would have no better luck locating Father Genly.

Pretty soon Wat and Armand were engaged in a close and confident conversation, which Hermitage couldn't hear. He thought about going over, but if Wat wanted to tackle this on his own then let him get on with it. At one point the weaver must have said something very offensive, as Brother Armand took a step back, turned very pale and said 'That's outrageous!' in a very loud voice.

Wat made calming gestures with his hands and then a couple of other gestures which Hermitage didn't recognise, but which he thought looked rather crude. He hoped Wat wasn't being aggressive with a monk of De'Ath's Dingle. Eventually the Brother threw his hands in the air and stomped off. The weaver returned to Hermitage with an even larger grin.

'Well?' Hermitage wanted to know what was going on.

'He was last seen in, erm, conversation with a Brother Segnar.'

'Brother Segnar?'

'You sound surprised.'

'Brother Segnar is a very strange fellow. Always flitting about in the middle of the night and never available for any chores in the day time. I think he may be touched as well.' Hermitage frowned as he tried to conceive what business Genly and Segnar would have together.

'I think you may be right,' Wat replied simply.

'What is it about you monks and names?' Wat hastily changed the subject, as they walked across the grounds to Segnar's cell. 'Some of you seem to have perfectly normal ones, some seem to be religious and yours doesn't make any sense at all.'

'Ah well, it's part of the order you see.' Hermitage forgot all about the conversations concerning Father Genly and Wat's unaccounted amusement. Here was an intellectual subject, much more to his liking,

'When you take orders you can choose a new name, a name which reflects the approach you will take to your enclosed life. Are you going to be poor or caring, look after the sick or preach the word of God and so forth? Depending what you're going to do you take an appropriate name. Of course you don't have to; you can keep your own name. Most older monks do that, as they're already known in the community. Suddenly changing name from Mark to Brother Paul could cause confusion.'

'And Hermitage? I don't recall seeing that in the Bible.'

'Ah no, well I was slightly different. You see I did want to take a new name when I joined the order. I thought about Brother John, rather like John the Baptist, you know, a humble follower.'

'So what happened?'

'Well the Abbot of my first monastery thought the best thing I could become for the sake of my Brothers was a hermit.'

'Really?'

'Yes. Apparently my power of prayer was so strong that I would do an enormous service to the entire order if I were to go off into a cave somewhere and pray on my own for the rest of my life.' Hermitage tried not to sound boastful, but he felt the glow of pride on his cheeks.

'I see.' Wat disguised his smirking laugh as a cough.

'They would send up food and make sure that I was still alive, but other than that they would leave me alone. After that the Abbot took to calling me Hermitage and the name seemed to sort of stick. I've got used to it now.' Hermitage drifted off in thought for a moment. 'And there are times when I wish I was a hermit, you know,' he said rather plaintively.

'I can imagine there are.' Wat said this with feeling, and he had witnessed only a small selection of the events which made up the life of Brother Hermitage. 'So what's your real name?'

'Oh, I don't have one. That life is gone and the name with it. I shall never speak it again.'

'Fair enough.' Wat accepted this with a nod.

All young men considered the monastic life at one time or another. It offered a way out of constantly fending for yourself all the time. Plenty of women and drink if that was your taste, and a bed of straw to sleep on. Thoughts of retreat were quickly dismissed if you achieved some success in the world. For instance by selling a very risqué tapestry for a huge amount of money.

During this conversation Hermitage had led them a roundabout route, which brought them back to the cells they had started from. Wat was getting used to the place as he showed very little confusion.

Leading through an archway into another block of door-less chambers, Hermitage wandered along looking carefully at each entrance.

'They all look the same,' Wat said with some irritation, as

Hermitage looked at each one as if they had doors with names on them.

'Oh, not at all. With no doors we have to make some indication of which is our cell. It's a very confusing place sometimes and you can find yourself in entirely the wrong building, let alone the wrong cell. There'll be an indication of Brother Segnar's presence somewhere, a little symbol of some sort – we all have them.'

'What are we looking for then?'

'If I recall correctly, Brother Segnar's badge is a Lamb of God sitting on a cross.'

'Pretty complicated picture.'

'Oh, it's very crude,' said Hermitage in all innocence.

'And what's your symbol?'

'Well, you won't believe it, but when I asked if anyone else was using a plain, ordinary cross, no one was.'

'Really?'

'I know, what good fortune. I expect a departed Brother had been using it and it had become vacant just at that moment.'

'Yes, I expect that was it. Is this the one we're looking for?' Wat pointed at a carving on the wall outside one entrance that put the word crude firmly in its place. Whatever this was an image of, it certainly wasn't the Lamb of God atop a cross. It was an animal of some sort and it was sitting on something, but there the similarity ended. Hermitage examined the image closely.

'Ah yes,' he said looking carefully, 'that's it. I don't recall it being that way up though.'

Hermitage entered the cell first and Wat followed. He walked straight into the back of the stationary monk who seemed to have become a solid piece of stone, firmly joined to the floor.

'What is it?' Wat asked trying to crane around Hermitage who was blocking the door. 'Is Father Genly there?'

'Oh, he's definitely here,' Hermitage paused. 'But I don't think he's going to be much help.' He stepped aside and let Wat see the room.

'Oh, bloody hell,' the weaver said as he gazed upon the scene before him.

For some reason Hermitage felt protective of his companion. As he thought about it though, he couldn't see why. Wat was more familiar with the world than he was. It was to be hoped that even he hadn't seen anything like this before.

Father Genly was naked. He was somehow even more naked than the day he was born. There were bits of him on display that any reasonable person should not be expected to see. He was lying on the straw pallet, if face down with your backside in the air can be called lying, and he wasn't moving.

Hermitage knew from his own experience that under the habit, monks were very pale. Faces and hands got scoured by the wind and weather, but the protected parts remained unblemished. The problem was that not all of Genly was unblemished. The cheeks of his backside, proudly presented to anyone entering the room, showed clear marks of chastisement.

'There's a turn up,' Wat added, quite matter of fact. 'I assume this is Father Genly we're looking at?'

Hermitage moved into the room and bent down to get a clear look at the face.

'Oh, yes,' he said, 'but what's happened? Why isn't he dressed?'

Wat's head sank to his chest in deep thought as he considered his reply.

'Brother Hermitage,' he said, with a heavy and weary tone.

'Yes?' came the bright reply.

'Perhaps this is the time.' Wat sounded like Hermitage's father, when he had told a horrified child all about the birds and the bees. And the animals. And the people. And sometimes the animals and the people.

'Time for what?' he asked in some trepidation.

'I have spent many years wandering the length and breadth

of the nation, and I have seen many things.'

'I'm sure.' Hermitage really wasn't getting anything out of this.

'Some of those things, I must confess, I have put into my works. They are works of which I am not particularly proud, but they are very lucrative.'

Wat paused, but Hermitage didn't know what was going on so he kept quiet.

'They are works which are commissioned by individuals who have very particular interests,' Wat hinted.

'Like Ambrosius and the wilderness?' Hermitage remained resolutely unhinted.

'No. Not like Ambrosius and the wilderness. Like Father Genly and his sleeping habits. My clientele, I'm afraid to say, are interested in the more physical aspects of human interaction.'

'You don't think?' Hermitage started and let the awful truth hang unspoken in the dismal cell.

Wat nodded encouragement to Hermitage to take the next step.

'You don't think he's been… robbed?' Hermitage found this hard to credit. This was a monastery after all.

Wat's exasperation snapped out, 'No, I don't think he's been robbed, Hermitage. Look, his habit is on the floor.'

'So it is,' said Hermitage in wonder. 'He surely wouldn't sleep that way, he'd freeze to death.'

'The carnal,' Wat said, very deliberately.

Now that didn't fit the discussion at all. Hermitage was starting to wonder if Wat was talking about something completely different.

'You mean?' said Hermitage, although he wasn't sure what Wat meant.

'That's right,' said the weaver in some relief, grateful that Hermitage had got it.

Except Hermitage hadn't got it, of course. He stared at Wat

for a while. And then stared at Genly.

'Perhaps he wasn't alone?' Wat suggested.

'It's possible, I suppose,' Hermitage admitted, thinking hard.

'Possible?' said Wat, in disbelief. 'In that position, with that look on his face, it's inevitable.'

'There is a woman who comes in to bring the donations from the poor sometimes, but she's an old crone.'

'God spare us,' said Wat. Hermitage frowned.

'So, Brother Hermitage, use your learning. If he wasn't alone and it wasn't a woman, who else could it be?' Wat asked in as innocent a voice as he could manage.

Hermitage's incisive mind took the necessary steps and there was a look of guilt in Wat's eyes as Hermitage drew the only possible conclusion.

When a person realises something to the good, it is often said that their eyes light up. The opposite is clearly not that their eyes go out, but whatever the opposite is, that is what happened to Hermitage. The light that was his innocent awe at the world and all of God's works, spluttered in the face of a gusty blow as he realised what the alternative was.

'You mean?' was all he could say, but it was clear that was exactly what Wat did mean. 'Oh, my goodness,' he said.

Just like in stories, Hermitage really did put his hand to his open mouth and sat down on a nearby stool.

'But he's a priest,' Hermitage said. The two ideas in his head were as contradictory as immovable objects and irresistible forces.

'*Was* a priest,' Wat corrected.

'I didn't, I mean I never, I mean he…' and Hermitage stumbled over thoughts and images that were as unwelcome as they were new. 'Oh Lord,' he came out with as he sat with his head shaking slightly, hoping that the movement would make these evil impressions fall out of his ears.

Wat shrugged. 'These things happen.'

But Hermitage was sure that they shouldn't.

'But only in the Bible,' Hermitage pleaded, 'and only in the Old Testament at that. What are we going to do?'

'That's better,' said Wat. 'An hour ago you would have been down on your knees praying for the soul of the departed. We probably straighten him up. It's not very dignified, is it?' He gestured at the prone priest.

'No,' Hermitage was actually cross. 'Not Genly. What are we going to do about another death? That's two. We were coming here to see if Father Genly could shed any light on the death of Ambrosius. Now we have to try and shed some light on the death of Father Genly.'

'Well, at least this one seems to have a fairly obvious cause.' Wat performed a most inappropriate little dance in front of the body on the bed. 'Exhaustion.'

'Mister Wat! We have to fetch the Investigator, this could all be connected.'

This time Wat was horrified. 'Hermitage, that is exactly what we don't have to do. You've seen the Investigator at work, he's useless. What did the Abbot say it meant?'

'What?'

'Investigate?'

'Oh, to track.'

'Well, this Investigator couldn't track a track across a field with one track and a sign saying 'track this way'. Show him another body and after he's finished throwing up he'll order you hung there and then. Look what happened the last time you were found with a dead body. It's starting to look like a habit, pardon the pun. What we do is just return Father Genly to a more normal position, dress him as best we can and then leave. Someone else can find out about this one.'

'But there must be erm ... someone out there.' Hermitage really couldn't bring himself to think that it might be another monk. 'Someone out there who was here at the time. Someone who knows that Father Genly is dead and has chosen not to tell anyone.'

'We don't know that. Whoever was here might be on their way to tell the Abbot or Athan right now.'

'I hardly think so. It looks like the Father has been in this state for some time. I'm sure we'd have heard by now.'

'So what do you suggest? We go and find Brother Simon and you say, excuse me Brother, but I've found another dead body. I know I was there when the last one was discovered and everyone thinks that I'm a killer, they want to hang me and everything, but I thought I'd better just mention it. And while I'm at it I think one of the Brothers is a sodomite so we'd better ask them?'

'Erm.' Hermitage was having too much for one day.

'What size noose do you take, Hermitage?'

'But he wouldn't.'

'Oh, come off it, of course he would. The man's an imbecile.'

This still didn't sit happily with Hermitage. How could important people with titles be imbeciles? 'What can we do then?'

'Just what I said.'

'But it's – it's dishonest.'

'So is what Father Genly was doing. I think he's going to have more explaining to do when he meets the Lord than you are. I really don't think you can rely on the integrity of either Simon or Athan to take the reasonable view of this, can you?'

Hermitage gave a great sigh. 'Probably not.'

'Far better, then, that you and I look into things further. We think Ambrosius died of natural causes. Genly here died of unnatural causes, but at least they're explicable – but it's all just too much of a coincidence.'

'What, two deaths?'

'And more. The arrival outside of a bunch of builders who have come to tear the place to pieces when no one inside seems to be expecting them.'

'I don't see any connection. Ambrosius and Genly weren't

even residents. They were only here as opponents in the Conclave.'

'Not much of a welcome, eh?' Wat's eyebrows rose as another thought occurred which he let straight out. 'And, of course, that's two of the people connected to the debate dead.'

'What?' Hermitage couldn't keep the tremor out of his voice. A tremor that could have brought down a fair share of masonry all on its own.

'Ambrosius and Genly, the main protagonists, both gone,' Wat said.

'What are you suggesting?' Hermitage really wanted to know.

'Nothing really, it's just another coincidence.' But Wat didn't sound like it was nothing.

'So if Brother Francis or Brother James or even I become co-incidentally dead?' Hermitage asked.

'It's definitely something to do with the debate,' Wat said, brightly.

The two men looked at each other and then once more at the semi-recumbent Father Genly before their unspoken agreement was signed. They moved to the bed to give the man what dignity they could.

'I think we need to find Brother Francis or James as a matter of urgency,' Wat said. Hermitage could see this was the priority. And with his new-found knowledge of some his Brothers, he considered that getting the person who last saw Father Genly alive to come forward voluntarily might be a bit of a problem.

Day Five Magna Missa

HE EARL OF NORTHUMBRIA was not a man to hurry. Neither was he a man to up his pace or get a bit of a move on. He would not speed things up or crack on, jump to it or leap into action. He was a man for whom a lifetime of unimaginable power over others had inculcated the conviction that the world moved at his pace, not vice versa.

The Earl's wealth brought him time. Most of it belonging to other people. He didn't have to do any of the boring chores that normal people did simply to survive, and so all of that time was his to play with. He didn't have to find food or build a house. He didn't have to maintain his dwelling or go out to work for someone else in order to get the necessities of life. He simply got up in the morning and went to bed at night. The period in between was full of stuff, but there were always people to deal with all of that. God knew why they wanted to, but they seemed willing enough.

He knew other people didn't live the way he did. He had servants and staff all around him, and it was obvious that they didn't have the same choices about their days that he did. But then they didn't matter.

Thus, as the Earl of Northumbria had decided that he needed to see the monastery as a matter of the utmost urgency, it was some half a day later they were nearly ready to set off.

Nicodemus observed the preparations from a distance, as his retinue was tiny compared to the Earl's. He could be ready to move in an hour or so. It had taken that long for the Earl's head man to take the register to make sure that none of his servants had run off.

Toksvar was as organised as Nicodemus, only in a far more alarming manner. He did have a large number of servants, but they had practiced every move required to get their master ready for travel. They packed to the sound of whistles while Toksvar paced up and down in front of them, slapping one around the ear and kicking another one on the shin when some tiny step went awry. When it wasn't done right, he made them unpack and do it again. At the end of each attempt they would line up and stand bolt upright, hands by their sides, to await the inspection. If there was a problem, they would all get into small huddles to discuss how to improve performance, but if it was favourable they would slap one another on their backs and sing some hearty song. It was unbearable.

Nicodemus's party would lead the way, as they knew where they were going, and Toksvar would bring up the rear – an ideal position for ensuring that the Earl's rabble didn't simply run off with all his goods and chattels.

Toksvar and Nicodemus had assumed that the short journey would be completed in one day. They had reckoned without an Earl. Northumbria declared before the outset that it was his intention to take in some of the more interesting sights on their journey. Nicodemus had assured Toksvar this wouldn't be an impediment, because there weren't any. It hadn't occurred to him that the Earl would want to visit the Roman fortress, which was only two hundred yards from where they started.

When the august noble instructed his hopeless staff to make camp when they had only walked across a cobbled courtyard, Toksvar stepped in. He told them that if any of them so much as unpacked a sock, he would hang them all from the Roman fortress's historic and highest tower as an entertainment for the Earl, whom they all knew liked that sort of thing.

The Earl expressed his disappointment by swearing, once again, that if his eldest son Vignar were to die, he would rather leave his entire estates to the bastard son of a Danish horn polisher than see one iota of grass on the arse of one of his lambs pass to Toksvar. His son responded that Vignar's death could be easily arranged, followed closely by the Earl's, and that he would rather suck the grass from a lamb's arse than accept the off-cuts of the Earl's small toenail. And so the small talk continued. At least they didn't stop to look at the fortress.

For a short while, the journey continued in relative peace. All that happened from Nicodemus's point of view was that there was some muttering and laughter from the Earl's portion of the line. Whenever he turned around to see what was going on, some piece of discarded food would drop from the Earl's carriage. Or a servant would wander off into the undergrowth for some undisclosed purpose.

The whole of the Earl's retinue wasn't so much travelling as meandering, with no connection between any of the people who were moving along. It was procession by coincidence rather than design. It was even hard to tell which direction they were going in, as the people involved could be seen all over the place.

✦   ✦   ✦

As the party wandered on, a figure drew up to the carriage of the Earl. The figure made sure it was unseen as it threw aside a curtain and stepped into the slowly moving vehicle.

'Master,' it said as it approached the recumbent figure of the Earl, who was dozing on a large number of expensive cushions.

'Eh, what?' The Earl woke with a start and clipped the nearest servant round the ear. 'Oh, it's you,' he said as the new arrival removed a very smart cowl from his head.

'It is, Master.' The figure bowed low from his kneeling position, presenting the top of his expertly shaven head to the Earl.

'What are you doing here, you idiot?' the Earl spat as he gained some of his senses.

'I was not seen, Master. I am never seen.'

'Oh, for goodness sake. And stop calling me Master; it draws attention and you should know that's not wanted.'

The figure simply nodded.

'Well?'

'I bring news, Mas– er, my Lord.'

'I should think you bloody well do. Can't have you creeping about into people's carriages without news. What is it?'

The figure glanced at the two servants who were perched on either side of the Earl. With a simple, two-elbow nudge the Earl deposited them both on the roadside.

'Go on.'

'The path continues,' the figure said.

'Is that it? You better have some more news than that for waking me up. I know the path continues. I'm on it.'

'Your men make their moves.'

'Which ones?'

'The men of,' the figure paused for emphasis, 'the Craft.'

'Oh, the builders.'

The figure grimaced slightly at this crudity.

'Sire.'

'And Master Nicodemus?'

'Continues on the…'

'Don't say he's on the path as well, tell me what he's up to.'

'He commissions the work as planned.'

'And he has no idea.'

'None.'

'Excellent. Now this death I've heard about. Some debate or other. How does this affect us?'

'Deaths, Master. Two.'

'Really? A dangerous place this monastery.'

'Oh no, Master, nothing like that. As you know we do have a man there who is our ears and eyes. Unfortunately he will be unable to report further.'

'For what reason?'

'Er, his death…'

'Oh, he's one of them? That's not good. Are we discovered?'

'A coincidence, Master. No connection at all. The man was in a vulnerable state. It seems he just chose the wrong moment to reach the end of his vulnerability.'

'I don't like coincidences. Don't believe in them. And the other one?'

'Another natural event.'

'That is going too far.'

'It is a goodly sized community. I imagine death is a regular visitor.'

'I'm not convinced.'

'It could be most helpful.'

'How?'

'Should keep the monastery authorities occupied. Nicodemus has sent a Brother Simon to deal with that side of events.'

'Do we know him?'

'We know of him, he has a reputation.'

'Really?' This gave the Earl some concern.

'An appalling one,' the figure comforted his master.

'Ha ha, marvellous. Muddy the waters completely while we crack on, eh?'

'Such is the intention.'

'Right. You go and keep an eye on things, make sure no one makes any progress. You're good at that.'

'Master.' The figure took the compliment.

'I'll keep Nicodemus on the straight and narrow until the time is right to dispense with him all together.'

The figure raised his cowl once more and made for the back of the carriage.

'And if, on the journey I manage to run over my son with a cart, so much the better.'

The Earl laughed heartily, but the figure was gone.

✦   ✦   ✦

One of the servants only recently discarded on to the road from the Earl's carriage stepped quickly up the road towards Toksvar.

The contrast between the Earl and Toksvar's line was startling, if not slightly disturbing. All of his people were marching in step and it looked like some of the horses were as well. Nicodemus was rather grateful that he had to lead the party. Being at the front meant that he didn't have to talk to either leading member of the Northumbria family. His relaxation was short-lived though as, with a clop of hooves, Toksvar approached and drew up alongside.

'Well, we are on our way at last,' he said with a loud and cheerful voice.

Oh well, thought Nicodemus, better the young madman than the old stinkpot.

'Indeed, sire, and it will not be a long journey if we go direct.'

'Oh I can't guarantee that, I'm afraid. The ghastly lump of flesh that calls itself my father seldom does anything with much purpose any more. I shall use my best tactic, though, to keep him moving.'

'And what is that?'

'I shall go and talk to him, that'll reinvigorate his purpose.'

'Ah.' Nicodemus didn't know what to say.

'I can see you don't know what to say.' Toksvar read his mind. 'Few people do. Anyone not familiar with our family intimacies, and that usually means anyone south of York, would be staggered by what goes on. It's always thus and always will be. My older brother Vignar will, of course, inherit everything.'

'Of course,' Nicodemus said, although he wondered why this topic had been brought up. Vignar was the eldest son: what was there to discuss?

'And I must take me to his service as is right and proper. I will probably be given some minor estate out of the way and if I keep my head down I can lead a long and comfortable life.'

It sounded ideal to Nicodemus.

'Except, of course, I've been brought up in an Earl's house and I want to be an Earl. In order to achieve this I can't have any brothers older than me and I need to have a dead father.'

Nicodemus looked shocked.

'You look shocked.' Perceptive chap, this.

Nicodemus wasn't shocked at the idea; that was perfectly reasonable. He was, though, shocked at being told all about it.

'It's all part of the selection process really. If I can get rid of my brother before my father dies, and then have that happen fairly quickly afterwards, it obviously shows that I'm cut out to be an Earl. I have all the necessary qualities, you see. Obviously if my father were to pop off now it would leave my brother as Earl and that would make things a lot more complicated. He would have all the power, the authority, the land and the men with pikes. Be much harder to get at.'

'But surely your father…?' Nicodemus's suspicion that familial affection might be buried beneath a surface of open hostility was being firmly put in its place.

'It would obviously be better for my brother that there were no younger sibling around either, but my father can't have that. We live in dangerous times and it's quite possible that my brother could meet with death by a myriad of different paths. He is terribly military, likes marching around shouting at people and hitting them. Loves nothing more than a trip to the coast with the King so that he can slaughter some Danes. That's where he is now, as a matter of fact. Risky business, though, and who would become the next Earl if my brother got caught on the wrong end of a long boat?

'So you see my father has a real dilemma. He wants me dead so that I'll stop bothering my brother, but he can't have me completely dead as I'm required as a standby Earl. There is an entirely sensible way out which would give the old gasser the arrangement he wants. He could do the decent thing and die. That way

Vignar becomes Earl as he wants. Trouble is the selfish bastard won't do even that for his family. I ask you, it's just me, me, me with him.'

'But surely if he were to die?' Nicodemus was puzzled. The argument was sound, but Toksvar's actions didn't match. 'As you say, that would make things difficult for you, why does it appear that you, erm …' He didn't quite know how to say it so he made a little mime with his hands, of a cart with an Earl in it being pushed into a river.

'Oh, I see,' said Toksvar, 'why would I try to kill my father when it would leave me in a worse position?'

'Exactly.'

'He's handy.' Toksvar shrugged as if he'd just decided to have the pork instead of the lamb and beamed in a most un-usual manner. Nicodemus wondered who would be next in line if there wasn't a member of the young man's own direct family nearby ready to be slaughtered. Was Toksvar's younger brother really off in the diplomatic service or had some accident already befallen that young man? Apart from having been born into this ghastly family in the first place, of course.

'So Father's latest wheeze is to have me take holy orders, for God's sake. Me, I ask you? Do I strike you as the religious type?' Toksvar's question seemed genuine.

Nicodemus had made his mind up that he wasn't going to let this man strike him as anything. He shrugged in what he hoped was a noncommittal sort of way.

A servant, far too scruffy to be one of Toksvar's, approached the side of the man's horse and whispered into his ear.

'And this monastery of yours appears to be the answer.' Toksvar took whatever the message was and continued the conversation. 'Very comfortable, but what else? Big high walls and guard dogs?'

'Oh no, sire, nothing like that – quite the opposite in fact.'

Toksvar raised his eyebrows.

'But I hear you've had some trouble there yourself?' The man said this in such a knowing and devious tone that it was clear he knew something from somewhere.

'A minor altercation. It'll all be sorted out by the time we get there.'

'A dead monk, I hear tell.'

'Nothing out of the ordinary. A harsh life, that of a monk.'

'But in the middle of the Conclave?'

'A routine event, I assure you. I've already dispatched a fellow to attend to all the necessary formalities.'

'I'm not sure I fancy a monastery where the death of the inmates, sorry, Brothers, is a matter of routine.'

'This was an elderly fellow who had reached the end of his allotted span, no cause for concern.'

'Yes, but what about the other one?'

'What other one?' Nicodemus gulped before he could stop himself.

◆   ◆   ◆

'Where else could Francis and James be?'

Wat was getting frustrated. The search for Genly had been overly complicated, but the next two targets were nowhere.

'I don't understand it. I mean, we've looked everywhere; it's almost as if they're moving around ahead of us, keeping out of our way.'

'It is, isn't it?' said Wat, with some interest.

'I suppose it will do no harm to go to the main entrance. Ask the gatekeeper if they've gone out somewhere?'

'Should they do that?' Wat asked, surprised.

'Oh, absolutely not. But we've been everywhere else.'

'Lead on.'

When they arrived at the gate there was a bit of a scene. The gatekeeper, a large linen bandage around his wound, stained red with the contents of his head, was holding quite a large log and waving it around as he sought to keep the King's Investigator at bay. Simon had his bag packed and was trying to leave the monastery as directly as he could. Whenever he made a beeline for the open gate, the keeper would hobble into his way and brandish his timber.

'Let's see how you like it,' the man said in a very calm but rather scary voice.

Handicapped by several private discussions with Athan, capped off by the sort of blow to the head that could have taken out one of the monastery's more robust towers, the man was not capable of co-ordinated physical action at all, let alone an attack on a moving target.

He repeatedly swung wildly from side to side more in hope than expectation. Such was the vigour and devotion to his task that if he had struck home he would have taken the King's Investigator's head clean off – at least that seemed to be the general idea.

Taking the situation in quickly, Hermitage and Wat moved forward to bring things to a halt. Simon reacted as if two more were coming to join in. He couldn't retreat now. His only way out was the small inner gate that stood open, the beauty of the outside world beckoning like a homely lantern.

Not wanting to be on the receiving end of the tree, Hermitage and Wat were cautious as they approached. They circled around, looking for an opening. Neither of them was inclined to risk their own limbs against the gatekeeper.

Simon was getting the measure of his damaged opponent. He feinted one way, waited until the hobbled gateman dragged himself in that direction and then sprang away, as if to enter the shack. For an oldish man he seemed remarkably adept at avoiding trouble. At the last moment he skipped away with the agility of one who had spent a lot of time skipping away from incoming blows and was two steps from escape.

The gatekeeper, seeing the move, used his momentum to spin

himself around and despite the agony this caused his battered body, raised his weapon for a merciless blow on the retreating Brother Simon.

The blow flew, the blow struck and the blow destroyed. Simon, with an instinctive avoidance of violence, ducked at just the right moment and let the wood strike the building behind him.

Thus the blow destroyed the humble shack of the gatekeeper in a single moment. The dumbstruck man could only stand and watch as first the walls, and then the roof of his home collapsed into a pile of shattered wood until it looked like nothing more than a bonfire.

'Nooo...,' he screamed and collapsed to his knees, 'you bastard, you absolute...' The stream of obscene invective which sprang from the monk's mouth would have shamed the famous Swearing Man of Grimsby – famous for having driven Vikings from the coast at Hull simply by telling them they couldn't leave their boats on the beach.

Seeing his moment to escape, Simon stepped up to the small door to leave. He bumped straight into, and bounced off, a huge tree of a man who was coming in the other direction. Fearing another attack, the King's Investigator scrambled quickly to his feet. He was assisted by two massive hands which lifted him bodily, brushed him down while his feet were still two inches off the ground and then planted him like sapling.

All present gaped at the huge shape that now blotted out the gate altogether. It raised its right hand, which held a large staff, decorated with strange and mysterious markings.

'I've come to measure up,' said Chirk the builder, proudly displaying his ruler for everyone to see.

Caput XIV

Day Five   Before Vespers

ROTHER ATHAN WAS A MAN with a mission. It wasn't a very nice mission, in fact it was positively sinful, but it gave him a purpose in life. Monks abroad within the precincts, who would have scuttled out of the way to avoid the man's gaze, let alone his blows, found that they were ignored. Athan was searching for something. They were all enormously grateful that it wasn't them.

Early in his expedition he asked one or two if they had seen Simon, the King's Investigator, and they answered that no, they hadn't. Everyone knew never to tell Athan that you didn't know what he was talking about. Here was Brother Snod. He was a nosy so and so, always prying into other people's business, and usually getting a punch in the eye for his trouble. He was bound to know.

'All right, Snod, hold it there.'

Brother Snod sniggered, but stopped very quickly.

'I want to know if you've seen someone,' Athan glared with eyes and voice.

'Oh yes,' said Snod, brightly, 'I've seen…'

'And I warn you,' Athan continued, 'that I am not in a good mood. So, if you give me any of your so-called wit, I shall wrap it round my fist and use it to rip your ears off.'

'Right,' said Snod in a suddenly sombre mood. 'Who might I have seen?'

'He's called Brother Simon and he's the King's Investigator.'

'Sounds impressive.'

'It isn't.'

'Well, it doesn't mean anything to me. What's he look like?'

'A weasel.'

'Hmm?' Brother Snod pondered. 'A bit more, perhaps?'

'He's a sneaky, shifty, weasel-faced cretin of a man. He has all the brains of a goat and smells like one as well. That's because he is the offspring of his mother's fornication with the runt of the flock. He is a deceitful, self-serving, underhanded sycophant who would sell his own grandmother for the chance to suck up to the third son of a second-rate noble. If his grandmother could be persuaded to own up to having anything to do with him, that is.' Athan paused for breath, and the colour of his face darkened.

'He is a creeping, slimy, crawling thing who has no more right to walk the surface of the earth than this bug.' Athan stamped with vigour on a beetle who just happened to be passing. 'He is not fit to wipe the soles of the feet of beggars, who have just walked through a dung heap, on their way to the annual stinking feet contest at Wickham.'

Snod's mouth opened once, but he clearly thought better of interrupting.

'He's a worm.' Athan was now almost screaming and Snod was backing off slightly. The poor monk looked around as if expecting some aid to come his way. Other Brothers who were nearby backed off completely.

'He is less than a worm, he is a worm's armpit. At least worms have some use. He is a destroyer of all that is good in the world. He takes men of worth and value and casts them aside as if they were nose droppings, simply to assuage an inflated view of his own importance. He is a crook and a liar and deserves to be roasted for eternity in the burning, fiery furnace.' Athan was rising to a crescendo now and Snod had a very worried look on his face.

Several other Brothers poked their heads around the walls they had hidden behind to watch the display. And perhaps to sympathise with Snod. And perhaps not.

'He was put on earth by the Serpent himself to wreak destruction on all that is good and true. And to do so in such a manner that the hatred of the entire human race is poured upon his head in a stream of filth from the very arse of the creator, without end.' Athan finished with a scream and took several deep breaths as he recovered himself.

Snod looked around the area at the watching faces.

'Er,' he said, pointing very carefully, 'is that him?'

Just at this moment Simon came around a corner with Wat, Hermitage and Chirk.

'Yes!' Athan yelled in triumph, and made straight for the Investigator with no good will in his heart. The distance between the two men, and the presence of witnesses, acted as some sort of control, however, and Athan's rage was bottled. A bit. He gripped his fists tight to his side and approached the group with what self-control he was capable of.

This gave sufficient time for Simon to hide behind Chirk.

'What?' said Wat.

'Yes, I know,' said Athan.

'No, I mean what's going on?' Wat's irritated tone was annoyed with monks and all things monastic.

'Going on?' said Athan, trying to sound all innocent. He was so successful that he sounded like a ferret trying to persuade a rabbit to pop out for lunch. 'What could be going on?' He hid his clenched fists behind his back, but the rage still shone from his face. 'I just need to have a word with the King's Investigator. In private.'

The reaction from Simon said that was the last thing that was going to happen. If it did happen, it probably would be the last thing.

'No, no,' said Wat, still snappy and ignoring the murderous intent of Brother Athan and the rapid cringing of Simon. 'What's this builder doing here?' he demanded. 'He says he's come to measure up.'

'What?' Athan had trouble with this. He stared open-mouthed at Wat and looked from one face to the other.

Wat spoke, gestured and made miming movements at the same time.

'This man builder,' Wat gestured at Chirk although there was little need, given the size of the man and the state of his clothing, 'why he here?'

'I'm not an idiot,' Athan said, his attention diverted from Investigator to builder.

'Excellent,' said Wat. 'I'm glad I've found the one person in this place who isn't.'

Watching monks gasped at this impudence and waited for the explosion. It didn't come.

'So why is there a builder here?' Wat repeated.

'Why does that matter?' Athan shook the nonsense from his head. He was dismissive of the question. 'We have one dead monk, a King's something or other who probably can't tell a corpse from a copse, and a priest whose death, while not exactly unexpected, is a bit of a bloody coincidence, and you want to know about the builders?'

'It could be important,' Wat said, very deliberately.

'Oh, could it? And what exactly does it have to do with you, Mister Wat? And why exactly are you still here?' The old Athan was back. He poked Wat in the chest.

There were nods of recognition and anticipation from the watching flock.

'Mister Wat accompanied us from Lincoln,' Hermitage put in, hoping that it would help. It didn't.

'I know,' Athan barked. 'So he's a suspect as well then?'

'Look,' Wat shouted. At Brother Athan. 'All I want to know is what the builder is doing here.'

Athan's familiar annoyance was bubbling to the surface. 'And we want to know why you want to know, and why you want to know.'

Everyone looked very puzzled at this, and there was no immediate answer.

'I've come to measure up,' said Chirk, who seemed to be terribly excited at the prospect.

'Yes, Chirk, we know.' In the short journey from the gate Hermitage had concluded that there was little point in trying to engage with the builder. There was also little point in getting him to do any building for you, let alone measuring up. He was sure that the man could adequately put one rock on top of another, but that was probably the extent of his value to the world of construction. That he would be able to read his ruler at all was doubtful.

'I need to know,' Wat addressed Athan as he got his head around the question, 'because there is something going on here. Then I need to know because no one else seems to be approaching this matter without having already leaped to their own conclusion in a single bound.'

'It's quite clear what's going on,' Athan said definitively and almost spat at the weaver. 'Brother Ambrosius died and was obviously murdered by this,' he gestured at Hermitage, 'as proved by the fact that he was there at the time. The King's personal do-dah agrees. Father Genly has then died, but he probably just died. That's what's going on and it's nothing to do with you.'

'How come you now think that the King's do-dah agreeing has any value? A moment ago you implied he was useless. And what do you want to see him in private about anyway?' Wat peered at the two men in turn through slitted eyes.

'A purely personal matter,' Athan said, sounding as aloof as he could. Which still gave the distinct impression that he wanted to do something very personal to the Investigator.

'I don't like coincidences,' Wat said as if this was supposed to explain everything.

'Oh dear,' said Athan, not caring less.

'I don't understand, Mister Wat,' Hermitage said. 'What

have the builders got to do with anything?'

'Exactly,' said Athan

Wat sighed as if some child-like explanation was required.

'The tradesmen in Lincoln said that there was a major piece of work about to start out here and they would all be heading this way. Hermitage doesn't know anything about this and he lives here.'

'Funnily enough,' said Athan, 'we tend not to share the long-term plans of the monastery with the least significant members of the community.'

'And no one else knows either,' Wat went on. 'When we get here we find the tent contractor putting the builders' village up. We find Chirk ready to measure up.'

Chirk proudly thrust his ruler forward for all to see and admire.

'I've had a quiet word with several of the monks and none of them know anything about builders either.'

Wat was obviously deeply intrigued by this.

Athan obviously wasn't. 'I really don't see what any of this has to do with anything. Or, and I ask the question again, why it is any of your business. Why don't I just get a couple of my very large Brothers to escort you to the door and make sure that you don't walk back through it again? Or be able to walk anywhere else for that matter?' Athan relished the prospect.

'It's my business because I bumped into a helpless and rather hopeless monk on the road to Lincoln.'

'I say,' said Hermitage

'Sorry, Hermitage,' said Wat, 'and when I get him home I find that his Brothers in God want to string him up for a crime he quite patently didn't commit.'

'Oh, didn't he?' said Athan

'Of course he didn't. For one thing he's not capable.'

Hermitage almost butted in with 'oh yes, I am', but realised that it wouldn't be helpful.

'And for another thing, you are too damn keen to see him hang and hang quickly. We've discovered that there were two other Brothers there at the time, but you haven't even attempted to find them and ask what went on. I will agree with you that the King's Investigator appears to be several sorts of fool all at the same time, and so we can't believe anything he says. Which tells a tale in itself. It's almost as if he was selected to simply agree with the right people.'

There was some incoherent muttering from Simon at this grievous insult. He wasn't prepared to take the issue up with the whole group though.

'And then there are the builders,' Wat said, as if this opened up a whole new bucket of worms.

Chirk felt it was sufficient just to nod towards his ruler at this reference. He looked around at the funny monks who appeared to be even more barking than the average.

Wat hadn't finished trying to get his point over. 'It would be strange enough if we simply had one dead monk and a monastery more than keen to execute one of their own number. But we have two dead monks.'

'One monk and a priest,' Hermitage corrected.

'We have one dead monk, and a priest, and a monastery leadership out for blood, and builders turning up that no one knows about.' said Athan, 'well now that you've got all that off your chest perhaps you can be on your way and leave us to get on with our work.'

'Just a minute.' Wat wasn't accepting this.

'I don't have to answer your questions, weaver.' Athan said the last word as if weaving were akin to indecent acts with animals of the forest. Probably dead animals.

'I'd better ask the Abbot then.'

'Ha.' Athan thought that was really funny.

'No, really,' Wat said, 'it was clear from our last conversation that he has no time for Brother Simon. He released Hermitage and said that he couldn't have killed Ambrosius.' A revelatory thought crossed his face. 'I wonder if he knows about the builders.' He asked this in that very sly tone of voice that says 'I know what you're up to.'

'The Abbot is the leader of our community, he knows all there is to know,' Athan said bluntly.

'Hmm.' Wat wasn't convinced.

'Anyway,' Athan was clearly about to dismiss Wat, 'you have made your views abundantly clear and rest assured that we will give them their due weight when coming to our final conclusion.' He paused for a very short moment. 'There we are, they've had their due weight. Now, the Investigator and I will retire and consider matters further.' Athan looked around. 'Where's he gone?' he screamed.

They all looked around and realised that Brother Simon was nowhere to be seen.

'Find him!' Athan yelled at all of the Brothers who had gathered around for the entertainment. They knew better than to wait for Athan to repeat himself and so they scattered to the corners of the monastery. Looking for someone or other apparently.

Athan himself stomped off leaving Wat, Hermitage and Chirk alone in the quad. The weaver and the monk exchanged looks, which varied from complete confusion at events to sympathy for the idiocy of mankind. There was clearly no point in trying to make sense of this at the moment and so mutual shrugs were exchanged. Hermitage was getting the hang of shrugging.

Chirk looked around him once and then set to measuring up, which he did by holding his ruler up against things, looking at it carefully and muttering before wandering on.

'We really, really need to find Brothers Francis and James,' Wat said eventually.

'I know, but how?' Hermitage was puzzled, given they had already searched the monastery completely.

'The time has come to use some more direct methods,' Wat said, and winked at Hermitage. Despite the friendly gesture, the young monk felt a bit of a shiver run down his back.

✦   ✦   ✦

Brother Simon's departure had been stealthy and unnoticed. He was a man who didn't want to be found by anyone. As he went, he tried his best to weigh up his options by repeating them out loud. He was even condescending and patronising when he talked to himself.

His wanderings along the corridors brought him with ear-shot of the routine of the monastery. The sound of a shovel and something soft being dropped into a bucket came round the convoluted turns, and more turns, of the stone.

'Aha,' he said, 'I shall stop some passing monk and instruct him to accompany me out of the monastery.' He paused for a thought about the exit. 'If that has to be through the main gate, my guide can negotiate with the gatekeeper, or at least act as some sort of shield. Better still, perhaps there is some secret back door where none of the inmates of this madhouse can obstruct my passage. Perhaps I can order the fellow to accompany me to Lincoln. The person of the King's Investigator must be protected.'

Walking down the passage – with which it was a shame Simon was not familiar, as it contained a number of the better known exit routes – he was brought up by a shadow that seemed to move of its own volition.

'Who's there?' he called, trying to sound demanding and powerful but achieving neither.

The shadow moved off to his left. It could be some monk about his normal business. It could be a trick of the light. It could some miscreant up to no good. Simon's instincts took over and he went right.

After a few more moments the shadow appeared again, this

THE HERETICS OF DEATH

time in front of him. It was the same shadow. A cowled head, but clearly visible legs. Not a monk in his habit then. The thought of cautiously investigating this apparition, of following it to see what it was didn't even approach Simon's head. He turned on his heels and walked away. Quickly.

Had he bothered to stay and watch he would have seen the shadow throw its hands up in despair and retreat rapidly down the corridor.

More random wanderings amongst the random corridors brought him to a bend around which the shadow was visible once more.

Simon stopped. Perhaps there was more than one shadow. Or it was the same one able to travel through walls. Either way it was after him and running away had done no good.

As he watched with mounting terror the shadow beckoned to him. One dark and withering arm stretched out and slowly called him towards it.

When Simon made no move at all the arm became a bit more impatient, and quickly indicated that Simon should move himself.

Still no movement, and so the shadow stood with hands on hips for a second or two before stamping one foot and beckoning again.

This time Simon moved. Very slowly and reluctantly, but he moved. He didn't really have anywhere else to go. As he approached the shadow it receded down the corridor, leading him on.

This gave Simon some confidence that he wasn't going to be set upon and so he quickened his pace.

He followed around corners and down turnings, the shadow always maintaining its distance but occasionally having to stop while Simon tested whether he was allowed to give up or not. Passing around one last corner, he saw that the shadow had gone.

There didn't seem to be anything particular about this place. It looked exactly the same as every other ghastly spot in this ghastly place. All he wanted was a way out and he cursed himself for being led astray by mysterious shadows.

He paused to get what bearings he could and then heard the hissing noise. It was the sort of hissing noise that only comes from someone who is trying not to attract attention to themselves, but in fact does so admirably simply by hissing, which no one else around them is doing.

'Who's there?' Simon asked to the walls in general.

'Oy!' one of the walls said and Simon nearly jumped out of his meagre skin as a monk unpeeled himself from the stonework. Even though this man was as grey and pasty as the wall and, like most monks of De'Ath's Dingle, thin enough to fit in the cracks between the stones, Simon was shocked and alarmed.

'Come with me,' the monk said.

'Certainly not,' Simon said. No one accompanied strange monks in dark places. This seemed doubly important in a place like De'Ath's Dingle.

'We know you're hiding,' the monk said, looking shiftily up and down the passage.

'We?' said Simon in some surprise. One monk in a dark place was risky enough, but two? You could say goodbye to whatever it was you had that they wanted.

'Brother Francis and I,' the strange monk whispered, as if the walls themselves could hear him and would go and tell the Abbot.

Francis? Simon frowned for a moment with some vague recognition. It soon passed.

'Have you been following me? Or leading me rather?'

'What?' the monk looked very shocked at this. 'We haven't moved. What have you seen?'

'The shadow of a man kept appearing on the wall. Of course, I chased after it to see what was going on.'

The monk wailed. 'You've seen the cowled shadow.'

'Well, it was a cowled shadow, I suppose.'

'Dead are those who see the cowled shadow.'

'I'm not dead.'

'Not yet you're not. The cowled shadow appears around the monastery. Some say it's the spirit of one of the builders of the place. Buried under his own masonry in some hideous accident, and left there to die.'

'Oh, really.'

'Or that it's the ghost of William De'Ath, come to wreak his horrible revenge.'

'It just beckoned me along the corridor. It looked like an ordinary man.'

'That's what it does. Good job Francis and I didn't see it.'

'And what exactly is it you and Brother Francis are up to?'

'Hiding.'

'Hiding from what? The cowled shadow?'

'The Serpent.'

'Ah.' Simon nodded, carefully. Two more madmen to add to the college of lunatics who wandered the precincts of this monastery as if it was their natural habitat. He backed away ever so slightly. There probably wasn't even a real Brother Francis; he would be one of those imaginary monks made up by the less willing novices to keep them company. Simon thought about running, but the thin and ghost-like fellow before him looked young enough to win.

'What?' came a voice from the darkness, which Simon assumed must be Brother Francis after all. He backed a bit further, not wanting to let himself get surrounded by them.

'It's another hiding monk,' the one in front of Simon answered to a piece of the wall.

'What do you mean, a hiding monk?' Simon blurted out. He was trying not to engage these people in conversation.

'We can tell,' the wall-monk said.

'Really?' Simon asked, still trying to sound frantically interested while looking for the quickest route of escape.

'Oh yes, it's in the walk.'

'Is it?'

'It is. And the look. It's in the walk and the look. A bit shifty, a bit too hurried, lots of looking around and examination of your surroundings. People going somewhere don't tend to look where they've been so much. They don't examine the route so closely. And someone without a destination is either out for a nice stroll, or is contemplating, or is getting away from something. Those getting away from something are usually looking for a quick escape route, like you are now.' He paused to let Simon take this in. 'Or they're looking for somewhere to get out of the way, while whatever it is they're getting away from goes by. Am I right?'

'What are you talking about? I've only just arrived.'

'Ah, but we've been watching you.'

'Then you saw the shadow as well and know that I was following that.'

'I've never seen the shadow,' the monk barked, most insistent. He forgot it straight away. 'Now the nice stroller can be subdivided into the idle moments, the interested examiner or the bored. The former is easy to spot you see. Lots of...'

'Yes, yes, right,' Simon said. The man was embarking on something of an exposition on the various motivations of walking and it seemed to be a bit of an obsession. Obsessed monks in dark places. It was getting worse.

'You, my friend, are a clear doesn't-want-to-be-founder?'

'Am I?'

'Oh yes. I said to Brother Francis I said, that gentlemen there is a clear...'

'All right.' Simon tried to wrap the explanation up.

The man had relaxed somewhat now and was turning out to be a rambling madman instead of a skulking one.

'So you can come and not be found with us. We've got a good

place we have. They won't find you here. The Serpent hasn't found us, so it must be safe.'

Before he could back away, the monk had grabbed Brother Simon by the arm and dragged him into the wall. Not literally into the wall, obviously. There was a turn in the masonry that was hard to spot from any distance. This led around a couple of corners until it reach a dead end, mostly surrounded by stone, in the middle of which sat another monk.

At least Simon could see from this one's face that there was no question about his sanity. He was as mad as a coot. He stared at Simon as if the Investigator had just trodden on the corpse of his dead mother. He cradled a small stone in his lap to which he kept mumbling. Little clues of madness that even Simon could pick up. Unfortunately, even though this madman was huddled almost double on the floor Simon could see that he was young, healthy and built like a keep.

'He's saving the rock for the Serpent,' the first monk explained. 'I'm Brother James, by the way, and this is Francis.'

'What,' said Francis in greeting. He held up his rock for Simon to admire.

'Very nice.' Simon nodded vigorously and smiled.

'Have you heard it?' James asked

'Erm, I don't think so.' Simon was noncommittal.

'Oh, you'd know if you had. Hisses it does.'

'Ah, the Serpent, of course.' Simon smiled reassuringly.

'We heard it, didn't we?' James spoke to Francis, who held up his rock again.

'Couldn't it have just been a, erm, snake?' said Simon, although he imagined that they had thought of this.

'In the refectory? And loud it was, hissed like the very Serpent itself, come to take us from the Garden of Eden.'

Simon's eyes widened at this. The monastery of De'Ath's Dingle wasn't even remotely connected to the dung heap at the bottom of Garden of Eden.

'Ah, that Serpent,' he said.

'The only one.'

'Of course. And erm … what was it doing here, do you think?' Simon asked. More out of politeness to a dangerous madman in a confined space than from any desire to actually know.

'Killed Brother Ambrosius, didn't it? And now it wants us.'

'Oh,' said Simon with some shock. 'How do you know it killed Brother Ambrosius?'

'And how do you know so much about the Serpent?' James asked with a narrowing of his eyes. Francis hefted his rock.

'I don't know anything about it,' Simon responded hurriedly, one eye firmly fixed on Francis's rock. 'You told me, remember?'

James thought long and hard. 'Right,' he eventually said grudgingly. The rock was returned to readiness. 'Why do you want to know though?' James wasn't completely satisfied.

Simon straightened his back, thrust out what little chest he had and lifted his chin just a fraction. 'I am the King's Investigator,' he announced.

'What?' said Francis.

'The King's own personal Investigator,' he ladled it on.

'And what's one of them?' James asked. He narrowed his eyes again. 'And what's it got to do with Serpents?'

'I have been sent here to look into the death of Ambrosius.'

'Yeuch,' said James

'Indeed,' said Simon, with a shiver and clenching of stomach muscles, 'but I can help you with the Serpent.'

'How?'

'Well, as I say, I am the King's Investigator.'

'We know,' said James, wanting something more.

'So,' said Simon, thinking very quickly, for him, 'I have the authority of the King.'

'And?'

'And the King is anointed by God.'

'So?' This man was never satisfied.

'So the anointed of God have authority over the beasts of the earth and the birds of the air.'

'Yeah, but this isn't just any Serpent, this is the real Serpent, The SERPENT, you know.'

'Don't fear, my son.' Simon was back to condescending normality.

'So you can fight the Serpent off.' It was a bald statement, and when it was put like this Simon wasn't keen on the sound of it.

'Well,' he responded, with some hesitation, 'first of all we have to be sure that it is the Serpent of the Bible you heard. Perhaps there is some misinterpretation of a natural event. It might be a perfectly normal serpent.'

'Well, that'd be easy to deal with then,' James responded.

The look on Simon's face said that he didn't fancy this option much.

'Unfortunately,' he continued, 'if it is a natural event and a natural Serpent, that isn't what King's Investigators are supposed to do. There are special people for that sort of thing.'

'King's people?' James was frowning. The rock was wobbling.

'Oh, absolutely,' Simon sounded enthusiastic. 'If we do come across a normal snake, I can get someone else to deal with it.

'But if it is the Serpent which tempted Eve…' James thought through the problem, 'it'll be a bit more impressive than your adder. For one thing, it can talk and pick fruit.'

Simon gave a noncommittal nod.

'Just a minute,' said James with high suspicion in his voice. 'You're a don't-want-to-be-founder? If you're God's Anointed King's High Investigator,' Simon beamed at that, 'and you can fight off the Serpent, what was you hiding from?' The rock rose again.

'I need to move without being seen,' Simon responded, with the universal sign of a knowing tap of the finger to the side of his nose.

'You mean, you was sneaking instead of hiding?'

'Exactly – you are an astute observer, my friend.'

James mused. 'Hmm, could work, I suppose. The characteristics are very similar.' He weighed up the possibilities in his head and eventually seemed satisfied with the explanation. 'We'd better get on with it then.'

'On with it?' Simon asked.

'Killing the Serpent. Now there's three of us – me, Francis with his rock and you with your anointment – he'll be no match for us. Just think, if we kill the Serpent heaven will reign on earth and we shall sit on the right hand of God.'

'About this Serpent,' the Investigator wanted more information. 'What makes you think it killed Ambrosius?'

'We was there,' said James proudly.

'Ah, now that's interesting. There at the time, eh? Have you told anyone else?'

'No, of course not. We ran off when he was struck down by the Serpent.'

'And erm, how exactly did, Hermitage, I mean the Serpent, cause Ambrosius's death?'

'He hissed at him,' James announced.

'Oh.' Simon was disappointed. 'No knife or a rope or a fight or anything? Hissing at people isn't generally considered to be one of the more violent types of assault. It certainly doesn't usually lead to death.'

'It hissed,' James insisted, 'kept on at it. All through the argument.'

'What argument?'

'The argument Ambrosius was having with the concave.'

'Conclave.'

'Yeah, that's it. Something about sand.'

Simon sighed as he prepared to explain to the less intelligent than himself.

'Ambrosius was to argue that the Lord did suffer the normal vexations of the human body when he was in the wilderness. He got sand in his shoes which would have been very uncomfortable. His Father in Heaven did not spare him the indignity, as he could have done; he wanted him to live as a normal man. That was Ambrosius's proposition.'

'Dirty devil.'

'Not that sort of proposition. It was his argument, that was what he was suggesting. Then it was up to someone else to argue the opposite and the Conclave would determine which of them was right.'

'So who was arguing against him? Hermitage?'

'No, no, it was supposed to be Father Genly.'

'Oh, the dead priest,' said James, without batting an eyelid.

'How did you know that?' Simon's eyes narrowed.

'Word travels fast among the hiding monks.' It was his turn to tap the side of his nose now.

'Are there many of you then?' he asked, with some incredulity.

'You've met Athan, have you?'

'Ah, take your point,' Simon mused for a moment. 'What do you mean hissing? Hermitage was hissing?' He couldn't understand this.

'Hermitage?' James was surprised almost to the point of laughter. 'No not Hermitage, he was listening carefully, that's the sort of thing he does. Funny bloke. No, the hissing was coming from nowhere, that's how we knew it was the Serpent. We couldn't see anyone.'

'Or any Serpents,' Simon suggested.

'Course not. Wouldn't be visible, would it, the Serpent?'

'Of course not, silly me.'

'Anyway, the hissing goes on and on and Ambrosius gets crosser and crosser, and then he shouts out and sits down.'

'He sat down? Is that it?'

'Yeah, but he sat down dead. We recognise someone when they sit down dead. So that's when we thought, time to go. Nick of the moment as well. We've got a method.' James winked again. It was most unnerving. 'I leg it at the first sign of trouble and then Francis comes at the second. Otherwise looks like we're up to something, doesn't it?'

'I imagine it would.' Simon nodded knowingly at this nonsense.

James hadn't finished. 'Who should walk in afterwards but Arsehole Athan, pardon my Latin.'

'So Hermitage didn't have anything to do with it?'

'What?'

'The death of Ambrosius.'

''Course not.' James shook his head that anyone could think such a thing of Hermitage. 'That's a funny monk. One chant short of a plainsong if you ask me. He was still thinking when we left him. Mind you, he does think a lot. Can't be good for you.'

'This is very bizarre.' Simon seemed to forget where he was or who he was talking to. 'Athan is convinced that Hermitage did it and has a very good case. The Abbot has concluded that Hermitage didn't do it, but that seems largely based on the old man's blatant prejudice against me rather than any lucid consideration of the facts. The weaver fellow appears to be on the Hermitage side of the moat. Why then is Athan so keen to get Hermitage convicted? It is all very puzzling and very confusing.'

'Right then,' James said, with a very blank look on his face, which said that Simon's little speech had gone in one ear and hadn't even made it out of other one. It had been swallowed in the intervening void.

Simon took a deep breath. He moved to follow James out of the cosy nook and back into the big bad world. As he did so he felt a tug at his habit, and turned quickly to Francis in case the imbecile was playing with his rock again. Francis beckoned and drew close to Simon's ear.

'Pay little heed,' Francis said.

Simon stepped back, shocked to hear lucid words coming out of the man's mouth,

'James is a little, you know ...' Francis made the familiar 'barking mad' sign with his finger against his head. 'Obviously unlikely to be the Biblical Serpent, but there's something going on. I'll keep close.'

With this he stepped after James but turned and winked at Simon, hoisting his rock ready for whatever they were going to face.

Day Five   Vespers

I F THE BIBLICAL FLOOD HAD COME at that very moment to wash the stain of De'Ath's Dingle from the face of the Earth, Hermitage would not have been the least surprised.

Wat's idea of direct methods involved making the most revolting accusations against any monk who passed their way. He threatened that if they didn't reveal the whereabouts of the missing monks, the revelations made about them would make the destruction of Sodom and Gomorrah look like mild rebuke from a lame duckling guarding a piece of rotten bread.

When they didn't know where the missing monks were, Wat demanded some piece of information about some other Brother. It always turned out to be information of a positively appalling nature.

Hermitage was well aware of the sins of man. He had read about them all in the Good Book. Yet he had never expected to discover so many carried out in such a place as this, and with such enthusiasm. He understood the principle of one or two rotten apples in the barrel, but this entire monastery seemed to have turned to cider. If it wasn't disgraceful behaviour such as that practised by Father Genly, it was business dealings that would have made the traders in the temple give a round of spontaneous applause.

Most shocking of all, he found that there was a group within the precincts who were dedicated to Epicureanism. He would never have believed that there was access to fine foods and wines, albeit on a very limited basis. That there was access to food and wine at all was a surprise. The smell of a ham alone would drive the monastery into a moderately sized riot. He took this information particularly badly as he still recalled his starvation-induced nightmares, when lack of food had brought him to fainting whenever he stood up.

'It's a good job the Abbot's not involved,' said Wat after the interrogation of a particularly surly Brother. He had eventually, reluctantly, indicated that he had seen James and Francis two days ago, headed for one of the passageways that wormed their way through the intestines of the monastery.

'Why?' Hermitage was coming to the conclusion that he was the only one in the place who had not been engaged in one sort of very un-monk-like behaviour or another.

'Because they wouldn't care then. Threatened with exposure to their Abbot they'd just have shrugged and said "go on then." When you say you'll tell the Abbot, at least this lot have the good grace to go very pale and look worried. That means there's a chance they're telling the truth.'

'You make it sound like you've done this sort of thing before.' Hermitage liked Wat, he seemed to be generally supportive, but he was displaying a rather doubtful side to his personality.

'Not this exactly, and certainly never in a monastery, but I'm sorry to say I've had my fair share of contact with the less pleasant end of society. Doesn't matter where they are or what they're up to especially, they all behave the same when there's something going on.' Wat shrugged and spotted a new victim across one of the ubiquitous quads.

'Oy, I want a word with you,' Wat called to a passing monk. Hermitage braced himself for another onslaught on his moral sensibilities.

'What's going on?' he squeaked in frustration, skipping after Wat. 'What could possibly be going on? Ambrosius, an old and excitable man, drops dead of natural causes, why does there have to be anything going on?'

'Damn.' Wat stopped as his monastic target vanished around a corner. He turned and looked his companion up and down. 'It is a shame to drag you into so much of the modern world all at once. Why do you think Athan and Simon are so keen to think that you did it?'

'Because they think I did.' It was obvious.

'No, no, no. We can all see you didn't, it's blindingly obvious. It may even be obvious that there was nothing done and it was all natural, as you say. So, give yourself that fact and then ask again … why does Simon, and more particularly Athan, want you guilty?'

'Why particularly Athan?'

'Because as far as I can tell Simon isn't capable of independent thought. He's just following where everyone else has already gone while doing his best to make it look original. It's a common enough ploy.'

'Perhaps Athan really believes I did it.' That's what Athan said, so Hermitage believed it.

'He's not stupid. Assume for the moment, for the sake of argument, that Athan knows you didn't do anything. Why would he say you did?'

Hermitage looked intently at Wat as his thought processes worked through the problem.

'Because he hates me?'

'He seems to hate everyone, why you? Why not Francis or James?'

'Because I was there.'

'God, you're making this hard work, Hermitage. Look, he knows Ambrosius is dead because he found him. In this discussion we're assuming he knows you didn't do it. Why would he say you did, if it wasn't pure and simple malice? What other reason could there be?'

New pathways in Hermitage's mind opened up. From the expressions that went over his face, they were narrow and wobbly pathways, subject to collapse at any moment.

He stumbled over the sentence. 'If he accuses me of murder, he must know that Ambrosius didn't die of natural causes.'

'Aha.'

'And perhaps accusing me takes attention away from whatever did happen?'

'Praise the Lord.'

'What a strange expression.' Hermitage paused in his exploration. 'Ah but, ah but, ah but,' he added.

'What?'

'Sorry, I get a bit carried away with arguments some times. I'm famous for my ah-buts.'

'I can imagine. What's this one about?'

'What if Athan knows that it is natural causes, but wants there to be a murder for some reason?'

'What reason?'

'I don't know. I've only just started thinking of a senior Brother of the monastery as a potential deceiver. Never mind the sins of the other Brothers. And I have you to thank for that.'

'Don't mention it.' Wat nodded in recognition of his role in Hermitage's growing maturity.

'The question is "why" to all of this. Why want a murder, why distract attention?'

They both looked at one another, then at the ground, then at the sky and then at the buildings that surrounded them. There was no revelation.

'What would happen if there was a murder?' Wat asked.

'Pretty much what has happened, I suppose. An investigator comes in, the culprit gets found and that's that.'

'I still think this building work is in the weave somewhere. It's too much of a coincidence. We need to know what that's all about. Francis, James and the builder. We've got three people to question now. I think we should split up.'

'Oh.' Hermitage didn't like the sound of this. There was no

telling if Athan was going to be waiting for him somewhere. He was convinced the man would be able to arrange a trial and execution in the blink of an eye.

'You'll be safe enough. You know what we're looking for, what we're trying to find out. If you find any of them just get as much information as you can. We'll meet back here in an hour in any case.'

Hermitage detected that the weaver didn't know where here was, or how to find it again from anywhere else.

'You just look for the third falling chimney.' He pointed up at the roofs above them.

'Right,' said Wat, and was gone.

'Now then, Hermitage,' Hermitage said to himself, 'gathering information and drawing conclusions should be right up your track.' No. Bracing talks didn't make the churning feeling in his stomach go away. Perhaps he could just wander around for an hour and then come back. Mister Wat was bound to have found something out. He seemed a very bright fellow. And a successful weaver. He must remember to ask more about his particular products, though. They still seemed shrouded in mystery for some reason.

Better still, perhaps he should simply go and hide for an hour, that way there was no chance of Athan finding him.

Slipping around a corner, scanning his surroundings for a suitable resting place he walked straight into the figure of Chirk.

'Oh, sorry,' said the builder, helping Hermitage up. He seemed to be doing this a lot recently.

'Ah. Just the man,' he said, disappointed that he couldn't run away and hide after all.

'Really?' said Chirk, pleased to be wanted.

'Yes. I wanted to ask you something.'

'Oh good, fire away.'

Here was the first problem. The idea of finding Chirk was clear. The notion he would have some information of value was understood. What that information might be, or how to get at it, was a complete blank. Whatever the link that Wat might perceive between the builders and events, it was a closed door behind a tapestry to Hermitage. 'What do you know about the murder of Ambrosius?' seemed a bit blunt. With all the plotting and scheming that might, or might not, be going on, it was likely Chirk didn't know anything about it anyway.

'Erm, what are you doing?' It was hopelessly weak, but at least it might buy him some time to come up with something a bit more penetrating.

'Measuring,' said Chirk with an enormous amount of pride. He held up his ruler once more.

'Ah,' said Hermitage. He hadn't had enough time yet.

'Measuring what?'

'The buildings.'

This was getting nowhere. Wat's conversations with monks went on a lot longer than this.

'Why?' Why was a very good question. It was not one he had used very much in his career to date. His work on biblical texts had included a lot of who, and where, and what, but very little why. He would have to try it out when he got back to work. If he ever did get back to work.

The simple word caused Chirk all sorts of problems. People didn't ask him why he measured. It was enough that he did. It was the sort of thing people expected. If you brought in the builders the first thing you wanted to see was some measuring going on.

As his old Dad had always said, 'The secret of success is to always look like you know what you're doing'. It was generally accepted among the building fraternity that if anyone looked like they knew what they were measuring, it was Chirk. At builders' parties, Chirk was always asked to bring his ruler.

'Why?' he repeated.

'Yes, why?' said Hermitage, kindly. 'Why are you measuring?'

'Well, you have to measure, don't you?' Chirk said with the enormous confidence of a specialist who could look like he knew what he was doing. He also added a dash of underlying contempt for people who were not builders, and so were incapable of understanding the fundamental elements of the job. Like measuring.

'I imagine so,' said Hermitage. He encouraged Chirk with a smile.

Chirk smiled back and nodded. That was that.

Hermitage realised his query needed to be more explicit. 'I don't mean why are you measuring as part of the overall construction process.'

Chirk looked worried.

'I mean, why are you measuring here, at this time?' Hermitage specified.

Chirk looked up at the sky and judged the time of day. Then he looked at the building he had been holding his ruler up against. He shrugged.

'Well,' said Chirk, gathering himself, 'you see this building's at the apex of the cross dimensions, which means that alterations to the substructure of the supporting trusses need to be co-ordinated with the uplift members.' He was very proud of his Builder-speak, the sub set of trades-talk used to confuse and disorientate clients.

'I'm sorry?' said Hermitage.

The clients usually were after that.

'I mean, why in this monastery at all? What building work is it that's going on? What have you been asked to do?' Hermitage was quite definite. Surely the question was clear enough now.

'Measure,' said Chirk, still dealing with one question at a time.

This was hard going, thought Hermitage. Mister Wat was able to get straight to the point and move on. Hermitage was even finding this conversation a little irritating.

'What work is going to happen here?' he asked slowly.

Again Chirk looked at the building.

'What, here?' he said, pointing to the spot.

'No, not here,' said Hermitage, pointing at the ground and hearing his own voice raised in unaccustomed frustration. 'Here,' he demanded, waving his arms about to indicate the whole of De'Ath's Dingle.

'Oh, right.' Chirk had finally twigged. 'Improvements.'

That wouldn't be hard to imagine, but it wasn't enough.

'What sort of improvements?' Hermitage pressed. He felt unsettled and restless with the responses he was getting. That he should have such thoughts about another person, rather than a recalcitrant piece of text, was unnerving.

'Various.' Chirk was discomforted by this inquisition.

Hermitage felt a small growl start at the back of his throat. If he opened his mouth too quickly it would come out as a shout. This was appalling. He couldn't be driven to rage by a simple builder. No matter how simple. Perhaps he should just give up. No, Mister Wat would not be impressed if he came back after his hour and Hermitage had got no information. A full explanation might help.

'There is a dead monk,' he said.

'Where?' Chirk jumped back and looked at the ground he had been standing on. 'Why don't you bury your dead in graveyards like everyone else?'

'No, no, not here,' Hermitage snapped rather testily. It didn't seem to affect Chirk. Perhaps he was used to people being testy with him. 'I'm trying to explain why I need to know what you're doing.' Hermitage was immediately ashamed of raising his voice. He had never done such a thing before. This discussion was getting to the core of him and wriggling about.

'Measuring,' said Chirk, holding up the ruler.

'I know you are measuring.' A flash of impatience snapped the words out of Hermitage. He was both ashamed and rather excited by it.

'Look,' he said, much more loudly than was necessary. He made eye contact with the builder to indicate that the man should shut up about measuring.

'Some time ago a monk called Ambrosius died while he was taking part in a debate.'

'Must have been very dull,' said Chirk.

'It was not,' Hermitage barked, 'it was a fascinating debate.' He stopped himself. This was not the point of the conversation. He breathed deeply a couple of times. 'It has been suggested that he was murdered.' Hermitage decided not to add that the main suspect was standing in front of the builder, as this would probably make him run a mile. A measured one.

'There appears to be no reason for the murder,' Hermitage went on before Chirk could move away. 'It was a very complex debate which wasn't going to have any major impact on anyone and the monk was not a very significant fellow. The only odd thing is that there is building work going on which no one seems to know about. Brother Athan won't tell us anything.'

As he reasoned this, Hermitage began to see what Wat might be getting at. Could there be any connection between the death of Ambrosius and the arrival of builders? It was very far-fetched and he couldn't conceive of anything that combined the suffering of Our Lord in the wilderness, with the knocking about of a ghastly place like De'Ath's Dingle.

Chirk didn't say anything. He looked at Hermitage and it wasn't clear the words had made any sense to the builder, let alone had any impact.

'So,' said Hermitage, thinking that anyone would be able to follow this, 'what we want to know is what building work is going on here and who is organising it?'

He waited and watched Chirk to see if any of this had sunk in. If the man said 'measuring' again, Hermitage would not be held responsible for his actions.

'I'm not building a graveyard.' Chirk was offended.

Hermitage really didn't know how to deal with this. When you debated or enquired of people, they answered. They didn't not answer. They didn't talk about something completely different. Or answer a question you hadn't asked. Granted, sometimes they just walked off. Well, quite often really, but when they were engaged they responded. The man before him didn't appear to understand the rules.

'I am not saying you are.' Hermitage spoke with quiet menace. For the first time, ever.

Chirk simply held his ruler up again.

'For heaven's sake, it's a simple question.' Hermitage was brusque. He had experienced many new emotions over the last few days. His respect for authority had taken a severe pounding, and he had discovered things about the world that he profoundly wished he could un-discover. He now had the urge to lash out at an ordinary builder. This was awful. He drove his words out through gritted teeth. 'I'm asking what it is you are building.'

'What's it got to do with a dead monk?'

'That's it!' Hermitage yelled in some triumph. 'At last I've got through. That's what I want to know.'

'Absolutely nothing.' Chirk was clearly offended. 'I have got absolutely nothing to do with some murder. Not after all that trouble with the cesspit.'

'What?' Hermitage was taken back. What did this have to do with anything?

'That wasn't my fault,' Chirk was agitated. 'Of course the sides were slippery. The daughter of the house hadn't been watching where she was going. Bloody nobles, they're always going off the deep end about the smallest thing. Never let anything go.'

Hermitage looked aghast. Of the two reactions open to him, giving up on a hopeless case or taking it the next level, his new instincts leapt him to the latter. His shameful shouting at this poor man seemed insufficient somehow.

'I'd have a more intelligent conversation with the ruler,' Hermitage muttered to himself as he paused for breath. His mind told him that this was getting nowhere. There was no point in examining the man who stood before him. The act of simply standing before him was probably taxing him to the limit.

It wasn't his mind in control now, though. It was the frustrations of Athan and Simon, of his journey to Lincoln and the accusation of murder. It had all built up in him like the old outer tower of the monastery. The poor builder was simply the crumbling stone that brought the whole thing down.

Perhaps mime would help.

'Mr Chirk. Do you even know why you're measuring?' Hermitage threw his arms around the limited view of the monastery trying to indicate measuring. He gestured his measuring impression at the floor. 'Do you know why you're here? Was it perhaps the case that someone told you to come and measure? Do you realise where you are? Perhaps you've come to completely the wrong place and are measuring all the wrong things?'

This bought a shameful look of some recognition to Chirk.

Hermitage made small building movements with his hands and fingers. He now paced up and down and tried to gesticulate great buildings into being.

'If you have actually measured anything with that stick of yours,' he said,

Chirk clutched his ruler defensively.

'Who are you reporting it to?' Hermitage continued. 'Who wants the measurements? What are they?'

'Your monk was already dead before I got here?' Chirk interrupted the stream.

'Well, yes,' said Hermitage, deflated. Had the man really got the point? Had the shouting and yelling all been worthwhile?

'Good,' said Chirk, 'nothing to do with me then.' He picked up his ruler to do some more measuring.

'No,' Hermitage now whined plaintively and jumped up and

down on the same spot.'Please try to listen to what I'm saying.'

After some frenzied time spent kicking small pebbles and trying to turn others to dust with the soles of his very thin shoes, Hermitage recovered his breath. His fists were clenched and his teeth were fixed together. He really, really wanted to take hold of the wretched man by the scruff of the neck and shake him until something horrible happened. Between panting gasps of recovery he looked Chirk up and down and weighed the evidence for the man either hiding something or being stupid. Stupid. It was definitely stupid.

'We are going to stay here until I understand what's going on. Even if takes all night,' Hermitage said, very seriously.

Chirk looked decidedly worried at that.

'Look who I've found.' Wat burst the moment by appearing around the corner with the scruff of Brother James's habit in one hand and that of Francis in the other. The King's Investigator followed at the back, looking rather surly.

'What?' said Francis.

'You found them,' Hermitage cried out. It was a huge relief that some progress had been made at last. It was slightly disappointing that Wat had managed to locate two missing monks and find the King's Investigator, while all Hermitage had managed to do was not get any answers from a builder. Still, he mustn't be selfish.

'I have,' Wat confirmed, 'and you're a monk so see what you make of what they say. Personally, I don't believe a word of it.'

Caput XVI

Day Five Vespers

NDER THE ORGANISATIONAL SKILLS of Toksvar, the caravan of the Earl of Northumbria made good progress from Lincoln. This organisation involved the carts and horses moving along at a pretty hectic pace, while everyone else simply had to keep up.

At a particularly damaged part of the road, one of the Earl's men tripped and fell into the adjacent bog. He sank immediately up to his waist and continued a slow descent, exacerbated by his struggling. His travelling companions sprang into action straight away, gathering around the spot to point and laugh. Bets were placed on how long the struggle would continue, and bids were made for ownership of the man's meagre possessions when he had no further use for them. Which would presumably be quite soon.

A fight almost broke out when a detachment from Toksvar's entourage barged through with ropes and logs. They set up a sophisticated ramp and pulley system and extricated the man from his muddy prison in no time at all. A far more prolonged and vicious fight broke out while the Earl's men debated whether the bets were null and void, or whether the bookkeeper should pay out on the time of the rescue. The journey resumed, but the score of bookkeepers was now bog one, train nil.

Toksvar's team were not immune to the attrition, despite its order and method. One man screamed out when his leg found a new pothole in the road. Toksvar examined the wound, found a break and decided there were only three options.

Firstly, the man could buy his way out of his Lord's service and do whatever he liked. Hobble away to a new life as a cripple, wait for rescue or take up begging there and then.

Secondly, he could let Toksvar's blacksmith have a go at setting the bone. Something he'd never done, but always wanted to try. After that he would still be left behind, but there was a chance he might be able to walk again. Eventually. Sort of.

Finally Toksvar was willing, on this occasion, to do the decent thing and put the man out of his misery straight away. After all, he was a very good swordsman and it probably wouldn't hurt much at all.

It was the Earl's men who came to the rescue on this occasion. Fussing Toksvar's legions out of the way, they lifted the injured man on to one of their carts where he was given something to drink. Next he was dosed with a special herb the Earl always carried, and which, within the space of ten minutes, had the injured man singing at the top of his voice and repeatedly declaring that the trees were really, really green. When one of the Earl's men had then set the leg with the minimum of effort, the injured man had simply giggled, before throwing up and passing out.

Despite these interruptions Toksvar's relentless pace meant it was only mid-afternoon when they arrived at De'Ath's Dingle.

The Earl took one look at the place and decided to make camp outside the walls. He set his staff to attend to this in their haphazard manner while Toksvar's method had his tents erected in about ten minutes.

Leaving them to their various organisational styles, Nicodemus approached the gate of the monastery. His steps, confidently carrying the authority of the Bishop, faltered as the smell of burning wood drifted in the breeze. It was not the familiar, comforting smell of the fire in a grate welcoming you in from the cold. This was more like the disturbing odour of a whole house going up. He ran the last few steps. God forbid that the place should burn down.

Knocking on the closed door he heard the crackle and pop of a fire not far away and saw smoke and sparks emerging from behind the entrance. The sparks floated away and away on the wind, happy to escape De'Ath's Dingle. Even if it did mean going up in flames.

'Ha ha.' A cackle now joined the crackle, so he knocked harder and the door swung open – revealing a combination of several horrible things. Nicodemus despised the lunatic fringes of the religious world, he had a real problem with nudity, even his own, and there was something about uncontrolled fire which sent shivers down his legs and brought sweat to his brow. The gatekeeper of De'Ath's Dingle was sitting, as naked as a body could get, in front of the burning wreckage of his hovel, throwing dust over himself and alternately mumbling and laughing.

'For God's sake, man, put some clothes on,' Nicodemus scolded, 'and tell me where I can find Brother Athan.'

✦   ✦   ✦

Brother Athan, unaware that he had a visitor, was engaged in a personal and difficult discussion with his leader and was just finishing a pertinent and personal anecdote.

'...how was I to know the naked monk was the youngest son of a cousin of the Earl of Wessex and the woman was his sister?'

'What? His own sister?'

'No,' Athan was shocked, 'the sister of the cousin.'

'Ah, his aunt,' said the Abbot. That was all right then.

'Yes,' grumbled Athan. That didn't make it all right at all.

'There was all hell to pay,' he went on. 'There was an official complaint and a demand for punishment. Not for them fornicating in public, but for me finding them out.' The outrage was still fresh and rampant in Athan. 'Several of my colleagues said things like this happened all the time and the punishment would be something nominal. They wouldn't want it to be public that the Earl's family were doing it to one another.'

'I can understand that,' the Abbot commented. 'I have come across similar situations in my travels.'

Athan had gone beyond listening. 'Then it turns out that the complaint is being handled by some incompetent, ineffective, sycophantic, petty-minded dolt of a monk.'

'Brother Simon?'

'Yes,' Athan barked and paused. The Abbot had reached that conclusion remarkably quickly.

'I can tell you my experiences of the Brother are of a very similar nature to your own.'

Athan had always felt an affinity with the Abbot. The mindless rages, the uncalled-for violence and the contempt for everyone and everything had always struck a chord. Now he felt positive companionship.

'And now,' he fumed, 'the stupendous, self-serving, arrogant fart bag is here, parading around as the King's Investigator when he's incapable of bending over without a map.'

'I think we are agreed on that,' the Abbot said, 'so why do you come to tell me this now? Why at this particular time?'

Athan sighed heavily. 'Because I have come to a decision about my future life and my place in the monastery. Even in the Church as a whole.'

'Really?' the Abbot asked, genuinely puzzled.

'Yes,' Athan said, calm once more. 'I have decided, and your opinion has only confirmed my resolve, that I am going to have to leave the religious life. This is because I am going to kill Brother Simon. Probably the next time I see him, but almost certainly today.'

'Athan,' the Abbot said, standing on his one leg and moving so close to Athan his aura was tangible. Athan's reaction was to step back from the most tangible bits of it, but he controlled himself. The Abbot went on.

'You are a violent man. Vindictive, spiteful, aggressive and unpleasant. You bear grudges and ill will such as I have not seen for a long time, and you have no friends at all to speak of. The other Brothers look on you with fear and loathing. They tremble in your presence and create the most imaginative fates for you in your absence. You have achieved the fine balance of being hated, while cowing all those around you such that none of them are prepared to do anything about it.'

'Thank you, Father.' Athan's chest swelled with pride.

'You are just the sort of person the modern Church needs. Who do you think is going to take the place of the likes of me when I am gone? The young men of the church today are mamby pamby soft heads, like that idiot Hermitage. He couldn't run a monastery. He couldn't run water. He'd have the monks engaged in conversations, producing manuscripts or some such wasteful nonsense.'

'You are too kind, Father.' Athan felt quite touched, he never knew the Abbot thought of him so highly

'And if not you or I, and if not Hermitage, then it will be the likes of Simon who steps in. Imagine anything run by him.' The Abbot left the awful thought to hang in the air, but Athan was resolute.

'I am grateful for your support, Father. It means a lot and I wholly agree with your assessment of the Church. I don't know what else I can do, though. I now realise Brother Simon has festered in my guts for all these years, and once he is gone I can rest easy. If I leave him be, I shall not be able to function normally. He will gnaw away at my soul until it is gone. Better to do it now, I think. I shall confess to the crime immediately, of course, and pray that the Church will find it in its heart to offer me mercy. Or at least a hanging instead of some ordeal or other.'

'Athan, Athan,' said the Abbot, coming even closer and putting his arm around Athan's shoulders, which wasn't very nice at all. 'I appreciate your feelings towards Brother Simon, believe me I do, but there is a different way to approach this.'

'There is?'

'Of course there is.' The Abbot looked around the room as if expecting someone else to be there listening to their conversation. 'Don't simply walk up to him and kill him.'

'No?'

'No. Wait until it's dark and then come up behind him. That way no one need know.'

'Father!' Athan was shocked and looked at his Abbot's face in genuine surprise and dismay. That such a figure could make such a suggestion. The look he got back was one of plain honesty and openness. Not a familiar one coming from the Abbot.

Athan turned and pondered the sinful suggestion in his mind. Not for long. It grew on him. What a marvellous idea it was. Athan grinned and the Abbot grinned back. That wasn't very nice either.

Caput XVII

Day Five   Before Compline

N THE ROAD FROM THE NORTH. From Stamford Bridge to be precise, a unit even better drilled than Toksvar's was making their way to the south. Passing through Lincolnshire, they had made a brief stop by the side of the Ermine Road while advance scouts moved ahead to find the night's camp ground.

One very impressive tent, guarded by some very impressive large men with lots of weapons, occupied an area of clear ground. Cleared specifically for the tent and the person inside it.

Galloping up the road at great speed, on a very nice horse, was a scout with a very interesting discovery.

◆   ◆   ◆

'What do you mean "Serpent"?' Wat asked with some incredulity as James and Francis told their tale. Hermitage was engrossed as well, as the two monks were interrogated round the back of the refectory.

Hermitage had recommended they return there as it was a place seldom visited by others. It also scared the wits out of most people and so might loosen tongues. Wat was impressed with his thinking. Brother Simon loitered towards the edge of the building, saying he had heard all of this before. If their attention was distracted for long enough, Hermitage suspected the man might run away.

'We heard it,' James insisted. It was clear to Hermitage that the man was sincere. He didn't seem the sort to be able to make up a tale like this, and then keep a straight face while repeating it.

'But how do you know it was The Serpent?' Hermitage thought it very unlikely the biblical Serpent had turned up without some sort of announcement.

'It was hissing,' said James

'Hissing,' said Francis, and they all looked at him in surprise.

'Hissing doesn't kill people,' Hermitage responded. 'Now, if the Serpent had appeared and bitten him, that would be something. Or had reared up and caused him to fall? That I could believe.' He came to himself and realised what he was saying. 'Just a minute, I was there and I never heard any Serpent.'

'Yeah,' said James in disdain. 'But then you was listening to Ambrosius, wasn't you?'

'Of course I was.' Hermitage was puzzled. If James and Francis had been there, surely they'd been listening as well.

'So you wouldn't have heard the Serpent 'cos he was hissing quietly,' James explained quietly. As if the Serpent could still hear them.

'This is ridiculous,' said Wat. 'How does some quiet hissing kill a man?'

James looked at him in some shock that his gruesome tale was being dismissed so lightly. 'I don't know, do I?' he said in irritation, 'I'm not a scholar. I'd have thought if the Serpent is hissing in your ear, you'd better watch out. We're not talking about a wasp or a frog, we're talking about the Serpent. It could have had the fruit of the Tree of Knowledge with it for all I know.'

'A frog?' Wat shook the idea of a hissing frog from his head. 'And the apple would have made the hissing more deadly, would it? Fruit-assisted hissing?' Wat shrugged hopelessly at Hermitage.

'You wouldn't understand, you're not a monk. What are you doing here anyway?' James suddenly realised who was questioning them.

'How did Ambrosius die though?' Hermitage wanted to know. 'If, as you say, the Serpent was hissing, what was it that actually happened to Ambrosius? Did you see that?'

"Course we did,' James said. Francis nodded vigorously.

'Well?'

James paused and looked around the space as if adding effect to what was going to be a momentous statement. 'He sat down,' he said with a flourish.

'Oh, brilliant,' said Wat, 'the quiet hissing of an unseen snake with an apple causes an aged monk to sit down. Well, it's obvious, isn't it? Deadly combination, a clear case of the most evil and violent murder I ever came across. Quick, arrest all the snakes in the vicinity and question them without mercy. If you find one with fresh fruit, kill it. Oh, and remove all the chairs in case anyone else sits down.' He seemed to be getting a bit hysterical.

'I'm still not clear, though,' said Hermitage. Wat gazed at him, marvelling at his patience in asking any more questions of these brainless cretins.

'Just sitting down wouldn't kill him. Some hissing on its own wouldn't kill him. There must have been something else?'

"Course there must have been,' said James.

'Ha,' said Wat throwing his hands to the air and stalking over to stare at Simon for a while. The Investigator had crept suspiciously close to the edge of the building. He took a smiling step back towards the conversation.

'We know there was something else, but we couldn't hear, could we?'

'Couldn't you?'

'No, of course we couldn't. If the Serpent was talking to Ambrosius we didn't want to hang around to join in the conversation.'

'What do you mean talking?' Hermitage said with interest. 'You said it was just hissing.'

'Well yes, obviously it was just hissing to us,' James said in a tone that made it quite clear Hermitage was some sort of fool. 'We was too far away to hear, but the Serpent was obviously talking to Ambrosius.'

'What was it saying?' Hermitage asked, unable to believe that he had just asked that question.

'Didn't I just say we was too far away to hear?' James rolled his eyes in despair at Hermitage's stupidity. 'Whatever it was, Ambrosius didn't like it.'

'How do you know?' Hermitage asked.

"Cos he was getting crosser and crosser.'

'Was he?' said Wat, with a very knowing slowness to his words.

'Yeah. I mean he was an excitable old boy at the best of times, but whatever the Serpent was hissing at him was getting him really annoyed.'

'And then he sat down?' Hermitage asked. He couldn't see the significance of Ambrosius getting cross. He rather thought he would get cross if he was trying to deliver an argument and kept getting hissed at. By a Serpent or anyone else.

'Well, yes,' said James, 'as I say, the Serpent was hissing. Ambrosius was talking. Then he was shouting and getting redder and redder and eventually he just shouts out loud and sits down. Dead. That's when I thought it was time to go. Didn't want to move before that in case the Serpent spotted me.'

'Is that what you recall, Hermitage?' Wat asked.

'Well, yes, I suppose it is really. Apart from the hissing Serpent, of course. I know that Ambrosius was getting very animated towards the conclusion of his case, but then I considered that to be only natural. Once he made his final declamation I heard him sit heavily in his chair. I didn't for one moment think that he was dead. I thought he was just exhausted. He was very old and had been shouting quite loud towards the end.'

'There we are, Mister Investigator,' said Wat, bringing Simon back into the conversation before he slipped around the edge of the building and away.

'There we are what?' said Simon, sulkily, patronisingly and

snappily, all at the same time. 'I've heard all this Serpent non-sense already, and can't see what it has to do with anything.'

'Witnesses who say that Ambrosius simply sat down dead after being hissed at for a bit?' Hermitage was incredulous that this solid reasoning was having no effect.

'So?'

'So, they say that Hermitage didn't do it,' Wat insisted. 'Don't you?' he added looking at James.

'Well, I suppose not,' James shrugged. 'Can't see how boring Hermitage could have been hissing and listening at the same time.'

'This proves nothing,' said Simon with his best air of superi-ority.

'What?' Wat said in utter disbelief.

'It doesn't prove that this man didn't have some hand in all of this. Who summoned the Serpent in the first place I'd like to know?' He was now very smug indeed.

Wat's mouth went up and down, but no words came out for quite a while.

'Right,' he said eventually, 'come on.' He physically man-handled James and Francis towards the builders' entrance to the back of the refectory.

'We ain't going in there again,' James fought back.

'Oh yes, we are. We're going to visit the scene of the so-called crime, then we can show this, this,' he was lost for a suitable word to describe Simon, 'this Investigator,' the word was spat with such venom that it might have come from the mouth of the Serpent itself, 'that most events in the world have explanations that are all too simple. Like him.'

He pushed and prodded James and Francis until they moved, and then ushered Hermitage and Simon towards the door. The King's Investigator went with a look on his face that was so con-descending it would have killed Wat on the spot if it had fallen on him.

'Get in there,' Wat said, and just resisted smacking the King's Investigator on the back of the head.

◆　◆　◆

'Oy, you!' Athan yelled at some innocuous monk who was passing on the other side of one quad. The monk looked up quickly before considering whether to run off or not. When he saw who it was, he realised that running away was futile. Bracing himself, he walked over to Athan.

'Where's the King's Investigator?' Athan spat as if the man was deliberately hiding the information.

'I don't know' was never a very sensible answer to give Athan, even when you didn't. It tended to have repercussions. Percussive repercussions.

'Erm,' said the monk. It was the standard holding ploy. Sometimes it prompted more information from Athan about what he was actually asking you. Sometimes it drew an exasperated sigh and a light blow to the head before Athan marched off. Only rarely did it generate a beating for the sin of hesitation.

'The King's Investigator!' Athan seemed to think that saying it louder would render it comprehensible. 'Weaselly-faced ferret of a man, always creeping about and causing trouble.'

The monk stared up into the sky, doing his best to look as if he was on the verge of recovering the very piece of information Athan wanted. It was in his mind somewhere, but would most definitely not be brought out of his head by it being hit in any way. The next moment he snapped his head down and stared at Athan with wide eyes.

'What?' said Athan, thinking that the man had gone mad.

'I've seen him,' the monk said in a delirious moment of joy as he realised that actually possessed a piece of information Athan wanted, when he wanted it. He was going to avoid a beating.

'And?'

'Yes, yes, I've seen him.' The joy was in the possession of the knowledge rather than the knowledge itself, and so the monk was sailing close to the fate he sought to avoid.

Athan stepped closer, and this brought the man back to earth with a bump.

'Yes, yes,' he babbled, 'weaselly fellow. Ferret. Trouble.'

'That's the one,' said Athan, with enough menace in his voice to alert a flock of lambs that spring was over.

'He was going round the back of the refectory with Hermitage and James and Francis and some stranger.'

At this news Athan stepped back as if he had been struck, and the monk was puzzled at the movement. His puzzlement was resolved as he realised Athan's step back had given him room. The blow which landed at least had the quality of being decisive, so there was no need for a follow up. When the monk woke up, he would wonder what he had said. There was no pleasing that man. Don't tell him what he wanted and he hit you. Tell him what he wanted and he hit you.

Athan strode with some pace towards the refectory. Matters now needed to be taken in hand with some speed. As he rounded one corner a figure stood in his way and, as was his normal manner, he attempted to walk straight through it. It would certainly be no one of any consequence, and it surprised him momentarily that the figure did not immediately leap out of his way. The Brothers knew the consequences of allowing themselves to be bumped into by Athan.

'Ah, there you are,' said the figure, in an incredibly impudent manner which, despite his current distractions, Athan was prepared to deal with in his usual direct way. As he took half a step backwards and adjusted his balance for his favourite right-footed low blow to the shins, he actually bothered to look at who it was he was about to kick.

'What the hell are you doing here?'

◆ ◆ ◆

Toksvar was genuinely shocked. 'What do you mean he's on his way here? What the bloody hell is that bastard doing coming to this God-forsaken hole?' His liveried servant had brought word from the outer guards of the camp of an impending arrival. He had received word, from advanced scouts, of another group moving down Ermine Street from the north.

'I know not, my Lord,' said the man, 'the scout I met simply said that they were travelling with haste to the south.'

'Ah well, not so bad then. If they're on their way to Canterbury down Ermine Street they might pass us by completely.'

'Erm.'

'What?' said Toksvar with a very weary tone in his voice, as there was obviously more bad news to come.

'It appears that one of the Earl's men was out scouting as well.'

'Don't be ridiculous, they couldn't scout a three-day-old corpse.'

'A couple of them had heard of a brewery not far away and were out looking for it.'

'Typical. And they bumped into the scout, I suppose. And told the scout who they were, where they were camping and so a decision was made to break the journey here instead of carrying on to somewhere more sensible like Stamford.'

'Almost exactly, sir,' the man said, impressed.

'Bloody hell.' Toksvar rubbed his chin in thought for a few moments.

'And does my father know?'

'He will do in a few moments, sir. I got back before the Earl's men who were making a leisurely pace.'

Toksvar sighed deeply. 'Oh well, could be worse. At least I'll have the two of them together in the same place for once. The presence of the rest of the ghastly crowd will make changes to the inheritance impossible. I presume we're all prepared?'

'As ever, sir.'

'Good. Then I think at least we can sit back and enjoy the spectacle of my father's camp receiving the news. You may go.'

The man left Toksvar's tent and ran to spread word to the rest of his fellows. Benches were gathered and seating places with good views reserved. The staff of the immaculately ordered camp of Toksvar sat down to watch what happened when the complete shambles that was the Earl's encampment received the news that the King was about to arrive.

The effect was as entertaining as anticipated. Two of the Earl's staff wandered into the camp and, after pausing for a drink from the main water butt, popped into the Earl's outer tent. The Earl was a relaxed man: he was a pleasure to work for as he really didn't care what you got up to as long as his bath was hot and his food chain endless. When he did rouse himself to action, though, he could be a complete pig. If there was one thing guaranteed to rouse him to action, it was anything to do with the King.

The roar that came from the Earl's tent, which must have been the moment he received the news, drew appreciative nods from the Toksvarian audience and the exchange of a few pieces of coin as the early bets were won and lost.

The Earl knew the King considered him a threat and he knew how to behave. Sycophantically obsequious usually did the trick. He also knew he wasn't a threat at all. He didn't want to be King: it looked like an awful lot of hard work. A lot of it dangerous. If the King believed he was a threat, though, that was that.

After a bit more blind panic in the Earl's camp, the first of the King's inner guard arrived. This lot were simply to make sure that there was no direct threat to the King's person. They did this by knocking down and turning over everything that had been put up and turned the right way up. Having failed to find any archers in the trees, or knife men in the water butt, they sent word back to the main body that the place was safe for the King to enter.

All of this time the Earl had been getting ready. The gentle-men of the chamber had been trying their level best to get him as clean as possible, and the special sealed trunk, which contained a full set of clothes, had been ceremoniously opened. This had been packed in Northumbria for just such an occasion, and its very existence was kept a secret from the Earl. He would only have opened it on the first day of their journey. Under strict instructions from his most trustworthy staff not to do anything in these clothes that shouldn't be done in clothes, the final layer was only put on when the King's own person was in sight.

The King's own person was not, of course, the person of the King. The King's person consisted of about fifty people, all of whom had very particular jobs. Most of these involved stopping anyone else getting anywhere near the actual King. They arrived in a single block and took over virtually everything in the Earl's camp, pushing his own staff out of the way as they were untrustworthy dogs who could get up to God knew what. Toksvar they left alone. He was known as a younger son and so no particular threat. They also knew he was a bit odd and unlikely to cause any trouble.

Eventually, after what seemed like endless to-ing and fro-ing, pushing, shoving, preparing and re-preparing, a lone tent was erected in the middle of the camp and a guard was posted around it.

A messenger went over to the Earl's tent, and with all due ceremony craved the Earl's attendance upon His Majesty. The option of declining the craving was simply out of the question. Unless you already had ten thousand troops ready for the war that would follow. As a second son Toksvar's presence was craved as well, and while he toyed with saying that actually he was a bit busy at the moment, just to see what happened, he decided discretion was the better part of getting his head cut off.

The Earl of Northumbria, together with his second son, were welcomed into the presence of King Harold.

'My noble Earl,' said the King, rising to his feet as if this was the most exciting thing that had happened to him in years.

'Your Majesty,' said the Earl, in so joyful an outburst that an observer might have looked around for the presents.

'And you, Toksvar,' said the King, approaching Toksvar and giving him a playful punch in the ribs.

'Your Majesty does us honour by visiting our humble encampment.' said Toksvar.

'I do, don't I?' agreed the King, 'And lo, I bring your brother.'

It seemed that one wall of the tent stepped forward and Toksvar recognised the great bulk that was his brother.

'Brother,' said Vignar, clapping Toksvar in a bear hug which would have had most bears choking for breath. 'And Father!' Vignar exclaimed, stepping forward to shake his father firmly by hand while kneeling at the Earl's feet, as was his duty. The Earl was sure that he felt a couple of small bones in his hand crack, but none the less he blessed his son and bid him rise.

'You come from a successful campaign in the north, Majesty?' the Earl asked. It was the sort of thing you had to ask Kings.

'Indeed, there's truth in what you say. The Terror of the North is despatched to a watery grave, is he not, Vignar?'

'Aye,' screamed Vignar and waved his fists about a lot. Toksvar raised his eyes to the roof of the tent and shook his head at the irritation of court talk and the true stupidity of his own brother.

'And now we are making all due haste to the south, as I hear that the liar William the Bastard makes plans to land in our beloved country. Near some place called Hastings. We will despatch him as we have the Dane and thereafter we can return to court and govern the country, instead of fighting to keep its borders clear.' The King nodded sagely, but Vignar looked very disappointed.

'When we heard that you were camped here we forestalled our journey to reacquaint ourselves with our most noble Earl,' the King beamed. The Earl cowered as he clearly heard what the King had said.

'What the hell are you up to?' Toksvar translated under his breath.

'But what brings you here, Earl – rather at the edges of your estates, are you not?' the King laughed, and clapped the Earl on the back.

'What are you doing out of your own lands, you bastard?' Toksvar whispered through clenched teeth.

'Ah, family business, your Majesty. You know my son Toksvar here longs for a place in the world where he may serve your Majesty.'

'No, he bloody well doesn't,' Toksvar mumbled.

'Ah, indeed, indeed,' said the King, as if this was blindingly obvious.

'And while his brother Vignar has so nobly chosen to serve your Majesty through might of his arms ...'

'Ahhr,' said Vignar, waving his mighty arms about some more.

'... young Toksvar takes more of the learned nature from his humble father.'

Toksvar coughed.

'And so he has turned to the Church.'

'My God!' The King let it out before he could control himself. 'Toksvar, in the Church, eh? God, erm, bless him. A noble ambition, young Toksvar. And so you visit this place to take your first steps into the seclusion of the cloisters?'

'I have been making arrangements on behalf of my son, and we do indeed visit, to see what our next steps should be. Once that is done I must attend a meeting in Warwick and then make haste back to my estates in the north. To make sure that the crops are being managed properly.'

'Excellent,' said the King, happy at this news. 'We have not visited one of our religious communities for far too long. We shall join you.'

'Marvellous,' said the Earl, with a tone that said, 'oh, bloody hell.'

Caput XVIII

Day Five   Finis

'VE COME TO FIND OUT WHAT PROGRESS has been made,' Nicodemus hissed at Athan, now that they were safely out of sight behind a fallen pile of stonework.

'I would send word,' Athan spat their agreement.

'You would if I didn't have the Earl of Northumbria and his son with me.'

'What?'

'They wanted to see the establishment they're investing in.'

'But that's ridiculous, we haven't even started yet.'

'Well, what do you suggest I tell them? Sorry, but I can't show it to you now. Oh, could you leave the money anyway?'

Athan looked puzzled.

'But this is a religious community, it's for the good of his soul. What does the man expect, miracles?'

'The man expects to see a monastery ready for development. I see the builders' tents are up, but what about the little internal difficulty?'

'Do you know who you sent?'

'Who?' Now it was Nicodemus's turn to wonder what was going on.

'Brother Simon.' Athan paused to let the name make its impact.

'I know, I chose him carefully, just the sort of person we need.'

'You did what?' Athan wasn't happy at this news and Nicodemus took a cautionary step back.

'Yes, he's just some bumptious idiot who hangs around the

Church all day telling people what to do. I told him he could be King's Investigator if he came over here and sorted out Ambrosius's death. Seemed a good idea, get things buttoned up officially as it were.'

'The only thing that's likely to get buttoned up is the Investigator himself. In a canvas bag all of his own,' Athan glowered.

'What are you babbling on about? Ambrosius's death was unforeseen. How were we to know that the old boy was on his last legs? It needed clearing up before we could start work. I assume you haven't explained everything to the Abbot.'

It was obvious Athan had not told the Abbot anything, 'I thought I'd leave that pleasure to you. You can tell him about Genly at the same time.'

'What about Genly?'

'He's dead.'

'Oh, so he's the other one. How did Toksvar know that?' Nicodemus shook his head to remove this latest imponderable. 'Less of a surprise, I suppose,' he shrugged. 'I'm very disappointed here, Athan. I thought that you had the best interests of the Church at heart, and that the Bishop's own instructions for the debate would have been sufficient.'

'I still don't know why the Bishop couldn't instruct the Abbot directly.'

'Because that is simply not the way anything works. You stick to your monastery and let me worry about who gets told what and when. Abbots are important and senior people, and don't need to be disturbed by fiddling small details. Once we have the plan fully developed, we can let the Abbot know. If we engage him at an early stage he'll only question everything, and the Bishop would be inconvenienced.'

'And we wouldn't want that,' said Athan sarcastically.

'No, we wouldn't,' said Nicodemus with a shiver. 'And neither would you. The Bishop might be far less inclined to give a new Abbot his own monastery, for instance.'

Athan said nothing, but he said it very reluctantly. 'At least your Investigator accepts the fact of the murder.'

'What?' Nicodemus was dumbstruck. 'I only hinted at that to scare him a bit. I didn't think he'd really believe it,' he paused for thought. 'Mind you, it is Brother Simon.'

'And he's convinced Brother Hermitage did it.' Athan considered this to be good news.

'Who?' Nicodemus frowned as he tried to recall the name. 'Oh, him. Really? He doesn't seem the type.'

Athan moved quickly on. 'The next complication is some weaver has turned up.'

'A weaver?' Nicodemus really didn't get this one. 'What's weaving got to do with anything?'

'He's not here to weave. He appears to be a friend of Hermitage and is asking all sorts of questions about Ambrosius.'

'Athan, this is all getting completely out of hand. It's quite a simple matter. Ambrosius popping off before the debate was ended should have been a hitch, nothing more. Now we have murders, dead priests, weavers and all sorts wandering around.'

Athan wasn't going to take this lying down.

'And King's Investigators and Earls of Northumbria cluttering the place up.' As he said this there was a rather unpleasant glint in his eye. Well, an extra one.

'Yes, yes,' Nicodemus answered automatically while thinking what their next step should be. 'Where's your weaver and his team now?'

'I was just looking for them myself, funnily enough.'

'Right, we'll go and find them, see what they're up to. I shall have to get everything sorted out before we let the Earl in. Even then we'll have to keep him away from the Abbot. No danger there?'

'No danger of anyone bumping into the Abbot. He'll stay in his cell and no one will go close to that out of choice.'

'So,' said Nicodemus, stepping out from behind the rubble

which concealed their conversation, 'Brother Simon and the weaver.'

＋　　　＋　　　＋

Having the King decide to pop in and see one of his monasteries is not a simple affair. Advisers on Church issues will wish to have their views heard. Military officials will have to make sure that the journey can be adequately managed. Victuallers will need to keep the party properly supported. Never mind just plain hangers-on, who go wherever the King goes in the hope that they'll get something out of it. Like a county, or a couple of major towns.

Then, of course, there was Vignar, who hoped above hope that a visit would give him the chance to fight someone. He was the only one of the party who was arming himself fully for a visit to a religious community. But then he armed himself fully wherever he went. He didn't have any other clothes.

The Earl had to move pretty quickly as he hadn't been prepared for an expedition, even if it was just a few feet up the track. He had his best court attire on, along with those awful shoes he could only just stand up in, let alone walk. He also spent a lot of time flustering about, asking where Nicodemus was. The King had a nasty habit of coming up with piercing questions and then getting all cross when you didn't know the answers.

The Earl didn't have a clue about most things, but as far as this monastery was concerned he knew pretty much less than nothing. Nicodemus was his source of information, and he wasn't there. Excusing yourself from the King's presence while you changed your shoes, or went to find someone who knew what was going on, was not the sort of thing even Earls did. As the King wanted to leave there and then, that was that.

Advisers, military men and victuallers were dismissed with a good natured wave of the royal hand while the King, the Earl, Vignar and Toksvar wandered alone up the roadway towards the monastery gate. Alone apart from a dozen or so heavily armed soldiers who accompanied Harold wherever he went.

'What's that, then?' the King asked, pointing off to the right towards the new builders' village.

'I don't know, your Majesty,' answered the Earl, who wouldn't have recognised a tradesman if he'd been eating one.

'Looks like builders,' said Harold.

'Shall I investigate, your Majesty?' Vignar drew his sword with some relish.

'No, no.' Harold gestured that the weapon should be put away. 'The last time I let you investigate something wholly innocent, the death toll was shocking and it cost me a small fortune in reparations. I'm sure we'll find out in due course. Now, does anyone know who the abbot of this place is?'

The question went unanswered as they came upon the open gate and bonfire which made up the entrance to the monastery. The King frowned and Vignar drew his sword. He grinned as he wasn't told to put it away.

The King nodded to his troops who advanced upon the opening. One of their number leapt through the gaping gate, sword in hand. A few moments later he emerged, none the worse for wear, indicating with a shrug that there didn't seem to be any trouble. The rest of the party approached and stepped through the small door.

As they entered and looked around, they caught a slight whimper on the breeze. Vignar jumped about, brandishing his weapon, while Toksvar turned his head this way and that until he identified the source. Kicking what looked like a burning hovel door to one side the naked figure of the gatekeeper was revealed as it scrabbled in the dust regularly beating its head on the floor.

'Ah, a madman given the shelter of the monastery, eh?' the King said, impressed by the charity. 'The builders are doubtless doing some repairs to the gate and the poor fellow believes it to be his house.' The entire party joined the King's laughter at the lunatic and went on their way.

After about half an hour of going on their way, and finding themselves back at the main gate for the third time, patience was wearing thin.

'The whole place cannot be deserted,' he said. 'Who feeds the madman?' A couple of soldiers were despatched in opposite directions to see what they could find.

'You're the visitor here, my lord Earl; what arrangements were made?'

The Earl, who had been far more concerned with his feet than finding monks, looked up from where he was rubbing his left sole while holding his court shoe in his hand. 'We are to be met by the Bishop's man, one Nicodemus. I can't think where the wretched fellow has got to.' Passing the blame to an under- ling was as natural as passing water.

'Sire,' one of the soldiers on monk-finding duty called and beckoned from the corner of one building. The party strode quickly over.

Across a couple of quads they could see the retreating backs of two figures, one of them in monastic garb, entering a large building set on its own.

'Over there, then,' said the King and led the way. Behind his bodyguard.

◆　　◆　　◆

Inside the large building set on its own, Hermitage had organ- ised what he called a reconstruction. James and Francis had been trembling ever since they re-entered the refectory, convinced that the Serpent was still there and was about to leap out and devour them.

Hermitage's patient explanation that Serpents couldn't leap had been of no comfort whatsoever. Something had to be done to bring them to their senses. Hermitage sat down where he had been at the time of Ambrosius's death, and suggested James and Francis go to their places as well.

Obviously Ambrosius couldn't be with them, although Hermitage did suggest going to fetch the remains to give the scene some authenticity. Wat pointed out that a days-old rotting corpse would be neither authentic nor pleasant, and so he would play the part of the old monk. Simon, as King's Investigator, should stand by and observe to see what conclusions he could draw. He tutted and fussed and humoured the fools.

'So,' said Wat, moving to the end of the building, 'I was here spouting on about sand and shoes and wilderness and stuff.'

'Hardly that,' said Hermitage, taking offence on behalf of Brother Ambrosius.

'Whatever,' said Wat, 'and you were there listening.'

'I was.'

'Well, listen then,' said Wat.

'Oh, right.' Hermitage adopted his crouched position with eyes shut as he imagined Ambrosius before him once more.

'And you two were there were you?'

'Yes,' said James in a shaky voice.

'Are you getting this?' Wat asked of Simon, who was looking around the room to see if there was a door he could leave by.

'Oh yes,' he replied, smilingly placating at the madman.

'Now,' said Hermitage, in a muffled voice from his hunched position, 'where was the Serpent?'

James simply blubbed.

'What?' said Francis.

'Come, come, Brothers, be bold,' Hermitage encouraged. 'Where did you hear the noise of the Serpent coming from?'

A very nervous James raised a shaking arm and pointed towards Wat.

'I was hissing?' Wat asked.

'No, you weren't here,' James said.

247

'I'm playing the part of Ambrosius.' Wat shook his head at the idiocy.

'Are you going to die as well?'

'No, I'm not. But I think someone else here might in a minute.'

The point was not lost on James.

'It was coming from behind you, I mean Ambrosius.'

'I see.' He looked over to Brother Simon to see if he had made any sense of this.

The King's Investigator was a lot closer to the door than he had been.

'Hermitage,' Wat said loudly. Simon stopped and looked up guiltily.

'Yes?'

'What do you see?'

'I can't see anything. I've got my eyes shut.'

'Open your eyes. Come over here and tell me what you see.'

'Ah.' Hermitage did as he was instructed. 'Of course. The builders' door.'

'The builders' door.'

'What have the builders got to do with anything?' James asked, still in a state of nervous collapse.

'How would the Serpent use the builders' door, eh? He's a Serpent. They don't have any hands.'

Hermitage's reasoning was lost on James, and so he looked to Simon. The Investigator actually had his hands on the door and looked as if he was about to open it. He wasn't prepared for it to be opened from the outside, and he fell through the opening on to the dirt as Athan and Nicodemus arrived.

Athan looked at the figure at his feet, grinned and lifted his right foot high. He looked around at the number of witnesses and put it down again. On Simon's hand.

Hermitage turned to look at the new arrivals. His stomach plunged at the sight of Athan, and was overtaken by puzzlement at the sight of Nicodemus.

'Master Nicodemus,' he said. 'What brings you here?'

Wat looked around at them all, eyebrows permanently raised.

'I have had to come and sort out what should have been a straightforward task. The death of poor Ambrosius seems to have got completely out of hand. I now hear tales of murder. Ridiculous.'

Hermitage was pleased to hear that, although Simon looked out of sorts. The reaction of Athan was hard to gauge as all he did was glare at Brother Simon. The Investigator was getting to his feet, rubbing his hand.

'The debate is inconclusive then,' Athan almost spat. He was talking to Nicodemus, although he never took his eyes off Simon.

They stepped into the room and closed the door behind him.

'Formally, I suppose one could say that, but perhaps there are other means of resolution we have not explored.'

This did make Athan turn to Nicodemus with a look of towering anger on his face. It was the look that was usually on his face, but he hadn't pointed it in that direction before.

'Other means?' Athan spoke the words very slowly and deliberately.

'Yes,' said Nicodemus, casually. 'I've been reviewing the regulations of the Conclave and we can desire the Bishop to extend his decision.'

'Extend his decision.' If Athan could have gritted his teeth any more, he would have been eating his own chin.

'That's right,' Hermitage agreed. 'If there is an inconclusive debate the Bishop can "extend his decision" – a sort of casting vote, if you like. He could hear the opposing argument to Ambrosius's and then decide for himself. Although that might be difficult as Father Genly is dead as well.'

'So are you telling me,' Athan growled, 'that it wasn't necessary to argue Ambrosius's point away?'

'Seems not,' said Nicodemus with a rather worried look on his face as he observed Athan. The man's fists were clenching and unclenching. He was swaying first towards Simon and then towards Nicodemus as if he didn't know which way to go first.

Hermitage frowned at them all as he turned ideas over in his mind.

The tension of the situation was broken as the door opened again. This time it was virtually flung off its hinges as a giant man in battle dress leapt through the door and waved a huge sword in all directions.

'Ha haaa,' he yelled and that was all that was necessary, as everyone quickly backed away.

Another figure strode quickly into the room afterwards.

'For goodness sake, Brother, this is a monastery, not a training camp.' This much smaller man stepped in front of the giant and glared at him until the sword was lowered.

'These people are monks,' he said glancing around the room before spotting Wat and Nicodemus.

'Mostly,' he added.

Vignar reluctantly sheathed his sword, but still glared daggers at everyone in turn, inviting them to provoke him into chopping something off.

Next through the door was a much smaller man than the rest, but much better dressed. The others seemed to make way for him, so he must be in charge. His demeanour and attire was so impressive that even Brother Francis stood up. The new arrival was unarmed, but had an intelligent look about him. He gave Hermitage a huge feeling of confidence. He thought that everything was going to be all right. He couldn't explain why, he just felt overwhelming security in this man's presence.

The small man was followed by a much, much bigger one dressed up as an Earl. Then came a large contingent of well-armed soldiers who took up station around the walls.

'Who are these people, and what's going on?' the man said. He gestured to Simon, who happened to be the nearest.

Simon recognised authority when he saw it and stepped forward to bathe in its glow.

'I am Brother Simon,' and he moved into declarative mode, striking what he thought was a noble pose. 'The King's Investigator,' he announced.

'That's odd,' said the man.

'Why?' Brother Simon demanded.

'Because I'm the King and I didn't know I had an Investigator.'

Simon's mouth dropped open and stayed there. He looked at the man who claimed to be the King. He looked at all the other people in the room he didn't recognise, and then he looked to Nicodemus for explanation. That humble servant was looking in every direction possible but Simon's.

It was Hermitage who was the first to kneel, a fact which did not go unnoticed, and the others all followed suit.

In the silence that followed it was clear no one actually knew what to do.

'I expect any minute,' the King said, 'that someone will answer my question.' It was a very mild comment, in a quiet voice, but it put the fear of God up everyone. 'A monastery with no gate and only a naked madman at the entrance. A man who claims to be the King's Investigator although the King has never heard of him. Where is the Abbot of this place?'

'Here I am,' the Abbot's voice called from behind Wat. An interruption so unexpected, and in so tense an atmosphere, that Hermitage actually screamed. Fortunately it was ignored as all the attention of the room focused on the Abbot as he hopped forward on a crutch which Hermitage was absolutely positive he had never seen before.

Those who knew the Abbot, or had heard of him by repute, would not believe that this was the same person. He was clean.

To Athan the miraculous crutch was as nothing compared to this revelation. The Abbot had found a new habit from somewhere, some water from somewhere and had washed himself virtually everywhere by the look of it. You could see the colour of his skin and each strand of his hair, rather than the mat it usually formed. Even more alarming as he hoisted himself into the knot of people was he didn't smell any more. How had he done that?

'My Lord Abbot.' The King clearly recognised the Abbot; this was a day of surprises.'I didn't expect to see you in this place.'

'Nor I you, your Majesty.' The Abbot bowed, and the King nodded in acknowledgement.

'There seem to be some goings on,' the King observed.

'Indeed there are. Several of them, all at the same time I believe.'

'And your presence here would be no coincidence.' the King said with some weight that meant nothing to anyone else.'Let us start with the King's Investigator, shall we. He intrigues me.'

'I think Master Nicodemus can help us there,' the Abbot replied.

If Nicodemus could have shrunk up his own nose, he would have.

The King followed the Abbot's gesture. 'So, Master Nicodemus, what's your tale?'

There was little information in all the stumbles and stutters which Nicodemus uttered before he finally got going, but his audience waited patiently.

'I, er, am the humble servant of the Bishop of Lincoln and news was brought to me of a death here in the monastery. It needed looking into and so I, erm, asked Brother Simon if he would carry out that duty.'

'And appointed him King's Investigator, eh? Is that within your power?'

Fortunately it was a rhetorical question and Nicodemus was

not called upon to answer. It clearly wasn't going to be in Nicodemus's power in the very near future. Very little would be.

'So, a death, eh?'

'A murder possibly,' the Abbot said with heavy weight.

'Really?'

'Or not,' said Hermitage speaking up for the first time, realising if he didn't do so now, in the presence of the King, it might
turn out to be his last opportunity lost.

'Ah, my loyal monk,' said the King with the emphasis on the
word loyal, and a piercing glance around the rest of the room.
'At least I assume you are a monk. Not a King's special monk or
anything. Not a murder, you say?'

'I am a monk, your Majesty. A humble monk,' Hermitage said, not without some pride. 'And no, your Majesty, not a
murder. Brother Ambrosius was an old man and in the excitement of the Conclave he simply passed away.'

'Did he?'

'No, your Majesty, he didn't.' Wat spoke up now from the
back of the room and stepped forward. Hermitage looked at
him with abject horror. How could his friend betray him, here
and now of all places?

The King had another look of recognition on his face.

'Master Wat, I trust you are well and your fingers nimble?'
The King grinned a most unhealthy grin.

'Indeed, sire,' Wat answered with a bow.

'I look forward to the latest instalment of my bathhouse ser-
ies.'

'In preparation by my apprentices as we speak, sire.'

'Excellent. So you say it was a murder then?'

'Possibly, sire. I think I know what happened, but I'm not
sure I know why.'

'Pray tell.' The King laughed at his own slightly monastic, but
very weak, joke. So did everyone else.

'Brother Ambrosius was proclaiming his argument from

here,' Wat took up the position, 'but at the back of the room there is a secret door, the builders' door. I maintain that someone came through that door and whispered to Brother Ambrosius.'

'Fiendish whispering, eh?' The King was enjoying this.

'Could be, sire. Brother Ambrosius was an excitable fellow, and a very old one as well. There are two witnesses who say that they heard hissing during the debate, which was making Ambrosius more and more angry. Whoever was whispering, and whatever it was that they were whispering, was enough to push poor Ambrosius into some sort of fit, of which he died.'

'But you don't know why, and presumably not who either?'

'No, sire. I understand that the subject of the debate was not one of great import. It could be that his opponent did it, but he too is dead.'

'Good Lord, a dangerous place to be, this monastery. Who was the dead opponent?'

'Father Genly.'

'What, the Father Genly?' The King was astounded.

'Indeed, your Majesty,' the Abbot confirmed.

'Oh well, good riddance, then. Anything else to go on?'

'Only the presence of builders, sire.'

'Do you think they did it?'

'No sire, in fact they aren't here yet.'

'Builders who aren't here yet, are here? You puzzle me, Master Wat.'

'I mean preparations are in hand for builders to start work, sire, but there is no knowledge of building among those here.'

'Is this true, Father Abbot?'

'It is, your Majesty.' The Abbot was good at confirming today.

'And our noble Earl of Northumbria is here as well, looking for a place for his youngest son. This hardly seems suitable, my Lord.'

The King glanced back at Northumbria.

'It appears not, your Majesty. It seems I have been grievously misled.' The Earl simply shrugged. He had dropped better men than Nicodemus in the most enormous piles of poo, and not caught a splash of it himself. All of this was nothing to do with him.

'Yes,' the King drawled; he obviously wasn't convinced by the Earl's declaration of heartfelt disappointment.

'We have a strange set of circumstances that require some explanation.' Being a King this wasn't a rhetorical question, even though it sounded like one. 'Brother monk, what is your conclusion?'

Hermitage stared at the King and then looked back over his own shoulder as he thought that there must be a monk standing behind him. When he saw there was no one, he turned back to the King. The look of innocent fear on his face would have brought a tear to the eye of Hengvar, Viking of Vikings, just after he had slaughtered an entire herd of extra-large-eyed fawns.

'Your Majesty?' he managed to get out.

'You seem a loyal and intelligent sort of fellow. Given the facts that we have before us, what would you conclude?'

Well, here was a marvellous opportunity. So often, when Hermitage tried to exercise his intellectual skills in front of people of note, they noted he should shut up and not be invited back again. This was the King, you didn't get much more noteworthy than the King. Well, you didn't get any more noteworthy at all. Perhaps that was causing Hermitage's mind to go all wobbly.

Not only was this man the King, but he looked the part. There was something in his bearing, his way of speaking, his simple assumption that he was the most important person in the room that put Hermitage off his stride. It did more than put him off his stride. It chopped his legs off and stopped him striding anywhere.

'Erm,' Hermitage managed. It wasn't very impressive and the King just stood there, expecting something a bit more illuminating. The look was gentle and encouraging, though, and Hermitage took some heart from it.

A lesson his father had taught him came flooding into his mind to fill up the space. Years ago, after another chasing around the village pond, followed by a beating and a ducking at the hands of the local children, Hermitage's father had spoken to him.

'For God's sake, lad,' it had started, and there had then followed the usual longwinded and explicit expressions of disappointment at virtually everything Hermitage had ever done. In the middle of it, though, had been a phrase which now came to life. 'The only thing you can do better than anyone else is debate. Pointlessly. Next time they start picking on you, debate with them. They'll all be bored rigid and bugger off to bother someone else.'

Hermitage thought that if he started debating the issue, an opening argument if you will, then something might occur to him.

'Well, your Majesty,' he began, and was very disconcerted to notice that the King and everyone else in the room was actually listening to him. He wasn't used to this.

'Let us consider the information we have before us. Brother Ambrosius we know is dead, and there is some dispute over the cause of that death. Master Wat has identified the unexplained presence of builders, and when I spoke to Chirk the builder myself all he could tell was that he was measuring up for improvements.'

At this point Hermitage's working mind, as opposed to his idling mind, sprang back into action. Rather like a waterwheel that keeps spinning when the sluice gates have been shut, he had been running on his own momentum and it wouldn't have been long before he stopped altogether. Now the gates had been opened, the water was flowing fast and strong and the wheel of Hermitage's thinking was powering along.

Unfortunately, being Hermitage, it had also come off its

spindle and was trundling down the hill heedless of whatever dangers lay in its path. It could either come to rest in a peaceful meadow or smash itself to bits against some rocks. The outcome was beyond Hermitage's control.

'But why would there be improvements in a place as austere as this?' he asked himself, disinterested in who else was in the room.

'Someone must be paying the builders to come and measure up. We have seen a tented village outside the walls to house a significant workforce. There are clearly detailed plans in someone's mind. Is it connected to Ambrosius's argument?' Hermitage paused at this point and everyone in the room thought it most impressive that he was increasing the tension like this. Hermitage had paused because he didn't know what came next. He knew his own mind well enough to realise it would come to him any second.

'And is it connected to any of the activities going on in the monastery that I have come across in my discussions with Master Wat and several of the Brothers?'

Brother James, thinking that this was some sort of quiz, almost put his hand up.

'Of course it is,' said Hermitage in his moment of revelation as all of his experiences over the last few days gelled together.

'How?' the King asked

'The Epicurean heresy.'

'Ah,' said the King, clearly not having a clue what this was. 'Perhaps you could explain it for those here who may not be familiar.'

'Wow,' thought Hermitage, a chance to explain some more.

'Well, sire. It is a given truth that those who take the religious path must endure suffering if they are to serve the Lord.'

'Of course.'

'And it is equally common that this suffering is achieved through physical discomfort. Cold cells, poor food, regular flog-

257

ging, that sort of thing.'

'Never did me any harm.'

'Well, the Epicurean heretics believe that's too easy.'

'Easy?'

'Yes, if you're already miserable because your surroundings are horrible and you are in considerable discomfort and pain, then it's easy to suffer. It doesn't take any effort at all.'

'I'm not sure where you're going with this,' the King said, 'but I think it's going to be bad.'

'On the other hand if you are living in comfort and warmth, with fine wine and food and servants to do all your work for you, then it would take a great deal more personal determination to suffer for your belief.'

Hermitage was oblivious of the inherent insult to the King's way of life.

'So the Epicureans want warm comfortable monasteries, where everyone has to work jolly hard to suffer at all?' the King asked, perfectly aware that this monk couldn't insult a Saracen.

'Exactly, your Majesty. Ambrosius's argument went to the core of this. If his position held sway at the Conclave, that the Lord in the Wilderness did suffer physical pain through his shoes, then the Epicurean Heresy is false. If the Lord's clothing caused physical discomfort, then of course we should suffer similarly. If Father Genly had won then it could be argued that poor living conditions are not part of religious suffering at all and so should be stopped. We could all wear nice shoes, I suppose.'

'And I imagine,' said the King, developing his own argument, 'that such a large, comfortable, warm and welcoming monastery would have the younger sons of the nobility queuing up to get in. They might even pay handsomely.'

Nicodemus moaned quietly in a corner.

'So the big question then is who, eh? Who would be involved in such a devious scheme?' the King said, casting his royal gaze around the room once more. 'Who do we have? Master Wat? I think not, already a rich enough man, eh, Wat?'

Wat simply blushed slightly and nodded acknowledgement. Hermitage looked at him in some surprise. He didn't know that he could like rich people.

'Brother monk here?' he gestured to Hermitage. 'Again, I think not. It is he who brings us this reasoning and it is hardly the sort of scheme he would be interested in. Who else do we have? Ah, my noble Investigator. You had not reached this conclusion?' He didn't wait for Simon to answer. 'No, I thought not. So, onward then. Master Nicodemus we have already met, and if he isn't in this up to his armpits I'm a Frenchman. Where does the funding for this sort of thing come from, apart from the coffers of the Church, and who better to have his cuffs in the coffers?' He turned to Brother Athan. 'Who are you?'

'Brother Athan, your Majesty,' Athan said, unable to think of anything more helpful to his cause.

'I see from the glances that you have been exchanging with Master Nic over there that you have some connection to all this.'

'I, erm ...'

'He would need an inside man, of course, as he couldn't be seen dirtying his hands himself. Someone who knows their way around the monastery, perhaps – who knows where all the doors and hidey holes are?' He let the question hang in the air with the clear indication that it wouldn't be the only thing hanging before long. 'And what might be in it for Brother Athan? Perhaps an offer of advancement? Your own monastery to command? Ha ha!' The King laughed long and loud as he saw from Athan's face that he had hit the monk on the head.

'Then we have the nobility here. Our noble Earl of Northumbria and his son come looking for a monastery. And Master Nicodemus is your introduction, my Lord.'

'Oh yes, your Majesty,' said the Earl, not satisfied with dropping Nicodemus in it until he had stood on him afterwards. 'Master Nicodemus put the proposal to me for a monastery such as the young monk here has described, and it seemed an interesting option.'

'I'm sure it did. I do hope you haven't put your money in yet because I fear the development is about to collapse.'

The King scanned the room to make sure he had covered everyone. Brothers James and Francis stood motionless in one corner.

'And who do we have here? More conspirators?'

'Brother James, your Majesty,' James said in barely a whisper. He had never seen a King before, let alone his own King, and talking to one was not something he had been prepared for.

'And you are a Brother here?'

James simply nodded with his mouth half open as if he expected the King magically to ascend to the ceiling, from where he would rain down fire on them all. James knew Kings could do that if they wanted. He thought that keeping silent might prevent this fate falling on him.

Wat spoke up. 'Majesty, these are the two Brothers who witnessed the whispering.'

'Ah whispering witnesses, wonderful,' said the King, as if this was all some party game.

'And the other fellow? Your name?'

Brother Francis looked around the company as if he was wondering who had spoken to him. He glanced at the Abbot.

'It's all right, Brother, you may speak,' the Abbot said. Poor fellow was obviously overcome by events. Francis took a step forward and knelt before the King.

'Brother Francis, your Majesty, Vatican special envoy.' From somewhere inside his habit he produced a small piece of parchment which he handed to the King. Harold unfolded it, read it and handed it back.

'Yours, I presume?' he asked of the Abbot.

'I'm afraid so, your Majesty. My Brother fears for my safety, of course, but Francis has been a most useful set of eyes and ears for me in this place.'

Athan just managed to stifle a loud 'Ha'. So that was how the Abbot always managed to know so bloody much.

'You are here to protect the Abbot?'

'I am, your Majesty,' Francis answered, still on his knees.

'Get up, man,' the King ordered with some irritation. 'I have to tell you that I do not like the agents of the Pope creeping about my Kingdom without my knowledge.'

'Indeed, your Majesty,' Francis said, 'and if it had become necessary to extend my activities beyond those of guarding Master Abbot in this place, then naturally I would have made myself known.'

'Naturally,' said the King, not believing a word of it. 'So you were witness to this whispering.'

'I was, your Majesty. It was hard to see, but it was fairly clear that there was someone at the back of the room whispering to Brother Ambrosius. The elderly man got more and more excited, and then simply expired.'

'And when were you going to raise this information? Before or after the execution of the wrong person?'

'Majesty, I immediately communicated to the Abbot who suggested that we should let matters progress so that the main protagonists would be exposed. I would have, of course, come forward to put matters right if they had been going awry.'

'Of course you would.' The King's tone was complete and utter contempt. 'And your brother would not have any connection with this exposure of heresy?' he asked of the Abbot.

This was going way over Hermitage's head. He was very proud of reaching his conclusion about events, while of course feeling very guilty about feeling very proud. All these people turning out to be not what they ought to be was too much. He would never understand people.

He did understand the stuff about the whispering, but what was Francis doing? More to the point, who was he? Hermitage had always thought he was some sort of idiot. Proved how wrong you could be. All the people who should be clever were turning out to be idiots, and the one who was certainly supposed to be an idiot was a papal agent. This was all going to take some working out afterwards. And who was the Abbot's brother, for goodness sake?

'My brother the Pope has obviously discussed the heresies that concern the Church as he would with any of his confidants.'

'I bet he has,' the King said. His voice didn't rise in volume, but it was clear that he was furious.

'The Pope,' thought Hermitage, 'I didn't know he had a brother. And anyway, I thought he was Italian.' It didn't occur to Hermitage that you could have a different parent and still be a brother, but then it wouldn't.

Nicodemus and Athan exchanged glances which carried very similar thoughts, although theirs were an awful lot ruder.

'And so he sends you here as some sort of carefully prepared scheme to defeat a rather obscure and harmless sounding heresy, on my territory and without my knowledge?'

'Your Majesty,' the Abbot exclaimed in a shocked voice. 'A complete coincidence I assure you. My brother requested an isolated and less demanding post for me after my mission to Jerusalem.'

'Jerusalem,' thought Hermitage. This was getting really interesting. Perhaps he should have spent more time with the Abbot, got to know him. On second thoughts, that wouldn't have been a good idea. The man might be the Pope's brother and have travelled to the Holy Land, but he was still a dangerous nut.

'The Pope doesn't send the feared Father Elick anywhere for a rest.' The King had ice in his voice.

'Oh, Jesus Christ,' slipped from Hermitage's lips before he could stop himself. No wonder he found the man terrifying. He crossed himself repeatedly while Brother James simply whimpered.

'I do assure your Majesty that the best interests of your kingdom and your people were paramount.'

'Yes,' the King stretched the word out. He clearly wasn't happy and was equally clearly going to do something about it.

'I did my best to protect the young Brother here by sending him out of harm's way to Lincoln.'

The King raised a questioning eyebrow at Hermitage.

'I was attacked before I got there. Mister Wat saved me.'

The Abbot shrugged. 'The heretics were on the verge of exposing themselves and their scheme, at which point I would have simply had them burned.'

'You bastard,' Athan muttered to himself, clearly feeling very let down.

As the King surveyed them all again, weighing up his options of what to do with them, the door was flung open once more. The King's uniformed messenger burst into the room and handed over a scroll. Harold unrolled it and read.

'Bollocks,' he said.

The others all waited to hear the news.

'As you will have gathered, I am not at all happy with the goings on in this place and I want to get to the bottom of it. What the Church gets up to on its own is its own business. Most of it's pretty odd anyway, but it's usually no concern of mine. When the Pope's relatives and agents start popping up in my country, it casts another light altogether. I will find out who the whisperer was, I will find out who is behind all of this and I will make an example of them.'

Nicodemus and Athan exchanged another glance as if it were their last.

'However,' the King said.

They breathed again.

'I have news here,' he waved the scroll about, 'that William the Bastard has actually landed at Hastings with a large force. This is not what we agreed at all. If he was coming, he should have sent word of the date. The man has no manners. Now I have to get down there as quickly as possible to see him off. I've done the Danes in the north and now I'll do the Normans in the south.' He cast a regal glare around the room which nailed everyone to their spot.

'After that I shall come back here, so I want nothing done until I return. No one is to leave. I shall instruct the local authorities to that effect. All I can say is that you're all bloody lucky there's a Norman invasion, or I'd probably string up most of you here and now. You.' He pointed to Hermitage, who was busy quaking in his habit.

He thought that the King had been quite a reasonable chap. Now there was talk of execution again.

'Your Majesty,' he managed to bleat.

'What's your name?'

'Hermitage, your Majesty.'

'Odd name for a monk,' the King frowned. 'Still nothing surprises me any more. Come here.'

Hermitage's shaky legs were only just sufficient to get him across the space to the King.

Harold put his hand on Hermitage's shoulders.

'Brother Hermitage,' he intoned with a purposeful look at Simon, 'I hereby appoint you the King's Investigator.'

'Majesty?'

'Well, until today I never knew there was such a position, but with all these goings on it seems I might need one. If I'm going to have one I shall make my own appointment.' This time the look went to Nicodemus.

'So,' the King spoke in his best regal voice, 'am I clear? No one leaves. Hermitage here is King's Investigator and I'll be back in a week to sort you all out.'

Various mumbles and nods greeted the King's instruction.

'Good. Now, Vignar, you're with me. We ride. To Hastings.'

'Yaarh,' Vignar waved his sword in joy.

'And Toksvar, you'd better come as well. If William has come with a large force I could probably use all the men I can get.'

The look on Toksvar's face changed during this instruction. It moved from horror at the thought of having to go and fight in a real battle to realisation that people do get killed in battles. All you probably have to do is make sure that it's the right people. He clapped his brother heartily on the shoulder.

'And noble Earl. A good job you are here at the time of your nation's peril. I will have you at my side as we drive the Normans from our shores.'

'Oh, good,' said the Earl.

'Master Wat,' the King called, 'walk with me. I have an idea for a work based on skirmishing band of soldiers accidentally crashing through a bathhouse, perhaps you can work on some preliminary sketches while I'm away. Once I've defeated William and taken his lands I have a mind to hang something insulting on the town hall in Bayeux. Never did like that place.'

The King swept from the room. 'To arms, to arms,' he could be heard yelling, as he left with Wat scurrying after.

There was a long silence while those left looked at one another, trying to decide what to do. Hermitage closed his eyes in silent, prayerful thanks that the nightmare he had lived through had ended. Had ended well, as it happened. He seemed to have been appointed King's Investigator. He would have to find out what his duties were.

When he opened his eyes again there were considerably fewer people. The Abbot and Francis had simply vanished, although Hermitage thought he could hear the sound of running feet. Well, three feet and a stick.

Brother James was hiding behind a column, probably thinking that he could stay in here for at least a day before anyone came looking for him.

Brother Simon's look spoke pages. His mind must be wandering about as if it didn't know which way to turn. Even through his thick skin the knowledge that he had not made a good impression on the King could be seen. He glanced repeatedly from Hermitage to Nicodemus, trying to weigh up which way his fortune lay. Nicodemus was in no fit state to be receiving visitors and so Simon wandered over to Hermitage.

'So, Brother Investigator,' he said.

Hermitage was too absorbed in his own experience to comprehend that he was being spoken to.

'This is particularly disappointing,' Simon said, mostly to himself, 'obviously that idiot Nicodemus has messed up the appointments procedure in some way. It probably was his right as the Bishop's man to appoint an Investigator. The King can't be expected to know all his own rules in detail.' Although he said this, it didn't sound like he really believed it. 'There are probably many of us. There could be Bishops up and down the country appointing Investigators.'

He paused for Hermitage to respond. Hermitage didn't.

'I did think about pointing this out to His Majesty, but he seemed engaged. And what was all that about the Epicurean heresy?' Simon was emboldened by Hermitage's daze. 'I've never heard of it, so it can't be true.' He paused again, waiting for Hermitage's response. It didn't come.

'Well, the King will be back in a week or so. We can sort out all the details then.' Simon frowned at Hermitage, demanding a response of some sort. 'I don't know why the King wanted two investigators when I was already in post.'

Hermitage stood and pondered his new-found role. Touched by the King. Wait until his father heard about this – perhaps he'd give him back his inheritance now. He would mark his new function by starting a journal in which he recorded all these events, and those which would come as he investigated for the King. He looked up as if recognising Simon for the first time. Somehow all of Simon's words had sunk in though.

'Oh, I don't think you are Investigator,' he said, calmly and with conviction. 'The King appointed me in your place.' He smiled broadly, assuming Simon would be as happy at the news as he was.

✦   ✦   ✦

Athan watched everyone go, apart from James, Hermitage and Simon who didn't matter, and then moved over to Nicodemus who was slumped on a chair.

'What do we do now?' Athan hissed.

'God knows,' all Nicodemus's pride and bearing had been washed away. 'You weren't supposed to kill him,' he spat.

'I didn't,' Athan said

'Oh, come off it.'

'He just died.'

'All you had to do was make sure that the argument was either lost or was at least equivocal. I would have done the rest with the Conclave, but oh no. You had to go too far.'

'All I was doing,' Athan whispered as quietly as he could, which was as loud as most people talk, 'was trying to put him off a bit. Get him to make a few mistakes so that you or that useless Genly could pick him off.'

'At least Genly had the decency to die.' It was clear Nicodemus thought that Athan should do the same.

'There was nothing decent about Genly,' Athan said. 'And anyway, how was I to know the old fool would get so excited about his stupid argument that he'd have a fit?'

'Well, he did, and you made it happen, and when the King comes back he's not likely to be impressed by "I didn't mean to".'

Athan recognised a threat when he heard one.

'Accomplices are no better.'

'Oh, don't worry about me, I know I've had it. The only option I had was running away, but now the King's made sure I can't even do that. We're just plain heretics, you and I. Burning will be a bit of a let off. At least we can rest in the knowledge that the Abbot and Francis are likely to be on the receiving end of much worse. If they can't run fast enough, that is.'

'There must be something,' Athan said, not at all keen on this forecast of events.

'We could pray that he loses the battle with William.'

'What?' Athan was shocked

'Well, if the King's not the King any more, he can hardly come back to sort us all out, can he?'

Athan thought for a long while. 'I'm sure it counts as treason, praying for the King's defeat.'

'Oh dear,' said Nicodemus, mockingly. 'I wonder which being executed for will hurt most, treason or heresy.' He lapsed into a thoughtful pause.

A dark shape detached itself from the wall at the back of the chamber and stepped silently up to the two men. It stood behind, head covered in a cowl, until Nicodemus got the uncomfortable feeling he was being watched. He turned around, puzzled, and almost leapt out of his skin.

'Bloody hell, what are you doing here?'

Even Athan, who couldn't normally be startled by anything, took a hasty step back.

'Things have gone awry,' the cowl muttered quietly.

'You're damn right they have.'

'Who the hell is this?' Athan looked around to make sure no one else had noticed this new arrival. 'And how long have you been here?'

'We are everywhere, always.'

'Oh, very mysterious, I'm sure. Well you're here now, and I can put a boot down your throat if you don't start explaining yourself.'

The cowl looked to Nicodemus for support.

'He will, you know,' Nicodemus simply nodded.

'I am a humble servant.'

'God, not another one. My experience of humble servants is

that they're nothing but trouble.'

'I am merely assisting in the progress of events.'

'Yes, well, we all thought we were doing that and look where it got us. What was your part in this shambles?'

'I am an organiser,' the cowl said slowly.

'Look, organiser,' Athan reached out and pulled the cowl down quickly so that it formed a neat ligature around the figure's throat, 'I am naturally a man of enormously bad temperament, so you can imagine what today is doing for me. Talk.' He released the makeshift noose just enough to allow speech.

'I'm a Mason. A Masonic agent,' the figure choked and squawked.

'Don't believe you.'

'He is,' Nicodemus chipped in. 'He's organising the trades for the building work.'

The figure had given up mystery and was nodding pleadingly.

'So you wanted this debate to fail as well.'

'Oh yes, I'm with you. There's a lot of money at stake. A lot of our members have turned down other work to get these contracts. Father Genly was our man on the inside; he was supposed to make sure things proceeded to plan, but he, er, came to an end.'

'He did, didn't he?' Athan said with heavy sarcasm. 'And what do you mean he was your man on the inside? What the bloody hell have I been doing all this time? Why didn't I know about this?' He turned to Nicodemus with no good intent in his heart.

'We had to make sure. Doubly sure. We all knew Genly's reputation. He was likely to come a cropper at any moment. Some jealous lover or other would eventually slice him up. The less you knew the better. Kept you safe that way.'

'Thank you very much. That will be an enormous comfort when they light the kindling. So you've been skulking about the place all along?' Athan turned to the Mason.

'Well, I've sized the job up, got Chirk from the local Lodge.

269

I've spent about a week on that bloody Lincoln road, riding backward and forward. I've hardly slept. I've engaged with Master Nicodemus here, and even the Earl...' He stopped quickly, but not quickly enough.

'What do you mean, the Earl?' Nicodemus asked. He gestured to Athan, who strangled the man once more.

'It's the Earl's men who are going to do the bulk of the work,' the Mason gurgled.

'His own men?'

'He's got a load of builders under tithe to him. He makes them work for nothing.'

'And so all the money he was investing was going straight back into his own pocket?'

'I couldn't possibly comment.'

'And all the other investors I'd lined up, they'd be paying the Earl as well.'

'Not entirely. As I say there are a number of key artisans who would be paid, but the labour was the Earl's.'

'God, I thought I was corrupt.' Nicodemus shook his head.

'So what happens now?' Athan was at a loss.

'If I might speak?' the Mason gestured at his throat. Athan released him.

'We all stand to lose out if this development is halted.'

'Some more than others.' Nicodemus gave a very realistic impression of a hanged man.

'The Earl has now departed and will take his men with him. The King has gone to battle.'

'Yes.'

'But the investors are still available, and the tradesmen will want their work.'

'Of course,' Nicodemus said with a new realisation. 'A large number of senior tradesmen who don't get the contracts they're expecting probably make a betrayed King look like a baby rabbit. They wouldn't be at all happy with the organiser, I imagine.'

'That's one possibility.' The organiser swallowed.

'Are you suggesting we just carry on? I suspect that the King might pile on a few extra punishments when he finds out we've ignored him completely.'

'Dangerous places, battles,' the Mason suggested, not very innocently.

'What do you mean?'

'The King might win, the King might lose. In either event it's quite possible he could suffer some fatal injury.'

'Possible, but not very likely. Kings don't tend to muck in with the arrow fodder. They stand at the back and give orders.'

'Yes, but the Masons are a very well represented organisation.'

'Get to the point before I get one for you,' Athan glowered.

'We have a number of experts on our roster who can be called upon to help their fellows out of difficult situations.'

'Such as?'

'Such as perhaps shooting an arrow rather haphazardly during a battle.'

'Are you saying what I think you're saying?'

'We do have one member who takes care of the most remarkable things for the right sum.'

'Really?'

'Yes, he's a phenomenal archer. Reckons he could take someone's eye out at two hundred paces. Being a Mason he's very discreet…'

FINIS

Post Scriptum: For further information on how things went for King Harold in Hastings, please refer to the Bayeux Tapestry or any reputable history of the period. (Hint: things could have gone better…)

Now available in The Chronicles of Brother Hermitage:

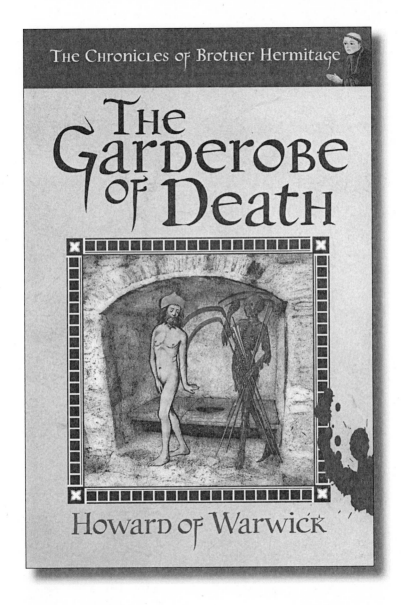

The Chronicles of Brother Hermitage

The Garderobe of Death

Howard of Warwick

ISBN 978-0-9929393-1-1

Find out more →

Now available:

Howard of Warwick's
"History as it might have happened – but probably didn't."

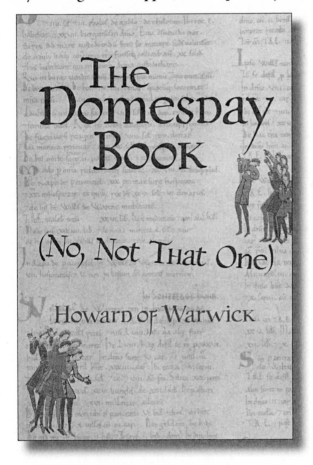

A book so epic it has a map.

Find out more →

The Domesday Book (No, Not That One)

William of Normandy ...

... has just won the Battle of Hastings but has lost something precious; so precious no one must even know it is missing. Reluctantly assembling a team of incompetents, he sends them on a mission of recovery. But his secret is out and another band is after the treasure. In a race across a savage land, through a population of confused misfits, against the clock and against one another, two forces hurtle towards a finale of cataclysmic proportions; all in 29 concise and entertaining chapters.

ISBN 978-0-9929393-2-8

And coming in 2015:

The Magna Carta (Or Is It?)

The Garderobe of Death

England 1067...

... and the King's favourite hunting companion has been murdered. How anyone actually did it is a mystery, given the intimately personal nature of the fatal wound. Robert Grosmal, a Norman of disordered mind, sends for a monk to investigate. Medieval monks are supposed to be good at this sort of thing. Brother Hermitage is a medieval monk but he's not very good at this sort of thing. Motivated by the point of a sword, he and his companion, Wat, weaver of adult tapestry, set off to solve the crime. Oh, and King William is arriving that night so they'd better get a move on ...

Read the first chapter →

Caput I

Midnight: Death Takes Norman

HESE WERE VERY DARK AGES. Thus mused Henri de Turold as he stumbled through one of the very darkest bits and stubbed his toes on a beam of worm-ridden English oak. Cursing the ghastly country and its truly awful people to an eternity of pain, he hobbled on down the corridor.

'But we're emerging from the darkness, sire; these are modern times,' learned men gabbled on all the time. To Henri's way of thinking, emergence from the dark would be a lot quicker if he set fire to England and all the learned men in it.

It had to be said that Henri's way of thinking was slow and laborious at the best of times. If anyone wanted goose feathers putting on their arrows, they would turn to Henri de Turold. If they wanted a decent conversation, they'd turn to the goose.

Yet the Norman made up for this absence of brain with a huge portion of good looks. Towering five foot nine if he was an inch, he had a chest like a barrel—the inside of one—and a stomach that couldn't muster the strength to reach his belt, let along hang over it. When he stood up straight his knees were so far apart that he didn't so much mount a horse as overwhelm it.

His face was normally an example of Norman power and grandeur, having been hit very hard, many times, by horses' hoofs. This had re-arranged his features into that pattern most favoured by the ladies of the Norman court. At this particular moment, however, his visage was contorted into a grimace of disdain that made him look almost English.

This strange moment of the night saw him stumbling through the very strange castle of his fellow Norman, and intellectual equal, Lord Robert Grosmal. Henri appreciated that Grosmal deserved the estate as reward for slaughtering the women and children of Hastings, but why had he filled it with darkness? England's darkness might not be actually darker than anywhere else, but he always felt it was ignoring him at best, if not actively conspiring against him. Not like Norman darkness, which was friendly and welcoming, and allowed you to get up to all sorts of things without being spotted.

To rid himself of this cursed gloom, Henri held a candle in front of him—one that seemed in league with the murk and strangely reluctant to help. It was admittedly a long, fat thing with a flame on top, but those were all the candle-like qualities it was prepared to accommodate.

The candle maker of Robert Grosmal had a reputation, and it wasn't a good one. The thing guttered and spluttered and dropped about enough light to illuminate its own shaft, which, being made of something truly unspeakable, was best not illuminated at all. No one knew quite what it was the man did to a candle, but they all knew it was horrible. They were the only variety that could make a moth leave a room.

'What the hell am I doing here?' Henri mumbled for about the third time. Drips of almost sentient wax did their best to cling on to the life of the candle before dropping towards the floor, swerving strangely as they went and landing with a soft, hot splash on his naked toes.

Walking naked through the halls of this disgusting house in January was clearly mad—but so was walking anywhere naked in January. Normally de Turold took off no clothes at all between October and May, and even then was considered outlandishly hardy. His only splash of common sense was the floppy yellow cloth hat on his head. Perhaps this would postpone the moment he froze to death.

For earlier that evening his desires, long dormant or satisfied by killing things, had taken control of his body, and he was only obeying orders.

Over dinner the Lady Foella, a Saxon beauty of such distinction she almost looked French, had hinted that if he were to walk naked from his chamber to hers there might be a warm welcome for him…

Henri's reverie was broken and dragged to the present by an odour, slinking out of the opening to Robert's new fangled garderobe. The Norman paused for a moment to consider his bowels, or rather they grabbed his attention by rattling like six squirrels in a sack of walnuts. Mindful of all the trouble he had been having down there lately, he decided to visit the facilities before descending, literally he hoped, on Lady Foella.

A testing clench of his muscles released a scent that would have made a pig of little discernment vomit, never mind a lady of refinement. The odour of ordure did brief battle with the scents drifting from the garderobe, but soon gave up an unequal battle and retired from the field. If Henri had been visiting a serving girl she could have been told to clean up afterwards, but Foella had class.

Nipping quickly into the room, he followed one of the garderobe night lights as its disgusting smoke seeped into the air. There were two planted on the stone paving by sides of two holes, badly knocked into the chamber floor. He could have sworn his candle flickered at the others, probably just the wind.

Above the holes, propped off the ground by lumps of wood, were two slabs of stone with matching holes, optimistically described as seats by Lord Robert. The candles burned in the room as a courtesy to light the way for visitors, or at least to stop them doing it on the floor by mistake.

Setting himself down on the nearest ice-trimmed hole, he prepared to let drop. He didn't need to prepare long as his lower intestine wanted rid of its contents faster than Henri wanted to get at Lady Foella's.

Henri put his own candle at a safe distance. Then he bent to move the other so the fumes would find some direction of travel other than up his nose. This candle had got firmly stuck to the floor by its own excreted wax, and so he gave it a tug. He frowned for a moment as below the noise of his own evacuation he could have sworn he heard something. One second later he was dead.

The Chronicles of Brother Hermitage
will meander on with:

The Tapestry of Death

Hermitage, Wat and Some Murder or Other

Notes pages for questions you might like to discuss
at your book group:

Why? Why not? Who and where? How come? Never again?

Notes pages for questions you might like to discuss
at your book group:

Why? Why not? Who and where? How come? Never again?

Notes pages for questions you might like to discuss
at your book group:

Why? Why not? Who and where? How come? Never again?

Notes pages for questions you might like to discuss
at your book group:

Why? Why not? Who and where? How come? Never again?

Notes pages for questions you might like to discuss
at your book group:

Why? Why not? Who and where? How come? Never again?

Notes pages for questions you might like to discuss
at your book group:

Why? Why not? Who and where? How come? Never again?